Dangerous Remedy

'Kat Dunn's captivating debut... is part
steampunk adventure, part historical thriller...
an enthralling, fast-paced adventure with
a cast of likeable characters.'
The Guardian

'An intelligent, lush and rollicking opener
to what promises to be your new YA obsession.
Vivid, dark, and complex...'
Kiran Millwood Hargrave, author of
A Secret of Birds and Bone

'Wonderfully atmospheric fill of strange science,
mysterious powers and fearless heroines.'
The Bookseller

'Lashings of lust, love, sacrifice, betrayal and horror.'
Melinda Salisbury, author of
Hold Back the Tide

'Dark, deadly and delicious. A thrilling adventure set
in a lavish but ruthless world, with a spirited cast of
characters you will root for instantly.'
Bex Hogan, author of *Viper*

MONSTROUS DESIGN

'The action is swashbuckling, the characters
believable... this is a no-holes-barred
read, gritty and exciting...'
Armadillo

'The Battalion of the Dead series has everything you
could want from a historical YA fantasy: adventure,
opulence, lies, science, magic and a captivating
band of rebellious characters at its heart.'
CultureFly

'Dashing young heroines and
a strong LGBTQ voice.'
British Fantasy Society

'Wonderful... tension and mystery... My 15-year-old
self would have loved it whole-heartedly.'
ParSec

'The plot is tight and totally believable, the characters
are strong... This is YA at its best. Recommended.'
Historical Novel Society

Glorious Poison

Kat Dunn grew up in London and has
lived in Japan, Australia and France.
She has written about mental health for
Mind and *The Guardian*, and worked
as a translator for Japanese television.
Her debut novel, *Dangerous Remedy*,
and second novel, *Monstrous Design*,
are both published by Zephyr.
She lives in London.

Also by Kat Dunn

Dangerous Remedy

Monstrous Design

KAT DUNN

GLORIOUS POISON

The revolution was her...

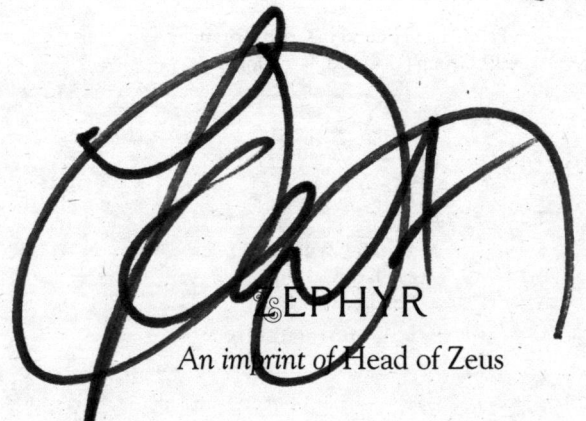

ZEPHYR

An imprint of Head of Zeus

First published in the UK in 2022 by Zephyr, an imprint of Head of Zeus
This Zephyr paperback edition first published in the UK in 2023 by Head of Zeus,
part of Bloomsbury Publishing Plc

9 7 5 3 1 2 4 6 8

A catalogue record for this book is available from
the British Library.

ISBN (PB): 9781789543742
ISBN (E): 9781789543711

Typeset by Ed Pickford
Cover design by Laura Brett

Printed and bound in Great Britain by
CPI Group (UK) Ltd, Croydon CRO 4YY

MIX
Paper | Supporting
responsible forestry
FSC® C171272

Head of Zeus Ltd
5–8 Hardwick Street
London EC1R 4RG

WWW.HEADOFZEUS.COM

For my found family

(though some of you are biologically related to me, it just took us a while to find family in each other)

Arrête! C'est ici l'Empire de la Mort

Inscription above the entrance to the
catacombs in Paris

Oh! pleasant exercise of hope and joy!

'The French Revolution as It Appeared
to Enthusiasts at Its Commencement'
William Wordsworth

The story so far...

It is six months since Camille and the Battalion of the Dead – her scientist girlfriend, Ada, deserting soldier Guil and disinherited aristocrat Al – were hired to rescue Olympe by the Duc de l'Aubespine, who was posing as her father. Olympe was the key part of his electrical experiments to find a weapon to topple the Revolution and restore the Bourbon dynasty to the throne. Olympe was held by Docteur Comtois, who had worked for the duc previously but taken the side of the Revolutionaries.

When the battalion found out the truth about Olympe, they refused to give her over to either side, instead determining to get her to safety. But before they could, Camille's English ex-fiancé, James, turned traitor and kidnapped Olympe.

Camille and Al pursued James and Olympe to England, while Guil and Ada stayed in Paris to anticipate the duc's next move. Secretly, Camille gave Ada her own mission: become a sleeper agent in the duc's household. To gain his trust, she would have to make him believe she had betrayed the battalion for good.

In England, Camille and Al went to James's family, pretending to be refugees from the Terror – and Camille still James's loving fiancée. She was welcomed home, and a date was set for the wedding. James was on the back foot. He had gone to Paris at the behest of his surgical tutor, Wickham, who had been conducting his own research into electricity and got word of Olympe's powers. James thought to take Olympe for himself and hand her over to his father, the Minister of War, to gain his favour, but his father didn't believe in her powers. James hid Olympe from both Camille and a furious Wickham out for revenge, but when James discovered Wickham had created his own electrical monster to hunt them down, he was forced to turn to Camille for help. Things came to a head at the wedding, when Wickham attacked, sending Camille and Olympe fleeing in a game of cat and mouse.

Meanwhile in France, Robespierre was overthrown and the duc sensed the moment would soon come to launch his coup. Ada secured a place for herself with him as his apprentice, claiming she had cut ties with the battalion. Then the duc revealed Olympe's mother, Clémentine, had been released from prison – and was his sister. Ada thought she might have found an ally and told Clémentine where Olympe was, but it proved to be a mistake. Clémentine was loyal to her brother, and when the duc discovered Ada's deceit, he dragged both her and Guil to England in pursuit of Camille and Olympe.

They arrived at the wedding in time to stop Wickham, but the danger wasn't over yet. Camille challenged the duc to settle their score in a duel, and for a brief moment it seemed as though the battalion could win.

Then Ada made her move.

She turned on the battalion and delivered Olympe to the duc.

Camille had known the duc would never stop hunting Olympe while she lived; to stop him for good, they had to play a long game. So she had instructed Ada to betray the battalion so drastically the duc could not doubt her loyalty to him. Their only chance was to convince the duc he had won and the battalion had fallen apart, to let his own arrogance blind him as they continued to work in secret to bring him down. And Ada, embedded in the heart of his operation, poised to strike when he would least expect.

Now, the duc's political allies rule Paris. With Ada and Clémentine at his side, and Olympe and Guil imprisoned, the duc thinks himself all but unstoppable, and Camille, Al and James have returned to France, broken and defeated.

But this is the Battalion of the Dead.

There is no fate. No destiny.

Everything is a choice.

What they choose next will change the course of history.

PART ONE

Bliss Was It in That Dawn to Be Alive

10 October 1794

1

A Cell Underground

A cell was not the worst prison Guil knew of. There was the narrow dugout in Spain he had been trapped in for three days, with the rotting bodies of his squadron for company. Any move was met by rifle fire; a prison he had no choice but to stay in, hour after hour, as the flies swarmed and the stink of putrefaction gathered like fog clinging to the inside of his mouth and nose.

Then there was the prison of a life half-lived. With no meaning, no hope, the only escape in death. A prison that closed around him when he deserted, disillusioned.

A cell, no, that was not so bad.

A cell had rules. Two square metres of freedom. Four walls of its own. The dream of escape.

He thought of Olympe enclosed within the iron mask. Her cell was visible by the narrow slot in his door through which guards posted him stale slices of bread, rinds of cheese. Once a day they would bring him a bucket of fresh water, and take out the previous day's bucket he had used for slop.

They came for Olympe more frequently.

Each day he watched as she was held still and spoonfuls of gruel were pushed through the twisted iron mouth so that she had to swallow or else choke. He thought of the way her head sagged to one side, the weight too great to bear. There were no eye slits in this mask. The duc had not thought it necessary. Blinkered like a horse, she was terrified, and malleable.

A cell was a far more benevolent prison.

His duty now was to watch over Olympe. Offer whatever protection he could.

A rattle of keys announced the guards and Guil took up position by the door, blinking as his eyes adjusted to the bright light of oil lamp they carried. Always two guards, stout and sturdy.

They knew she would fight.

She always fought.

This time was no different. A scuffle, the bark of metal on stone and her voice, a muffled howl, as the fight spilled from the cell. Olympe had grown as thin as he had, her arms too easily enclosed by the men's hands. She struggled all the same, wielding her mask as a weapon. She caught one in the face and he fell back, blood streaming from his mouth and a snapped tooth in his hand.

Snarling, he raised his baton high.

'Wait!'

At the sound of Guil's voice, Olympe turned the bulbous horror of her head towards him.

Guil's mouth was dry. He had tried to intervene before. There was a narrow line to walk between getting the guards' attention and angering them more. But he had a plan.

'Take me too.'

'They don't want you,' sneered the guard with the baton. 'Only her.'

'How much use is she to them if you cannot deliver her in one piece?'

'If they cared what state she was in they wouldn't keep her down here,' the guard laughed, but the other man seemed less sure.

'*He* might not care, but *she* would.'

Guil listened closely. They were talking about the duc and – no, he couldn't even think her name. He was still too furious, and if he got distracted by his anger this wouldn't work.

'So?' said the man with the baton.

'He listens to her. What if she decides we don't have jobs any more?'

Guil spoke up, 'Olympe will go peacefully if she has me with her. Is that not so, Olympe?'

Slowly, the heavy head nodded.

'Oh, for— Fine.' The guard holding her tossed a set of keys to the other man, who unlocked Guil's door.

'Turn around and keep your hands up.'

The door opened with a rush of damp air. Guil's arms were wrenched behind his back and tied tightly.

'You have to explain this to them,' grumbled Olympe's guard. 'I'm not taking the flack for letting prisoners out without authorisation.'

The men led them from the cellar, throwing a cloth bag over the iron mask. Guil's shoulder brushed against Olympe's as they mounted the stairs and the contact was a moment of respite. She was still here, alive, as safe as he could make her.

At the top of the stairs the house was cold with the chill of winter. Servants passed back and forth carrying pails of soapy water, buckets of coal, the running of a grand estate like a city in miniature. Guil stumbled, blinking against the whitewashed walls and the clatter of shoes on tiles. It was momentarily disorientating to be in space so open and light after many months confined to his cell. The guard jerked him upright and he staggered along, keeping pace.

So the battalion had come to this: bound and clumsy and trailing Olympe's skirts like a loyal dog. Perhaps that's all family really meant: staying with someone through the suffering. Bearing witness to their worst moments, and not turning away from pain.

Perhaps that was what the battalion had always been about.

The palace was busy with workmen too. Dust sheets had been laid over the parquet to create criss-crossing paths; people carrying sheets of metal and planks of wood, disassembled scaffolding and boxes of screws and nails and rolls of tools moved back and forth in a constant traffic. Their little party of prisoners and guards was given little attention. After the last five years of turmoil, only the most foolhardy asked questions.

The work centred on a vast ballroom set into the heart of the building; through the open doors Guil caught a glimpse of a space larger than seemed possible.

Then he realised part of the ceiling had been panelled with sheets of highly polished metal, giving the effect of a mirror hung overhead.

Before he could see more, they were pushed through another doorway and up a servants' staircase. Olympe, blinded by her mask, shuffled behind. Every now and then his elbow would nudge her arm, or his hip bump hers in some paltry gesture of comfort.

Finally they were brought to a halt outside a grand set of Rococo double doors decorated in white and gold fleur-de-lis and curlicues. One guard knocked, and a voice bid them enter.

The doors opened onto a large study where the Rococo excess continued, illuminated by dull autumn light that spilled in through floor to ceiling windows. A ceramic stove the height of a person radiated heat from one corner, and drawn close to it was a desk covered in neat stacks of paperwork. The Duc de l'Aubespine's crest of arms had been carved into the front, golden fleur-de-lis on a sable field bisected by an azure band, and above, the crown of a duc.

There was a single figure in the room, seated behind the desk.

'Prisoners for the duc,' announced the guard.

Ada folded her hands before her and regarded Guil and Olympe impassively.

'The duc is occupied. I will be conducting the tests today.'

The Palais Royal

The Palais Royal was back.

Five years of revolution had been snuffed out between one drink and the next. The Palais de l'Égalité had been a crucible of thought, new ideas simmering between sweating bodies and brimming glasses, new dawns declared from tabletops. But the paint on the sign was peeling, showing the old name beneath. Politics had been swapped for wealth, the new dawn sliding back into the lugubrious evening of the night before.

Al strolled through the gates like the devil returning to hell.

In a new silk suit, lace spilling from his cuffs and a silver-topped cane in his hand, he passed through the shaded colonnades towards the Théâtre Montansier; here and there a head turned, eyes following his progress.

The Café de Chartres sprawled across a back corner of the Palais. The bend in the river of humanity flowing from the theatres and gaming tables, where the current slowed and revellers washed up on the banks of tables and chairs to pass the time of day, watch the crowds and skim the scattered pamphlets and news sheets.

Al took a table under the shade of a beech tree and ordered a pot of coffee. His pocket watch marked it to be just after one. The matinées wouldn't have started yet. On the far side of the colonnades, a sans-culottes was being ejected from another café by the owner, who was shouting about an aunt lost to Robespierre and the Terror. Only yesterday, Al had read reports of a mob chasing Jacobin Revolutionaries through Nîmes until they were forced to jump into the river to escape being bludgeoned to death.

He took out a box of snuff and brought a pinch to his nose. Then another.

The coffee arrived. Al checked his watch again. Quarter past one.

It was a fine watch that had once belonged to his father. Imported from Geneva, it had delicate filigree engraving across the case and his family coat of arms at the centre. When his family had tried to join the other emigrés fleeing the Revolution, their hôtel particulier – the grand city palaces every aristocrat occupied – in Paris had been seized along with all their other lands and assets. But the attempted sale by the government had become mired in legal complications due to an incredibly boring story about a mill owner, twenty sacks of flour and the daughter of a local magistrate. Returning to France after the overthrow of Robespierre, it had only taken a little wrangling to get the execution warrant for his name thrown out as a miscarriage of justice. And so Al found himself in possession of the inheritance his parents insisted would never reach him.

The watch had still been on his father's desk when Al had let himself into his childhood home for the first time in two years.

He had thought about smashing it.

Then he had thought about the twist of his father's mouth when he had told Al in great detail what sort of punishment should be dealt to *men like him* and he pocketed the watch instead. The weight of it now in his waistcoat brought a bitter smile to his face.

A rowdy party of drinkers broke apart, scattering to their different destinations, and in the clearing stood Léon. Al's breath caught and he looked down at his coffee in careful indifference. The line of Léon's jaw, the column of his throat, were too beautiful.

Al didn't look up again until he heard the scrape of the chair at the next table, and sensed the body behind him.

'What were you smirking about?' asked Léon. They were almost back to back, their chairs set at an angle away from each other. Léon studied the sign of a print shop in the floor above them. To anyone passing, they would look like nothing more than two strangers taking coffee alone at separate tables.

'My incredible charm and wit,' said Al. 'And your incredible luck for knowing me.'

But his words held no weight. His palms were sweaty and he tried to discreetly wipe them on his breeches.

'My incredible misfortune, you mean.' Léon shifted in his seat and elbowed Al in the back.

'What do you mean? I'm here, aren't I? I came back.'

Léon said nothing for a moment, a muscle working in his jaw.

'You left without telling me you were safe. I saw your name on the execution lists and then the next thing I knew, you'd vanished—' He broke off. 'That was cruel of you.'

Al let the comment lie. His guilt turned the coffee bitter, made the grey clouds too low and close. Léon was right. If he were a good man, he would apologise. Or he would leave. But he was selfish and if Léon still wanted him after the way he'd behaved, he would let Léon stay and be hurt again.

That was all Al could offer: difficulty, and pain.

Maybe Camille was right. He needed to sort himself out.

First, he had a job to finish.

'Do you have it?' he asked.

Behind their chairs, Léon's hand brushed his. Al took the folded paper between them and put it into his pocket without looking.

'I've dug up all sorts of strange information for Cam,' said Léon. 'But *him*? What does she want with him? Has she lost the plot?'

'Oh, quite probably,' said Al. This was the polite version of what he had told Camille when she had given him his instructions for Léon. Most of it couldn't be repeated in public.

Léon's fingers touched Al's again, and Al let his

smallest finger link with Léon's. A hidden moment of intimacy concealed from the crowds of the Palais Royal.

Selfish. He was so selfish.

Léon's voice was rough with emotion. 'Don't be brave for her. Don't do something stupid. I need you to make it out on the other side of this.'

Al stole a moment, taking another sip of coffee. He didn't like this guilt, and he liked the rush of warmth – of *love* – even less.

Love was complicated. Love was frightening. Love was a trick.

'Don't worry,' he said. 'You know me. No bigger coward.'

But Léon didn't laugh.

Only curled his finger tighter around Al's, and said, 'You're not a coward. And that's what frightens me.'

3

The Duc's Palace

'Why is he here?' Ada didn't look at Guil when she spoke.

The guard haltingly explained. 'We can take him back if you want.'

Olympe began to struggle at once, flailing an elbow in the direction of the voice and the guard yanked her arms back so sharply she let out a yelp muffled by the mask.

Ada conceded. 'No. Leave him. It doesn't matter either way.'

'Yes, mademoiselle, as you say.' The guards both bowed, hurrying to obey her orders.

This was the woman the guards had spoken of. The person the duc listened to. The person the guards worried could end their careers.

Guil had seen Ada since her betrayal of the battalion in England. He had seen her far too many times: on their journey back to Paris, sitting with the duc and Clémentine sharing a meal, talking over documents, heads close together. He'd seen her from a distance, sweeping through the palace in silk gowns while he had been hauled from his cell for his weekly exercise in the stable yard that stank of horse manure and the chamber pots being scrubbed by a scullery maid.

No matter how many times he had seen her, his anger never dimmed.

Ada gave her orders. 'Set the test. Scenario three, test subject gamma.'

From an adjoining room a cluster of men in shirtsleeves and aprons arrived. Scientists, Guil thought. Ada's subordinates.

Olympe became as tense as a drawn bow. She was steered into an adjoining room and, as if an afterthought, one man chivvied Guil behind them.

Ada took a pencil from behind her ear and began to make notes on a sheaf of schematics, deep in concentration. He had always known she wanted more than the battalion could give her. Now she had it, with the duc.

In his first days of captivity, Guil had lashed out at Ada whatever chance he got, sending his fury and humiliation into the frigid air between them. He had begged her to rethink, to remember Camille, their home together as the battalion. Laid her crimes before her, listed the pain she had caused, the wrong she had put her hand to.

None of it touched her. It was as though a different woman walked among them. When she had struck the blow against him that had placed her alongside the duc, his Ada – the woman he had fought beside, schemed with, rescued and been rescued by – had dissipated like smoke from a snuffed candle. That life had been extinguished, and all he could catch was the faint traces on the air.

No, Guil would not talk to her now. If Ada thought nothing of him, then nothing he would be. Let them underestimate him. The soldier, solid, direct, unthinking. He had learned the value of silence.

This next room was decorated much like the first, white and gold panelling lining the walls, frothing with fleur-de-lis and vines, and vast windows overlooking the bony autumn forest. But it had been emptied of the usual furniture of a salon, and instead held a few heavy desks, trestle tables covered in bundles of wire and rubber, and glass jars filled with acid. The parquet floor was scuffed from heavy objects being dragged across it, and on the far side Guil saw the culprit: an electrostatic generator. A glass cylinder the size of his torso set within a frame to be spun to generate a current. It was as though the duc's laboratory of old had been stripped of its grisly specimens and reduced to something cold, clinical. Inhuman.

In the centre was a metal cage. One sheet of copper as the floor, another as the ceiling, and thin wooden bars supporting the structure like the lathes within walls. A memory stirred in Guil's mind but before he could place it, a door opened and a goat was led in on a rope. One of the slats in the side of the cage was removed and the goat led inside.

He shifted closer to Olympe.

Ada stood in the centre in her white linen dress, expressionless. She gestured towards Olympe and two men dressed in silk took her to the side of the cage. The sudden loss of warmth from her arm pressed against him made Guil feel more alone than he had in his cell.

Then he saw why they wore silk.

The men took coils of rubber-coated wire from where they were attached to the metal cell and unfurled them. The coils ended in a metal cuff. Each man took one of Olympe's arms and unbuttoned the sleeves.

'Everyone back!' ordered Ada. 'Onto the mat.'

Guil was jostled along with the room's occupants onto a stretch of rubber matting.

One cuff was closed around Olympe's wrist, and then the other.

Guil saw what was about to happen a moment too late.

Olympe panicked at the touch of metal. She couldn't see the cage or the wires. Smothered by the mask and cuffed, a wave of blue sparks ricocheted over the bare skin of her arms in fear. One man touched her wrist to adjust the cuff, and the contact was too much.

'Olympe – no!' yelled Guil.

An almighty crack rang out. A burst of blue light and the air turned sharp and prickling as Olympe let out a shock strong enough to send the man flying, stronger than anything that could ever be generated by the glass cylinders and sulphur globes Guil had seen put to use.

But the cuffs had done their job. The current ran along the wiring to the cage and grounded from the top plate of copper to the bottom.

Through the goat.

It made no sound. Only went rigid as the current ran through it. Its fur curled and smoked, the wet jelly of its eyes melted down its jaw. Its tail caught fire.

The current stopped.

Olympe swung the blind lump of her head around in confusion.

The charred corpse of the goat dropped to the ground.

It had all taken a matter of seconds.

The memory came to Guil now: rats, the catacombs. Ada solving the duc's difficulties in harnessing electricity to kill.

She had just solved one more.

Olympe's voice came muffled from inside the mask; Guil couldn't make out what she said but her panic and confusion were clear. The men in silk removed the cuffs and pulled down her silk sleeves, before binding her arms again. A murmur of delight passed round Ada's staff; some took notes, others went to examine the carcass, others the cuffs.

Ada alone stayed on the mat, eyes closed. Her nose wrinkled as the acrid smell reached her. 'Clear the mess.'

Some began to heft the remains of the goat onto a sheet, and guards reappeared to haul Olympe away, who slumped limply in their arms.

In that moment, Guil hated Ada. Purely and totally.

She had become far more of a monster than he had ever been as a deserter.

He had tried to understand her in the long, dark

hours alone in his cell. Tried to feel sympathy for her. He had betrayed his friends once too. But her mask hadn't cracked once.

Maybe it was time he accepted there was no mask. This was who she was.

'Tell me,' said Guil. 'Is he proud of you? When you kill for him?'

Ada opened her eyes. They were blank.

'I did what I had to do.'

'Everyone tells themselves that. It's so much easier when you don't have a choice. But you did. Everything is a choice, Ada. You chose *this*,' he spat.

For the first time, she looked at him. There was something unreadable in her expression. For a moment, he thought she was about to say something.

Then the door swung open and Clémentine swept in. The men carrying the goat passed her and she pulled her skirts away in disgust.

'Ada! Darling.' Unbuttoning her rain-speckled pelisse, she dipped her head to receive a kiss on both cheeks. 'Success?'

Ada nodded.

'Wonderful. Philippe will be back shortly and you can tell him about it.' Her gaze landed on Guil and turned cold. Tugging off her gloves, she asked lightly, 'Why is this one here?'

'No reason at all.'

Guil took a step towards her, hands balled into fists where they were tied behind him. 'You chose this. Remember that every time there's blood on your hands. You chose this.'

Ada's blank demeanour had returned. 'I did what I had to do,' she said again.

Clémentine smiled from behind Ada's shoulder.

Guards yanked him away and he was hauled from the room.

Then so will I, thought Guil. *So will I.*

4

Hôtel de Landrieu

The row of glass bottles gave no glint in the dull, clouded day. James set them on a card table in the salon that they had turned into a new headquarters for what remained of the battalion. Four bottles, ranging from the size of his little finger to the size of his hand. Cod liver oil, vinegar, turpentine and laudanum. He wanted to sweep them all to the floor. He was supposed to be training to become a *doctor*, but medicine offered little more than the contents of a painter's studio or the nursery room.

He could not help his mother escape the palsy that swallowed her mobility, and now he was powerless to help Camille.

The truth was he had been in Paris for four months and he had been powerless to do anything at all. He had failed Olympe, Guil was captured, Ada was at terrifying risk and Camille pushed herself on despite her illness. What had James contributed? Nothing. His wrongs were piling up, and still he failed to right them.

James packed away the bottles. He couldn't bear to look at them any longer.

There was at least one way he could be useful.

A bundle of correspondence, which he had picked up from the entrance hall, lay on the card table beside the bottles. He took the letters over to Camille's desk and began to sort through bills from chandlers and butchers, credit notes from tailors and bookbinders, an order for ink that had been rejected due to lack of supply, letters and invitations, and at the bottom, a folded stack of news-sheets, which Camille would pore over every evening by the light of a tallow candle. They had moved into Al's extravagant home, had at their disposal all his family's lines of credit and bank accounts, and yet Camille still watched their money like a hawk. Darned torn stockings and collected candle stubs and watered down her ink. What she had endured in the past few years would not wear off so easily, and each action drew thicker the line between the girl James had been engaged to and the one he loved now.

The bills and credit notes went into one stack, invitations and letters another; Camille left her desk in a state each night and James quietly took it upon himself to tidy it each morning, arrange their affairs and take on the day-to-day running of the household that neither Camille nor Al had any interest in. It was hardly glamorous, but it needed to happen and if that was all he could offer, so be it.

He took a tray of lunch as the bells rang the hour, and Al arrived back shortly after. The rain had come with him, sweeping across the rooftops like net closing around them.

'Isn't Paris beautiful in the rain?' said Al, shaking the water from his hair. 'It really brings out the smell of dog turds and rotting sewage. I've changed my mind, bring Robespierre back and let him burn it all down and start again.'

'Hello to you too.' James poured an extra cup of coffee.

Al fit in to the opulence of the hôtel like a second skin. James was no stranger to wealth, but the sheer excess and the gilt, vast, impractical spaces made suddenly clear the gap between his own family's money and true ancient wealth. There were times, when he got lost looking for the dining room, or searched chest after chest of silk stockings and velvet coats in search of a simple shirt, that James understood the urge to line societal parasites up against a wall and shoot them.

He supposed none of that had made it any easier for Al to cope with his family's rejection. None of it replaced love. None of that hurt could be rectified by watching them all be killed.

Still. He wore it well. This was the world he was from, and now he wielded it like a weapon.

'Where's Cam?' asked Al, as he took the coffee.

'Out.'

'Doing what?'

James shrugged. 'Nefarious deeds. Intrigue. Camille things.'

Al snorted, drained the cup and dropped it onto the desk with no regard to the splashes of coffee spraying the paperwork. James mopped it up with a sheet of blotting paper. He knew it was no use saying anything to Al about it.

'Should she be out? You know, in her ... health?' asked Al, a note of concern creeping in beneath his casual attitude.

'Do you really think I could stop her?'

'Fair point.'

James slit open an invitation to the opening of a new play and tossed it into the discard pile. At the next, he paused with the blade of the letter opener still held to the paper.

'What's a "Bal des Victimes"?' he asked. The card was edged in black and the typeface red. Woven into the border were bones and blades, the sharp beak of a crow and the empty eyes of a skull.

Al's nose wrinkled in distaste. 'Tacky. It's a ball where the guest list is exclusively made up of people who've lost someone to the guillotine. So, absolutely everyone. Just the usual crowd looking for a reason to be melodramatic.' He flung himself onto a chaise longue and threw an arm over his eyes. 'I think I'll die if I have to pretend to enjoy this new trend of plain dressing. Do you know I saw *five* men at the Palais Royal wearing that miserable all black get-up you English favour?'

James's mouth quirked. 'How lucky we are that you don't want anything to do with melodrama.' James discarded the invitation. 'You and Cam were invited but that's an easy no, then.'

Al sprang up and fished the card from the refuse. 'Oooh, are we? I'm surprised they'd let riff-raff like

Cam in. I suppose they might be feeling inclined to get a few petit bourgeois on side these days.'

'I thought you called it tacky?'

'Oh, extremely tacky. Look at the dress code – all black. I'll have to borrow something from you. I need to make an entrance.'

Smiling to himself, James went through the rest of the post and organised Camille's paperwork ready for her return. Al was infuriating, but James was sorely glad of the company. With the battalion split in half, his days were too quiet.

'When Cam gets back, I'll see if she's got anything suitable we can chuck in a vat of dye. Though I suppose her wan and ailing look will go down well. Where *is* she? Sends me out to get details from Léon, at great personal cost to us both, I might add, and then doesn't have the decency to be around when I've finished her silly little mission.'

James glanced at the clock. Al was right. Camille was in no state to exert herself, though naturally she paid his medical opinion no heed.

'I still think this is an awful plan. Of all people, why *him*?'

Al looked at James darkly. 'Battalion of the Bad Plans, remember? We have a reputation to live down to.'

James had hated the name since he'd heard it. Battalion of the Dead.

It felt too much like a prophesy.

5

The Duc's Palace

The smell of smoke tasted like home.

Ada closed her eyes and breathed in the scent of burning hair and flesh.

Well, something like home.

In her childhood there had always been wood fires to cook food. Bonfires stacked up on the land out of the back of their house, burning through the waste from the garden, burning for the beauty of the flames. At home, there had always been smoke.

Then she had come to Paris with its coal and the smog from the refineries. Always cold, always huddling too close to the ceramic stove so she singed her skirts, dried out her skin and hair.

Perhaps home had never been here. Home was with her mother and the maggots deep in the loamy earth.

Perhaps home had died with her.

'I've told Philippe a hundred times to keep your … practical experiments to the outbuildings.' Clémentine examined the mud stains on the hem of her dress and tutted. 'It's impossible to get rid of the smells.'

'What have you told me about smells?' The duc appeared in the doorway, just as spattered with mud and rain.

'That you have spent too much time alone and have forgotten that in polite society we keep the butchery to the kitchens.'

The duc laughed. 'Since when did you concern yourself with polite society?'

Clémentine snapped the end of her shawl at him with a edged smile. 'Since I spent three years rotting in a prison. It rather focuses one's mind on comfortable living.'

'Women care about a welcoming home, it is in their nature,' said a second man, who joined them, handing his coat to a footman.

Of average height and with red hair and beard that lent him a vulpine look, Charles Delacourt had arrived like an ill wind on Ada's return to Paris with the duc. A former colleague, he had worked with the duc and Comtois before the Revolution, then slunk into the shadows and kept his head low while France navigated the Scylla and Charybdis of political tumult. But with Robespierre gone, he had scented the shift in power and presented himself as an ally.

The duc had been only too happy to accept the adulation Charles had lavished upon him; the world was righting itself to the duc's mind, and of course this would mean men flocking to his side. Ada viewed his addition less rosily. She thought him a parasite, a man who swam with the current and was quick to sense its movements. That he had come back to the duc made her anxious in more ways than one: the struggle hadn't ended with her betrayal of the battalion in England. She had risked everything to position herself as a sleeper agent within the duc's operation, but now Ada had a rival for his confidences. Someone he would more readily trust.

Ada opened her eyes, considering the deep scratches in the parquet. This was what she did. Train her mind on some small thing – the tick of a clock, the rime of dust on a skirting board – and let the stomach-churning enormity of her situation slide by beyond her.

Charles was flicking through the notes taken by one of Ada's assistants during the experiment.

'I take it we attempted scenario three?' asked the duc. He braced his hands on her shoulders and they pressed kisses to each cheek.

'Subject gamma,' replied Ada.

The duc flashed a look at Clémentine. 'Ah. Well. I understand the complaints about the smell. Come, I'll have something sent to the orangery. A hot drink is called for in this weather.'

The lowering sky had broken and sullen rain fell across the gardens and the forest beyond. The stinking heat of summer and the muggy air of the battalion's rooms above the Au Petit Suisse seemed a long time ago. The duc's palace stretched from horizon to horizon, and behind it lay a maze of gardens – formal, kitchen and walled rose – several acres of hunting forest, an ice-house, stables, a lake, and at the back of the house, in two storeys of wrought iron and glass, the orangery.

It was in a sorry state after years of neglect during

the Revolution, but now an army of gardeners had revived one corner, growing more than simply oranges. Fronds and vines reached to the ceiling, the loamy damp earth mixing with the vegetal smell of crushed leaves and ruptured stems. A small iron table and chairs were set out ready for them, a servant bringing a pot of tea and a plate of madeleines. It was still cool in the orangery despite the network of clanking pipes sending heat from the furnaces and Ada was glad of the warm porcelain cup.

The duc was talking and Ada realised it was directed at her. He, Clémentine and Charles were looking expectantly and Ada smiled in apology.

'I was distracted. Forgive me.'

'The results are distracting, indeed,' said the duc. 'With the mechanics confirmed, it is simply a matter of coordination, and the vermin infesting our home will be eradicated.' The duc gave her a look of genuine warmth.

Charles cleared his throat. 'It is well done, I grant, but we must still investigate further the loss of current strength around the peripheries. I would kindly suggest you should consider your insulators before any flashy shows.' He directed the last towards Ada.

She forced a smile. 'You are quite right, thank you for the suggestion.' Her politeness was the only weapon she had to hand.

Charles led no experiments of his own, but made himself present in whatever work was being undertaken, dropping vapid comments and empty suggestions as though he were a medieval king distributing alms.

Today, Ada's star was brighter, drawing the duc's attention back to her despite Charles's efforts.

'And without you, my dear, we would never have achieved so much in so little time.' The duc reached across and clasped her hand. 'I was never fortunate enough to have children of my own, but I am glad to have had an experience such as this before my years came to a close.'

The sense of distance expanded like a telescope. At one end, the scene of Ada and the duc, hands joined among the decadent greenery; at the other, the misty vagueness of her own being, indistinct and numb.

'As am I,' Ada heard herself say.

There was more tea and tiny morsels of patisserie and other things that six months ago she would have been astonished to see available. But she felt none of it. Saw none of it.

When the duc, Charles and Clémentine rose, she came back to herself in a rush. The light had changed outside the glass walls: afternoon into evening. Ada frowned. Surely they had not sat for so long. The duc and Charles were in conversation now, Clémentine listening with the carefully crafted, inscrutable expression she so often wore. Charles and the duc led them back through the palace towards the ballroom. Ada had been losing time more and more. Sometimes she would rouse from a daydream and find her coffee cold, candles burned to stubs. Others, she would pause on the edge of her bed in the middle of dressing and only realise she had never finished when the maid came to summon her for luncheon.

At the entrance to the ballroom they stopped, and Ada forced herself to listen to what Charles was saying.

'… look over the schematics and take a view on how to install the cuffs…'

Behind a discreet curtain, ropes of wires snaked down from the ceiling where they emerged from a hole drilled into the wall between the ballroom and antechamber.

One of her team of gentlemen scientists was in shirtsleeves, working on the point where the wires ended. The duc and Charles directed a question to him, and Clémentine drew Ada aside.

'Tell me,' she said softly. 'How was she?'

It took Ada a moment to orientate herself. She thought of Olympe, head drooping in the heavy mask, lashing out with a charge of electricity, the consequences of which she could never have known.

'She will come round,' Ada lied. 'Leave it with me.'

Clémentine squeezed her hand in gratitude, and then the towering doors opened and the four of them went inside.

The floor was metal. Countless sheets of beaten and polished copper welded and riveted together to create a single surface that stretched from wall to wall. Above, another tide of copper ebbed across the ceiling, all but finished. The effect was astonishing, the melée of sound and light and noise, two golden reflections spinning away into infinity.

The work was almost done.

From some distant safe viewpoint in her mind, Ada was aware she felt sick.

This was a cage grand enough to fit many hundreds of people.

And she had designed the perfect mechanism to kill them all.

6

The Streets of Paris

It was the darkest moment of the Parisian night. The oil burned low in the lamps strung across the streets and a thick bank of autumn cloud covered the moon and stars. Dawn would arrive reluctantly in several hours' time.

For now, Paris was a city in shadow.

A figure unfurled from the blank mouth of an alley. It stood tall and shrouded in a heavy cloak. A mist had rolled in from the Seine, rippling around the silhouette as it crossed the rue des Prêcheurs to the inauspicious row of fourteenth-century buildings on the other side. The only sound was the tap of footsteps across cobbles. Like half of Paris, the medieval city clung on through fire and famine, collapsing under the weight of time. Bowed timbers sagged under jumbled roofs, small mean squares of windows punched out from the whitewashed walls.

A door stood among many. Unremarkable, warped from centuries of rain and humidity and set with an iron knocker.

The figure glanced each way along the deserted street, then knocked once. The bells of a deconsecrated church rang the hour. The shutter at one window twitched, easing open far enough for the occupant to assess their visitor. Then it closed, and the door opened. A man of middling height, narrow as a pole and all in black. His pale hair was cropped close to his head in the Revolutionary style and the bones of his face stood out in the manner of a man long deprived of good sleep. He held a basket with an empty bottle and a discarded wrapper marked with the last crumbs of cheese.

'You're late. I've had nothing to eat since yesterday.'

The figure lowered their hood and the man stopped speaking at once. Panic crossed his face.

'What are you doing here?'

Camille Laroche smiled wide enough for her incisors to show. 'My dear Docteur Comtois. I have come to make you a deal.'

PART TWO

Les Victimes

11 October 1794

1

Hôtel de Landrieu

'This is a terrible idea.' Al assessed the thin man in the dark suit, who was sitting in a Louis XIV chair and examining his nails as though he couldn't hear everything being said.

'This is our best option,' said Camille.

'No, this is unhinged, even for you. When you said you wanted me to find him, I thought you meant to squeeze him for information then toss him to the wolves, not offer him a bloody hand of friendship.' Al spoke lightly but he leaned against the wall, stiff as a corpse and radiating anger.

Camille ignored him. She was at her desk making a pretence of attending to the stack of correspondence laid out for her. Docteur Comtois was in the salon, behind a set of double doors that separated Camille's office. She had come home as dawn broke, accompanied by a figure wrapped heavily in a cloak.

James looked warily between them. 'Cam ... I'm inclined to agree. Can we trust him?'

She sliced through the flap of the envelope in one vicious movement. 'The bigger question is, can he trust us? He's wanted as an ally of Robespierre. He'll do anything to save his neck now.'

'And when he sells us out to do that?'

'Sells us out to who? This isn't the Paris we left. He has no friends and fewer allies. We're his only hope.'

Al narrowed his eyes. 'Only hope for what exactly? What did you promise him?'

'Safe passage.'

'To where?'

'That's his decision. I offered our unique skills and experience at removing people from trouble and he saw that it was the best offer he was going to get.'

At that, Al snapped. 'Why does he get any offer at all? Let them string him up.'

'You're being led by your emotions,' said Camille coolly.

'Damn right I am! That man presided over the execution of my family, do you think I'm going to be relaxed about it? I might have hated them but that doesn't mean I want to play nice with their murderer.'

Camille sliced open another letter. 'My parents were executed too. Comtois's regime killed them. You think the duc's regime will be any kinder?'

'Find anyone else but him.'

'We don't have enough allies to be choosy. He knows the duc. He knows the duc's work. We need him.' Camille held Al's gaze. 'You know what Ada has sacrificed. Where Guil and Olympe are right now. We can manage this.'

Al seethed, but bit back whatever had been on his tongue, and quietly said instead, 'You should have told me.'

James moved between them before the heat could build further. 'It's done now. We'll figure out how to get him away from the Revolutionaries and in return he'll help us to – ' James glanced to Camille – 'this is the bit where you come in.'

The Camille he had known would have rolled her eyes, made a show of annoyance at being forced to explain herself. But she was different now. Behind the desk, she sat too upright and too still, her skin so pale and thin he could see the filagree of veins at her temples and throat.

She regarded them coldly. 'We need a scientist.'

'Why?' pressed Al. 'Nothing stopping us blowing up everything the duc owns. We'll hit something useful eventually.'

'We need a scientist,' she repeated.

James wondered at the meaning beneath her words. She needed *Ada*.

Al pulled the whisky from the shelf and poured himself a finger.

'It's not even midday,' said Camille.

'It's always midnight in my soul,' said Al flatly, and knocked back the drink. He called to Comtois, 'Go on, Monsieur Scientist, be terribly clever and impress us all.'

The docteur swivelled in his chair as though he hadn't been listening the entire time.

'Present me with a problem and I shall endeavour to solve it.'

James had seen nothing of the docteur in person when he had been an enemy of the battalion, but now he didn't seem a threat to anything but clean water and soap. A straggly beard did little to disguise the narrow, pinched aspect of his face, nor did the fresh clothes he had been given after he arrived do anything to counteract months of hunger.

'I imagine you understand the problem far better than we do,' said Camille. 'You held Olympe captive for a reason, you knew the danger her abilities posed. What did *you* aim to do with them?'

'Absolutely nothing. We held the girl for her own protection.'

'I saw the manner in which you imprisoned her. Tell me again you did that for *her*.' Camille's voice was too cold.

'Oh, spare me the moral posturing, or take me back to that miserable hovel. You said you needed a scientist so give me something scientific to deal with.'

'Fine.' Camille rose and moved to the seats near the docteur. Al and James followed suit. 'Let's pretend you had no plans to utilise Olympe's gift. But if you *did*, what would they be?'

Comtois's features fell into a frown. 'You mean, what would the duc's plans be?'

Camille said nothing, her pale face and glittering eyes giving her an inhuman aspect.

'Unless he can coerce her to do as he wants, he will struggle. Otherwise she is little more than a power source. He will need some method of conducting the electrical current...' Comtois's frown deepened.

'There was an experiment he had begun to explore when I last worked with him. It was proving difficult to replicate Olympe, so he had tasked us with testing the limits of electricity. We know that lightning can kill, and yet the tricks one sees performed onstage come nowhere near that potency. The further we run a current, the more the electricity leaks and the weaker it becomes.'

'What are you thinking?' James prompted.

Comtois tapped a finger on the arm of his chair. 'Have you any indication of his current activities? Any allies he has been seen with?'

'There's a man. Delacourt,' offered Al reluctantly. 'All but moved in a few months ago. We think he is directing a portion of their work.'

Comtois sneered. 'Charles Delacourt. I knew him. A slippery specimen not much concerned with morality. It confirms my suspicions; he worked on that research. What else? What reports do you have from inside the palace?'

James exchanged a look with Al. They had no reports but what intelligence Al could source through Léon. From Ada, there could come nothing.

'We know he plans a coup. There's been building work going on at the palace. That's all we've been able to observe without getting inside. Perhaps he's simply redecorating...'

Al folded his arms. 'Or perhaps not.'

Comtois shook his head. 'I'm going to need a lot more to work with than that. For all his arrogance he is a practical man. If he has Olympe, he's no fool; he will want results quickly, and on a scale large enough to secure his victory for ever.'

'What do you need?' asked Camille.

Comtois sat forward, attention narrowed on the gaunt figure opposite. 'Schematics. Hell, I need to *see* what he's actually built. Everything we understand about using electricity relies on the flow of a current. Your best luck will be to break that flow. But I need to know exactly what he has built to tell you how.'

'Our fate would lie entirely in your hands, then. You tell us the wrong thing and we are mice in a trap.'

'Of course. But you knew that before you came to me, so you are desperate enough to take that risk. And you know that my betraying you would serve no purpose. The duc is likely enough to kill me if he sees me again. Half of Paris is baying for my blood. We are *both* in a desperate corner.'

After a beat, Camille gave a single nod of agreement.

'Tell me one thing I don't understand,' said Comtois. 'Why go to all this bother to sabotage his research? Why not just take Olympe from him again?'

'Because it's too obvious,' said Camille. 'The duc will expect us to target her; she will be guarded more securely than ever. We have to try something different. Something the duc won't expect.'

'But, Cam – we have to try, don't we?' James spoke softly. 'We can't leave her there. We have no idea what the duc might be doing to her.'

The sharp cut of Camille's gaze landed on him. 'We are all making sacrifices.' She turned back to Comtois. 'This is the end game. I must stop him now, or there may not be another chance—' She cut herself off.

Comtois had been considering Camille's words. 'He wouldn't expect you to be clever enough to understand how he intends to use Olympe – and he's right, you're not without me. But I need schematics to have a chance. If he's constructing this apparatus in his palace then there must be designs on site.'

Al arched an eyebrow. 'If it were as simple as sauntering into the duc's headquarters, don't you think we would have done that already? He knows our faces.'

Comtois shrugged. 'You didn't ask me to solve that part.'

Camille crossed to the desk, picked up the invitation to the Bal des Victimes and tossed it to Al. 'Find out if the duc is attending. Make sure he is.'

'How do you expect me to make him—' Al started, but Camille interrupted.

'I don't care. I don't care what you do. I don't care if you drain the Seine or marry an heiress or burn down the Louvre. Get it done.'

Camille had always been driven by a fire James didn't understand, but now it was burning out of control beneath her skin. Like a seam of coal ignited underground, it flared out in the glitter of her eyes and the high colour in her cheeks.

Before he could reply, she had gone, shutting the doors to her study.

'I hate it when she does that,' said Al.

James's gaze lingered on the closed doors. 'I suppose we have our next mission.'

Al caught his eye over the docteur's head and they exchanged a look.

Camille was losing control.

2

The Cells Beneath the Duc's Palace

The slot in the cell door snapped open. Guil sprang up, hands moving to catch whatever scraps of food would be flung through.

Nothing came. A lamp shone in the gap, and he squinted between his fingers. He thought he recognised the features behind the light.

Wood scraped against wood as the slot was pushed shut.

'Wait! Wait!' He jammed his hand in the gap to bar it open. 'Clémentine. Don't leave.'

In the corridor between Guil and Olympe's cells, Clémentine stood in her slippers and delicate housecoat, collecting dust and dirt around the hem. She held a candle in one hand and set of keys in another; her face was half in shadow, one eye bright and wary, the other lost in darkness.

'You haven't come before.' It was a guess. In those early days he had been barely aware of what was going on, lost in his anger and despair.

Guilt flashed across Clémentine's face and he knew

his jab had landed. Before she could reply, he asked, 'Where are the others? Don't they want to gloat over their victory?'

'I've not come to gloat,' she snapped. 'My brother and Ada are attending a debate at the National Convention. I never did care for politics.'

'Then what have you come for? All alone, in the dark, treading so softly.'

Clémentine did not respond, but turned to Olympe's cell, sending the shadows across her face.

'Be careful. She'll fight if she doesn't know who's coming in. Well, she might fight you anyway after what you've done.'

Clémentine bristled. 'I did what I had to in order to keep my daughter safe.'

'You think this safe?'

'Safer than with you and your so-called battalion.'

Clémentine unlocked the door, and it slammed open, Olympe barrelling out to collide with whoever she would find waiting. Clémentine side-stepped, narrowly avoiding losing a few teeth to the metal mask.

'Stop – Olympe. It's me.'

Olympe smacked her fist into her mother's chest, tearing at the silk of her housecoat. A muffled yell came from behind the metal. Clémentine grabbed her wrists, held her as she struggled. 'Olympe. I am your mother and I am ordering you to *calm down*.'

She fought on, thrashing against her mother's grip, but wore herself out. Dropping like a rag doll, she sank down, dragging Clémentine with her. Olympe sobbed, the sound damp and thick.

Clémentine held her close, and over her shoulder, Clémentine's gaze went to the cell behind: the dirt floor, the bucket, the lightlessness.

She turned to Guil. 'Why are the cells so dirty?'

Guil pressed his face against the slot in the door, mind racing.

It had been months, and Camille and the battalion hadn't come for them. He wanted to believe she was planning something, but for all he knew Camille had tried and failed to rescue them and she and the others were held captive by the duc somewhere else. In the darkest moments after Ada's betrayal he had wondered if Ada had broken Camille's heart too badly.

Perhaps Camille wasn't coming at all.

He could wait no longer. Ada had finalised the technology the duc needed to enact his coup. Stuck in these cells he had run out of options.

If he could get them somewhere else, then maybe they'd stand a chance.

Guil snorted. 'They are cells. I believe sluicing them out once a week is deemed satisfactory for prisoners.'

Her nose wrinkled. Guil let the silence stretch out, the guilt steep.

'I saw where the Revolutionaries kept her in the Conciergerie. It was nicer than this.'

Clémentine's eyes blazed. 'You kidnapped my daughter. What right do you have to criticise *me*?'

'Saved her,' Guil corrected.

'No, my brother tried to save her. Charged you with her rescue and you tricked him. He told me you pretended to kill her. How sick.'

Guil's pride flared. Clémentine might be their key to escape, but he could not pretend to agree with such lies.

'Perhaps if you had explained to Olympe that the man who had tortured her from birth was her *uncle* she wouldn't have begged us to take her away from him,' he said coolly. 'Or perhaps she would have begged *more*.'

Olympe spoke, unintelligible and furious. Clémentine pulled her closer, searching the blank, scuffed face of the metal.

'At least take that mask off her,' said Guil. 'If anything is "sick", it is that horror. You must keep her hidden, I understand that, but does it have to be here? Like this? I have seen your palace. I know this is a choice, not a necessity.'

Clémentine's face was pinched. 'We cannot take any risks. There are too many people who—'

'So you will lock her up for the rest of her life?'

'No. Only until … until…'

'There will always be something more. There will always be a reason to take the coward's route.' He shook his head in sorrow. 'I do not know who will survive this, but it may not be the daughter you knew.'

He had crossed a line.

Clémentine disentangled herself from Olympe, fumbled for the candle. 'I must go.'

'Wait—'

'No, I have listened to your poison words enough. She is my daughter. I will think of her first, and only.'

'And I think of her too. Which is why I am asking this: put us together. You know Olympe trusts me. You know it is cruel to leave her in isolation. If you must keep her in a place like this, at least let her know she isn't alone.'

Clémentine shut her eyes, fingers closing tightly around the keys.

Guil spoke softly. 'Can you imagine it? To live so completely at the mercy of strangers? But then, you were imprisoned too. You know exactly how it must feel.'

'Stop. Stop.'

Clémentine unlocked Guil's cell hurriedly, almost as though she could deny what she had chosen to do, if only she moved quickly enough.

He stood back, hands raised, until the door opened and he felt the stirring of fresh air against his face.

'Quick, then.' She stood to one side. 'I will explain it to Philippe. He will see.'

Guil didn't hesitate. He helped Olympe up and took her into her cell. Three seconds of freedom, and then the lock turned and it was done. Clémentine's slippers were so soft against the flagstones, he barely heard her leave.

So that was it. This was how he had used his opportunity. He could have run, but he had taken the risk of trusting Clémentine.

God help him if he was wrong.

He took Olympe's hand and squeezed, and she squeezed back. He hadn't been lying. The isolation was too painful to bear.

Olympe spoke again, but even in the quiet of the cell her voice was inaudible.

'I don't understand. I'm so sorry, I don't know what you're saying.'

She felt for his hand again, uncurled his fingers to trace something on his palm. Letters. An H to start and then three more.

The ghost of a smile curled his lip. 'Hope?'

Olympe shook her head, and moved her finger again, slower, more precise. This time the letters were clear.

The smile fell from his lips as he understood.

Hate.

3

The Steps of the Salle du Manège

As quickly as the rain had come, it passed, leaving Paris slick and bright and cold. Under a cloudless sky the National Convention gathered to debate France and its future in this new, empty world, free of Robespierre and so many other erstwhile leaders.

Al stood outside the Salle du Manège, the old riding school of the Ancien Régime, turning an enamel snuff box between his fingers. He had faint childhood memories of watching his elder brothers learn to ride in the long hall strewn with sawdust and rank with horse urine, before the Revolution had taken the building for a meeting hall for the people's new government.

The bells tolled three. The debate would halt soon, spilling politicians and observers alike into the Jardin des Tuileries. A minute later Léon swung round the corner of rue Saint-Florentin, wearing his usual eclectic mix of fashion dug from the costume box at the Théâtre

Patriotique. Today, a heavily embroidered frock coat from Al's grandfather's time, the plain black breeches favoured in London and a loose shirt unfastened at the throat, exposing a flash of Adam's apple and clavicle.

Al swallowed.

Léon stopped a little too close, the warmth of his breath ghosting over Al's lips.

Al's fingers tightened around the snuff box.

'You made it,' he said.

'Meeting me in the open now, is it? I thought you needed to be "discreet".'

'This is discreet. There are hundreds of people here, why shouldn't you be one of them?'

Léon's lopsided grin widened and Al felt his stomach flip. 'Hmm. But there's only one you *want* here.'

Stepping closer, Léon traced his fingers over the inside of Al's wrist – but then the doors to the National Convention were flung open and a tide washed down the steps.

Al looked away, hiding the blush creeping up his neck, and fished a folded scrap of paper from his pocket. 'Here. In a moment, Ada will come out of that door. I want you to pass her this – so no one sees.'

Léon's expression fell. 'When you said you wanted to see me, I was a fool to think it meant you really wanted to see me,' he sneered. 'Of course it's a job.'

Guilt curled through Al's gut but he ignored it.

'It's important. We need access to his palace when we can be sure he's out. Ada has to make sure he attends the Bal des Victimes tomorrow. I can't pass it to her, the duc knows me. It would be too suspicious.'

Léon said nothing, but he plucked the note from Al's fingers and slipped it in his pocket.

'No one wants to spend time with me if they don't have to, at least the battalion pays you to.' The joke died as soon as it left Al's lips. Léon looked him up and down in disgust.

'This is the last time.'

Before Al could say anything else, Léon crossed towards the Convention, where Ada and the duc had emerged. He joined the swirling crowd, hands shoved in his pockets, moving from group to group as though he was just another hanger-on coming to find out the latest political gossip. Ada and the duc paused, whether waiting for their carriage or to hail a cab, Al didn't know, but the crowd left a healthy space around the duc in his finery.

Still Léon couldn't get close enough.

So Al strode out, swinging his stick, a mask of feckless insouciance sliding into place. He let the crowd bring him to the steps, and as though distracted by something he'd just stepped in, smacked into the duc's shoulder.

'Excuse me – oh!' Al stopped in practised shock.

The duc narrowed his eyes. 'I know you.'

Al clicked his heels together and gave a short bow. Over Ada's shoulder, Léon watched in concern.

'Aloysious de Landrieu. Comte de Périgord, now that the rest of my family have perished.'

The duc sniffed. 'Yes. I did hear that you had taken up your family's residence again. I'm sure they'd be glad to know you are safe.'

His voice was sharp edged and Al heard the jab beneath the words. Anyone who had known anything about his family well knew what they would think of him having the run of the place.

Al smiled blandly. 'Oh, yes, didn't you hear? We're back.' Ada shot him an alarmed look, but Al continued, 'Camille and I, that is. Not much use for the battalion with Robespierre gone. It's all over now. Your side won.'

The duc considered him, icy blue eyes examining every thread of his jacket, every strand of hair. Al held his ground, letting his gaze wander to an attractive lawyer walking past. The duc's expression shifted, the muscles around his jaw and eyes relaxed. It was almost too easy, Al thought. No one wanted to take him seriously. All he had to do was hand them the scraps they needed to confirm their prejudices.

'You can see Camille yourself at the ball tomorrow,' he continued. '"Bal des Victimes". They're getting quite creative with the themes these days, don't you think?'

'I can't say I was planning to go,' said the duc.

Al laughed. 'Surely you wouldn't give up the chance to gloat over your victory? Ah, well, I suppose it's not really your world, is it? You may have won, but the future is for the young. None of this will belong to you, one way or another.'

Behind them, Léon drifted closer, enough to brush his hand against Ada's. She started almost imperceptibly, and Léon melted back into the crowd with one final pleading look at Al.

Ada got there first. Slipping the note into her pocket with one hand, she hooked the other through the duc's arm. 'I'm sure we have no interest in how you occupy your time. Of course you must attend balls. Are you not heroes of the resistance in your own way?' She smiled sweetly. 'Liberating all those people from the guillotine, I am not surprised you are first on the invitation list of any society event.'

It was true. They had gone from outlaws to heroes in a matter of months.

Ada bobbed a curtsey and led the duc to their waiting carriage.

As Al watched them go, a hand grasped his elbow and hauled him behind a shrubbery.

'What the hell was that? I thought you said they couldn't see you?' Léon was bright with anger and worry.

Al pulled his arm free. 'No, I said it would look suspicious if I tried to pass Ada a note. But I can do a perfectly good job at running cover.'

'Are you forgetting this man would happily see you dead?'

Al gave a hollow laugh. 'That's hardly a threat, my own mother felt the same way.'

'Stop, just stop. You have a clever little retort for everything. What are you running from? Me?'

Al closed his eyes. 'Maybe.'

Léon softened, and reached for Al again. 'You really think we're the first people like us? The first people who had to make something impossible work?'

'I know we're not.'

'Exactly. We've always found a way to make a life we want. So can we. You have money, resources. We could go somewhere...'

He trailed off as Al shook his head. Something caught in his throat. The words he wanted to say to Léon, the fears that stood in his way, the tangled mess of memories that hounded him.

Al searched Léon's face. 'For too long I thought I was going to die. I couldn't see anything else in my future. And now I'm not, and I'm terrified everything will be ripped away from me again if I'm stupid enough to want openly. To want a future. Can you understand that?'

Léon's mouth drew taut. 'You fear a future you cannot be certain of. Is that it?'

Al shrugged, helpless.

'I've been an actor since I was old enough to be useful and hold props,' said Léon slowly. 'I have had to work and fight and put myself on show night after night. I love it, god, I don't pretend I don't, but I have never known safety. Certainty.'

Giving Al a final look of pity and disgust, he said, 'If you are waiting to be *sure* of a future before you reach for it, you will be waiting for ever,' and walked on.

4

The Duc's Palace

The duc threw open the doors to the drawing room, a wash of cold air meeting the warmth of the stove-heated room where Clémentine sat in her housedress, feet drawn up onto the settee. Ada clasped her hands around her reticule to stop herself reaching for the note Léon had slipped her.

'Ah! There you are, my dear,' said the duc.

Clémentine startled.

'What's wrong?'

Ada closed the doors behind them gently, watching from the corner of her eye. Clémentine looked worn, thin lines drawn at the downturned edges of her mouth and between her eyes.

'Nothing.' She stretched, reached for a cold cup of tea discarded on the end table beside her.

'Are you sure? A problem shared is a problem halved.'

'Oh, Philippe, do shut up,' she snapped. 'You do not know best about everything. Give me my peace in this one moment.'

The duc looked at his sister, perplexed. 'What has got into you today?'

Clémentine pinched the bridge of her nose. 'I'm sorry. I haven't been sleeping well.'

The duc sat beside her.

'You worry about her.'

'Of course I worry, Phillipe. She has been through so much and still you ask more of her.'

Ada thought of Olympe in her mask, hauled into handcuffs to Ada's experiments. When, in any of that, did Clémentine think something had been *asked* of Olympe?

The duc knew only how to take.

'I followed you to keep her safe. But I find myself asking – at what cost?'

The duc took Clémentine's hands, held them firmly between his. 'We all have a dear cost to pay if we are to rescue France from such dire straits. Do not imagine this is easy for me.'

'She's not a monster.'

'I agree. But she is behaving like one – you have seen half our men return with bloodied noses. We have little choice but to restrain her.'

Clémentine made a noncommittal noise.

Ada took the post that was waiting for her on a silver tray and sat at her writing desk in a show of giving the siblings their privacy. Clémentine's face lingered in her mind. She had misjudged Clémentine before, but perhaps there was something here she could use. Some wedge she could drive between them. She slipped the note from Léon in among her post and began to work through the letters, opening and sorting things into neat piles.

At a hand so familiar it made her heart clench, she stopped. The ink was carefully blotted and ran evenly across the page, but the seal was a smear of wax, smudged from being hurriedly thrown on a stack of other post.

She had stopped reading her father's letters a month after she'd come back to Paris with the duc.

At first they were angry. Insisting she come home at once, that what she did was not proper. The duc had gone to him and explained Ada would not be returning, that Clémentine was her chaperone and all he wanted was for her to fulfil her potential. After that her father's letters had become long and rambling, begging her to visit, asking her opinion on a manuscript he had acquired, telling her about his day. She understood then how lonely he was. She hadn't seen it before when she had been with Camille and the battalion; furious at his betrayals and too caught up in her own sense of abandonment to see that he could feel abandoned too.

She ran her fingers over the edges of the letter, tucked her thumb under the flap to pull at the seal.

Then she dropped it unopened into the wastepaper basket.

What she was doing hurt *everyone* she loved.

The note was next. It was small and innocuous, but the message must be important for Al to have risked himself so openly. She'd hardly had more communication than this since the duel at Henley

House. She had sacrificed too much to get where she was – she couldn't risk dropping her façade for a second.

There were only a few words: a time and a place in a simple code the battalion used to coordinate jobs. She recognised Al's handwriting. He had doodled a skull with hollow, staring eyes next to it, but she didn't need the hint to understand.

The Bal des Victimes. Al had mentioned it too. They needed her there, and, she had to assume, the duc. She wasn't sure why, but she had her next mission to complete.

'What have you there?'

The duc appeared behind her and Ada startled, collecting herself quickly. 'Aren't we all to have our peace today?'

She tucked the paper into the neckline of her dress.

From the settee Clémentine laughed. 'Yes, Philippe, leave your poor women alone for one day. Go and bother Charles in the laboratory if you must bother someone.'

The duc smiled indulgently at both of their laughter. 'Indeed, a man's lot is learning how to appease his women for an easy life.'

Before, Ada would have feared the duc, but she knew him better now. Knew he needed to believe her his creature, for the sake of his pride.

After Olympe, she was his greatest achievement.

Ada stood and stretched. 'I'm glad we're not going to that ball. It sounds dreadful.'

A cloud crossed the duc's face but he said nothing.

'Imagine, all those eyes on us, wondering what we're up to.' She shook her head, closing and locking the lid of her desk. 'Those places are just to see and be seen. All those people strutting around like they own Paris, when *we* have the real power.'

She wondered if she'd laid it on too thick, but when she turned back, the duc was frowning, rifling through the mess of invitation cards on the side table.

'I think we will attend after all. Ah, here it is.'

He plucked out the black-rimmed card.

'We will?' asked Ada.

'Why not? We are invited. I am one of the great names of this city. I have seen and endured far more than any of these children running around playing at death.' He flicked the invitation, the black ink of the bones flat and dull in the autumn light. 'It is time they are reminded whose city they play in.'

Clémentine unfurled from the couch, and said a little too casually, 'I for one have no interest in coquetting around. Take Ada, if you must, she is your protégée after all. I have far better things to do here.' She flashed a nervous look at the duc, but he was too preoccupied to notice.

Curiouser and curiouser.

'Oh, very well,' said Ada, taking the invite from him. 'I must have something in black that will suit. A change of scenery will be good.'

'Better than that – we will go there as though we are studying one of our experiments.'

'How so?'

'Our electrostatic cage is nearly ready. A rat cannot

be forced to drink poison. But secrete it in something alluring, and the poison is irresistible.'

Understanding dawned on her.

'You mean to throw a party,' said Ada. 'And invite your targets.'

'Apparently a ball is an event no one can turn down,' said the duc wryly, enjoying his own cleverness. 'Charles has been assisting me to formulate this strategy. We must strike with one blow, so it is imperative we bring our enemies together. Charles suggests an electrical demonstration as a ruse – clever, I'm sure you will agree.'

It *was* clever, and Ada didn't like that Charles had thought of it. In every subtle way she tried to slow the duc down, Charles was there like some equal and opposite reaction.

'It is the eleventh today – why not the sixteenth? Fitting, don't you think? In commemoration of our dear queen's death we will enact justice.'

'But for such an event we will be forced to invite more than just the Convention men.' Ada's voice was weak.

'All wars have casualties.' The duc's face was devoid of emotion, a rigid death mask like those displayed by Madame Tussaud.

The duc had power, money, status and connections that meant something in a world after Robespierre. There was nothing she could do but acquiesce.

But he was a man.

Fragile. Human. Fervent in the belief that he was correct.

He was not without weaknesses.

Weaknesses she must exploit.

Ada thought of him sleeping in his palace amid the wreckage of a failing revolution. The rough stubble of neck, the jugular rushing with blood beneath.

Thought of taking a knife to his room and slicing his throat like Charlotte Corday with Marat in the bathtub.

Ada pinched her thigh through her dress against the wave of nausea.

To her surprise, Clémentine looked as disturbed as she felt. She might not have Olympe's stormy complexion, but her upset was easy to read.

Ada wanted to touch the note hidden in her dress for comfort. But there could be none. Their attendance at the Bal des Victimes was even more important now. She had to tell them that the duc had set a date.

There was so little time for the battalion to act.

And if they failed, she was terrified what she would be forced to do.

Camille's Bedroom, Hôtel de Landrieu

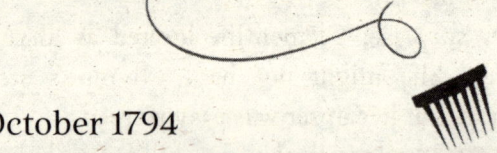

12 October 1794

Her hair hung around her like a shroud. Golden and shimmering and heavy, and masking the scent of death.

Camille picked up a hairbrush to pull it through the lock that fell over her breast. She sat at a dressing table, in front of a mirror old enough to have spotted in the corners. The hairbrush was also heavy, solid wood and carved with the initials of someone she did not know. Al's sister, perhaps. She slept in a dead woman's rooms and used a dead woman's things.

She was a dead woman too.

Camille said nothing to James or Al but she was not stupid. She saw the way her face had hollowed, the shock of scarlet in her cheeks. The brittleness of her nails and the wet, sluggish sound of her lungs. Evidence of the decay she carried inside her. The rot.

Unlike the battalion's headquarters over the Au Petit Suisse, Al's hôtel was quiet. No noise could reach the house, which sat cloaked in orchards and formal gardens on three sides, and a sprawling, paved courtyard on the fourth with its colonnades and iron-studded street doors. A castle in the heart of the city, a defensible bastion by an army of soft-footed servants, who appeared and disappeared without her notice. She was dimly aware of James with his ledgers and promissory notes and credit lines. Running a household seemed alien in its mundanity, as though she had already crossed a threshold to a place where food, fuel, laundry held no meaning.

Camille set down the brush and took up the knife. It was sharp and long, lifted from the kitchens and kept in her bedside drawer since they had arrived in Paris. She had learned never to sleep without a weapon. After her duel with the duc, she had given her pistol to James. It was tainted now. Her own blood marred the pearl handle, and the weight of it brought back the pain of the bullet grazing her hip. The wound had healed, but she had gained another nightmare.

In one hand Camille gathered up her hair and with the knife in the other, sliced it clean through.

A rainfall of gold shimmered in the air, and then it was done; her hair lay in hanks on the parquet floor and fanned around her head, shorn and wild. In the mirror she watched it settle, at her jaw on one side, the other touching her shoulder.

It wasn't enough.

She hacked away, sawing as close to the skin as she dared.

Trembling, Camille returned the knife to the table.

The face in the mirror was not the stranger she expected.

It was her mother looking back.

Her mother prepared for the guillotine, in her thin shift and bare face, staring down death.

Camille threw open the balcony doors and stepped outside. The wind was cold against her scalp, an unfamiliar sensation.

Paris glittered under the stars. The pinpricks of candles in windows, streetlights, and the fires that burned from clashes between those who had backed the terror and those who revelled in its downfall.

Retribution was coming. France was weak. Directionless. Easy prey.

Above, the winter sky blazed cold and unchanging. The stars had seen countless kings rule and die, countless revolutions founder. The tide had turned on Robespierre and his faction. Six months ago, it would have been all she wanted. Revenge for her mother, the Revolution rescued from darkness. But what had followed was a power vacuum in which the fragility of the world seemed so exposed.

Her parents hadn't died for their principles, as she'd thought. They'd died because of the petty jealousies and desires that poisoned life everywhere.

The Revolution was no different.

She thought of Ada then. Across the city in another palace, submitting to such terrible risk because Camille had told her it was worth the sacrifice. Whatever Camille did now, whatever choices she made in the time she had left, they would be for her. For Guil, Al, James. Olympe. She would stop the duc for *them*.

'Are you planning to jump?'

Al appeared beside her on the balcony, tailcoat thrown over his arm and neat black waistcoat buttoned tight over his flowing shirt. He had the knife in one hand.

'I came to ask if you were ready for the ball, but it turns out you've decided to star in a solo performance of Woman Losing the Plot. What on earth are you doing?'

They went back inside, and Camille indicated the fashion magazine laid out on the dressing table. 'I thought I would try something new.'

Al pulled it towards him and his nose wrinkled. 'Coiffure à la Titus. Hmm. Not entirely sure fashion-forward is the direction I would have suggested for you.'

The plate showed a young woman wearing a white dress and blue sash under her bust; her face was in profile to show a long, aquiline nose, and her hair shorn to short, choppy locks that curled around her temples in a style reminiscent of statues of Roman Emperors.

'Can you fix it?' she asked.

'I'm not God, I'm not in the business of miracles.'

But he took the knife and gingerly tidied up the ragged mess she'd made.

Camille watched him work, and felt nothing. With her hair cropped, there was no hiding the way illness had changed her.

'There. I suppose you'll turn a few heads, but I imagine that was what you were aiming for.'

She reached for his hand, squeezed it. 'Thank you.'

Al held her gaze in the mirror in a rare moment of sincerity. 'My pleasure.'

Camille opened a jewellery box, from which she drew a length of narrow red ribbon. Wordlessly she held it out to Al, who tied it around her throat. A single red line to mark where the guillotine blade fell.

Once he had brushed the last of the hair from her shoulders, Al stepped to one side, tucked an arm behind his back and extended the other to her, lowering in the beginning of a bow. 'Shall we?'

Camille rose. She felt light. Her tether had been snipped, and now she floated free, the world narrowing to a pinpoint below.

There was nothing else she could think of. Nothing else she could consider.

There was only the mission, and her will to see it through.

6

Bal des Victimes

In an hôtel particulier, at the heart of the once-fine Marais, the old world was returning to life. The street gates were flung open, and a procession of carriages teemed from the cour d'honneur, spilling out an unending crowd of black-clad guests, in silks and brocade, powdered wigs, ostrich feathers, military uniforms and furs. A torch-lined path led them through the hôtel to the ballroom that had been hung with swags of black fabric to cover the expensive frescos and mirrors, the gold and white Rococo furniture swapped out for heavy medieval wood and black lacquer. Crystal glasses of dark red wine were served on coffins, the shutters were folded back to the inky sky above and a string quartet played arias and fugues.

Around all of the guests' throats: red ribbons.

The victims of the Terror, risen again for one night more.

Ada stood among them, rigid with discomfort. She had not lost family to the guillotine, as prescribed on the invitation, but as the duc's protégée, the door was opened to her. She wore a simple silk and organza black dress in the modern style, the waist marked loosely under the bust. Her hair was not cut short like some of the women, and she did not wear an executioner's mark. Her only concession was a pair of guillotine earrings that Clémentine had bought in vicious delight, a ruby drop of blood hanging at the bottom of each.

As she walked the room on the duc's arm, the crowd parted with snatched looks and whispered words. She was used to it by now. The duc's status and reputation set him apart, even among guests as rich and titled as this. Her position in his household raised more eyebrows.

'A cadet branch of the Bourbons five generations back, I heard…'

'Owns half of Provence, or near enough…'

'Line dies with him. That girl…'

Ada ignored them all.

They were stopped by a man she recognised from the National Convention, small eyes and fleshy jowls set in a too pink, sweaty face. He had been on the front benches for some faction she could not keep track of.

'Citoyen.' He bowed deeply. 'Louis Marchand. Deputy for section Lepeletier. I believe I saw you in attendance at the debate yesterday? Let me say that I for one am delighted to see our great families returned to public life.'

'I thank you for your generous welcome.' The duc smiled but Ada recognised the narrowing of his eyes.

The memory of the goat in the electrostatic cage

haunted her. The smell of burning flesh. The body locked too rigidly to scream.

'This is my protégée, Ada Rousset.' She curtseyed.

Marchand looked her over. 'How charming. Wherever did you find her?'

'Somewhere most unexpected,' replied the duc, with a knowing raise of an eyebrow directed at Ada.

She repressed a shudder.

'I trust we will see you with us on the sixteenth?' continued the duc.

'I received your invitation just this morning. Why, of course.'

Ada had arranged the invitations. A rush print job the duc had agreed to give her father as a sop. They were a little sloppy, printed like a playbill or pleasure garden programme – but then she had designed them that way. A PRIVATE EVENING OF ELECTRICAL WONDERMENT styled after the advertisements for scientific displays and touring electromagnetists. An exclusive event to demonstrate the potential of electricity for France's future, the specifics of which she had left carefully vague.

She'd worked fast while the duc and Charles were in meetings with their allies – meetings Ada was not invited to by unspoken agreement.

The duc's trust had its limits.

So she used the time instead to control the invites and the guest list, while Charles was busy carrying the duc's coat and cane in salons and drawing rooms across the city. He scored one point, she scored another in return.

The invitations had been delivered after dawn to four hundred of Paris's leading figures.

Ada thought of four hundred bodies burning at once, and Olympe in chains.

They exchanged a few more pleasantries, then Marchand moved off, looking pleased with himself.

'I thought he was sympathetic to our cause?' asked Ada. She took the duc's arm again, feeling the strength of his muscles. The physicality of their research kept him spry, despite his age.

It would not be easy to overpower him.

The duc's lip curled in the edge of a sneer. 'He voted for the king's trial. He commits treason by sitting in the Convention at all. He is a usurper, like the rest.'

Ada felt faint. The ball retreated into a roar of noise, a wall of faces, that Ada watched from a far distance. Several more turns of the room and they had gathered another dozen confirmed attendees.

Charles had arrived a little after them and launched his own charm offensive to secure guests. Every so often she caught a flash of his sharp eyes and closely clipped beard that came to a point at his chin; when they washed up near the banquet table by the entrance, Charles joined them to report back his progress.

A crowd had gathered near the table, pinning them in; it was time for the monstrous egg to be served and the guests watched on in horror and revulsion. Among the spread of turtle soup, black bread, caviar, mule steaks, roast venison in chocolate sauce, truffles in jelly and hundreds of cups of coffee was a pig's bladder that had been dyed black, with forty eggs boiled inside. They burst forth one by one as guests took turns to squeeze the bladder to disgorge its treasure. The sulphurous smell turned her stomach.

Ada brought her fan to her nose.

'Excuse me, I need—'

Before she could finish her sentence, a footman stepped forward to announce a new arrival.

'Aloysious de Landrieu, Comte de Périgord, and Camille du Bugue.'

A hush fell across the ballroom, followed by a rush of whispers more forceful than those that had met Ada and the duc. Al, a pretender to his family's fortune. Camille, whose parents too closely skirted the line between visionary and vandal. And the work of the battalion that had helped so many in that room.

But Ada was paying no attention.

Her breath caught. She hadn't seen Camille since that awful day in Henley House – and even then it had only been a brief reunion after a month of separation.

Camille's hair was cut short, and the bones of her face and collar stood out too sharply. She looked beautiful, but like a wraith. Like one of the dead come back.

The duc swept forward; Ada and Charles hastened after him.

'We must welcome you,' said the duc. 'How many here owe their lives, or the lives of their family, to you?'

Al bowed, and the duc kissed Camille's hand as she curtseyed.

This was his world, his victory for the taking. He was ascendant, and they were struggling to stay afloat in his wake.

The duc turned to the room and presented them both. 'Our heroes, mesdames and messieurs.'

A ripple of applause washed through the crowd, glasses raised in toast.

The battalion had returned as heroes.

And enemies of the Revolution.

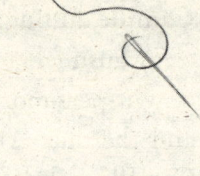

7

The Cells Beneath the Duc's Palace

Anoise like grinding metal, and the door slammed open, flooding the cell with light from an oil lamp. Weak, but blinding after the darkness Guil and Olympe had sat in for hours.

A shadow detached from the blur behind the lamp, hands outreached. Something sharp, held firmly.

Too many thoughts raced through his mind: they had been found out, they were going to be separated again, they were going to be punished.

The figure resolved itself and Clémentine kneeled beside them proffering a key. Her hair was tied back loosely and she wore a silk bedgown wrapped over her shift.

She was not supposed to be here.

'Let me,' she said. With the light behind her, it was impossible to clearly see her face.

Guil hesitated, then moved to one side so Olympe and her hideous mask were exposed.

A month or so after they had arrived back in France

her first mask, which had neat eyeholes and carefully smoothed edges, had been replaced. Olympe had used it as a battering ram so many times it had become misshapen and fragile at the hinges, and she sent skittering charges through the metal to shock anyone who touched it. Guil hadn't seen the switch. Olympe had been taken from her cell one morning and returned hours later with a heavy, crude thing shut like a clamshell over her head. Featureless, coarse, with only the mouth ripped open like some twist of scrap metal.

Clémentine unlocked the heavy padlock and pulled the two halves open. Underneath, there was a silk bag over her head, filthy and crusted with food. Olympe held herself so still she trembled with the effort. Guil grasped her hand as Clémentine gently unpeeled the bag from where it had scabbed against her mouth with spit and weeping sores. The smell was powerful.

Then the bag was gone and Olympe was revealed. Hair lank and plastered close to her skull, thick with grease and sweat. Eyes hollow and sunken.

Guil recoiled.

He had witnessed worse only in war. Soldiers trapped in horrors. The wide-eyed staring fixed on nothing.

The storm cloud of her skin was completely blank. Ash and still like the remains of a pyre. The array of stars in her inky eyes had been snuffed out.

He could not help but think that something of her had died.

Clémentine burst into tears and cupped her face. 'My girl. I'm sorry, I'm so, so sorry I let them do this to you. Can you ever forgive me?'

Olympe drew her grey lips taut over her teeth in a snarl, sharp incisors bared and face twisted in fury. Never had she looked more like the monster she was called.

Clémentine didn't flinch, only looked at her with the same love as before.

Olympe's eyes began to focus. Her shoulders lowered a fraction. Her mother kneeled in front of her, pleading. For a moment, Guil wasn't sure what Olympe would do. He was poised on his heels, ready to hold her back if she attacked.

The thread of tension between mother and daughter drew tight – then snapped. Olympe sank into Clémentine's arms with a howl. Clémentine gathered her up firmly, with the familiarity of a mother rocking her child.

He was silent in disbelief.

He had done it.

He had won some small victory against the duc. Turned Clémentine to their side, if only by a few degrees.

Olympe was free from that mask because of him.

A doubt snaked in. Something felt wrong.

Guil could see the sores on Olympe's neck and shoulders where the mask had rubbed her skin raw. But still she clung to Clémentine, like a lost child found.

Because wasn't that what she was?

Guil saw the puzzle pieces shift, the picture become more complicated.

His first step had been obvious.

But now, he was not sure where to tread next.

8

The Duc's Palace

J ames pulled his battered felt hat low over his face and broke from the treeline towards the servants' entrance at the side of the house.

Even grander than Al's, the duc's palace lay outside of Paris proper, set in huge lands of forest and tenant farms. Comtois moved along with him, the sound of leaves crunching underfoot too loud in the hush. The wait for the duc to leave had been unpleasant. They had dug through pawnshops that afternoon for workman's clothes, and the threadbare fabric and worn-through shoes did little to protect against the cold night. Their breath clouded before them. No moon shone above, only dense cloud cover that threatened rain and trees, too soon stripped of their canopy, crowded around the house.

Winter hurried ever closer, as though it could feel Paris's time running out.

At the stable block there were signs of life, grooms raking out stalls, tack being polished and stowed away. Unneeded footmen sat around a fire playing cards and smoking pipes. James and Comtois skirted along the shadows towards the door to the kitchens. It stood open, propped by an unattended bucket and mop.

A voice rang out as soon as they stepped inside.

'What are you lot doing back here at this hour? You were told not to get underfoot.'

James turned smoothly, a sheepish grin already on his face as he pulled his hat from his head. A woman – the cook, not the housekeeper, judging by her apron and lack of the great iron ring of keys all housekeepers guarded jealously.

'I know, I know,' he said. 'But we left our tools, see, and if any of them go missing it's out of my pay and I can't spare that.'

The woman didn't budge. 'And it's out of my pay if I let workmen trample the carpets and steal the silverware. The state you men leave the place in. If my boy were still alive today, I would have raised him to be a damn sight tidier.'

James willed Comtois to say nothing. He hovered awkwardly behind James; he didn't know how to do this work. If James hadn't needed him to assess the duc's invention, he would have far rather run the job alone.

'We'll keep the carpets tidy, I promise. Take our shoes off and everything.' Then he let some of the smile fall from his eyes, worrying at the brim of his hat. 'My little girl, she's not well. Please. I can't lose this money.'

It was a cheap shot, after the woman had mentioned her dead son – but it worked. She nodded once, curt.

'Go on, then. Tidy, I said!' she called after them, but James was already dragging along Comtois behind him.

'Where now?' James hissed.

Of the two of them, Comtois was the only one to have seen inside the palace, albeit several years ago, before the Revolution stopped the duc's work. Comtois indicated left up a flight of stairs – but in the end it was easy. A trail of dust sheets covered the floors, covered in scuffs and boot marks. They followed its route, ducking behind console tables and into doorways to avoid servants passing through the halls. It took a monstrous effort to maintain a place like this, James knew all too well from the lessons his father had tried to impart to him about running the family estate, and as he had learned himself in the past few months trying to run Al's family hôtel. Even with the duc away they would never truly have the place to themselves.

The path finally brought them to double doors easily twice their height. A mess of trestle tables covered in paper, coils of wire, sheets of metal, rivets, bolts and rubber mats took up the anteroom before them.

'The ballroom,' said Comtois. 'I remember this.'

'There must be plans around here that they're working from.'

They split up and took a table each, riffling through a mess of scraps and paper, news-sheets, equipment lists, pay dockets and order sheets. Nothing that looked anything like schematics.

'You know she's dying, don't you?' Comtois was so matter of fact it took James a moment to fully register the words.

His jaw tightened. 'Yes.'

'Do the others know?'

'Why are you asking me this?'

Comtois looked thoughtful. 'I made a deal with a dying woman. I want to make sure I get what I was promised if she goes before we expect.'

'If you think you can use this to your advantage—'

'What advantage? I told you before, I am a man with his back against the wall. Mistrust me if you will, but if I betray you, I betray myself too. All I want is what I am owed.'

James glared but said nothing. They returned to their search – at one point freezing in place at the distant sound of voices that came close, then veered off in another direction.

Eventually, James said, 'Al knows. The others … there wasn't time.'

'I see. Then tell me something I don't understand: if you know, why are you still here doing this? Take her away, to Switzerland. Al has the money. Why not take her somewhere with good air and less stress?'

'Camille isn't mine to take anywhere. She does what she wants.'

'Yes, she does, doesn't she? Perhaps she wants to die. I hope she doesn't plan to take us all with her.'

James wanted to lash out in return but the words didn't come to him. Comtois was right. He was failing Camille as a friend, and as her doctor. Just as he had failed his mother. He was useless to everyone he loved.

Comtois cast aside the papers and was instead drawing back a curtain of hessian that hung over a portion of the wall. He let out a low whistle.

'What is it?'

Set into the wall was a square wooden panel housing an ordered array of wires that were bundled together in silk insulation and ended in two dangling metal cuffs.

'It's an electrostatic generator … but not like any I've ever seen before. There's no glass cylinder or sulphur ball. Only…'

Their eyes went to the cuffs.

Only room for a human source.

'So this is where they generate the charge,' said James, unable to bring himself to say Olympe's name. 'But what are they doing with it?'

Comtois examined the composition of wires, how they ran into the wall. James stepped back and his foot knocked into something. Hidden by the hessian curtain was a large portfolio. He set it on the floor and untied the ribbon holding the leather covers closed.

'Comtois.' James summoned the docteur. 'Found them.'

Comtois crouched beside him and ran his fingers over the elaborate architectural plans, showing cross-sections and elevations, measurements and materials.

'It is the path for a current. Like the human chains you see in demonstrations, where the current passes from the generator to each person in turn. Only … the wires end here at the ceiling. The ceiling is … metal? And the floor … I do not understand…'

James rose and tried the handle of the ballroom doors. They opened on perfectly oiled hinges to reveal a vast space, blocked by scaffolding and the floor covered in protective sheeting.

Above, the polished copper ceiling reflected the room, and the glints of copper peeking through the fabric below.

'I do,' said James softly. 'I know what completes the chain.'

Comtois came to the door, and swore.

'Ah.'

With the space cleaned and tidied, it would be a ballroom to rival any grand palace. Many hundreds could fit inside with no bother.

Hundreds of human points to complete the chain.

9

Bal des Victimes

'Our heroes, mesdames and messieurs.'

The duc held his arms open wide and Camille and Al were buried in thunderous applause. She reached for Al's arm at the same moment he reached for her, an unconscious union as they stepped into a new and frightening arena.

Only then did Camille understand how totally the world had shifted on its axis. The battalion weren't outlaws. She had meant to sit the fence between Royalists and Revolutionaries, frightened by both their actions, but in her indecision the choice had been made for her. Robespierre had fallen and now she lived in the duc's world. Yes, the National Convention continued, there was no king on the throne. But whatever she had been fighting for, she had already lost.

Camille smiled, at once cold with dread and hot with fever.

'Thank you for the welcome, Monsieur le Duc. Much has changed since we last met. This time you have not put me on my back.'

The duc's eyes glittered with amusement. 'How is your hip? A nasty shooting injury. You young people should take more care with your violent pastimes.'

She held his gaze. She wanted to retaliate, but that was not the role she and Al could play any more. The duc thought her neutralised. She could do nothing to disabuse him of that notion.

'Healed, thank you. I seem to have quite lost my taste for the hunt.'

'Most sensible.'

Various great and grand figures, all sharp eyes and black clothes, came to thank them for saving their cousin, their sister, their son. The duc seemed to have picked up a new hanger-on, a plain man with a neatly tailored beard who introduced himself with a calculating look. Another variable Camille barely had the energy to understand. So many ways this could go wrong. So many ways she could fail.

And Ada, haunting the periphery as though to spare her the pain of a full reunion.

Her Ada, side by side with the duc.

God, she was beautiful. How long since the world had been as simple as Ada's hand on hers, the crook of her smile, her patience and her curiosity? Now she was severe and cool, regarding Camille with boredom.

This had been a mistake. She had asked Ada to hate her, to betray them, but it was too much. The heat, the lights, the smell of people. Like being crushed in a crowd before the guillotine. All eyes were on her, a thousand little needles picking at her skin; her skin that felt on fire, like she would burn up like a twist of biscuit paper held against candle flame, spiralling to the ceiling.

Al pinched the inside of her arm and she came back to herself abruptly. Someone had said something and they were all waiting for her to contribute. A wrinkle of concern appeared between Ada's eyebrows that had not been there before.

Camille made some anodyne response and the conversation moved on.

Everything was fracturing into pieces. She was falling apart.

When the flood slowed to a trickle, the duc held out his hand. 'May I have your company for the next dance? I trust your card is not yet full.'

There was no way to refuse him. Her skin prickled at the touch of his flesh against hers, and the duc swept her into the couples assembling for a quadrille. The ballroom was too hot, and she had been standing for too long. James had offered her laudanum before they had left, and she had been a fool to reject it. She had wanted to stay alert, but the exhaustion was its own fog. The duc's arm was firm around her waist, her hand clamped in his.

The music struck up, and they danced.

'How is your health, mademoiselle?'

'Quite well, thank you.'

Camille's head spun as they moved through the steps. How much had the duc noticed? Was he still watching them closely? She'd thought they'd integrated themselves into Paris society convincingly on their return from England.

'Your friend, Guillaume, is in tolerable health, I am told.'

Camille tripped over her next step and the duc had to yank her into place to stop a collision with their neighbouring couple.

'Is that so?'

She didn't know which feeling was stronger: relief or fear.

'For now.' The duc's smile was cold. 'I am pleased to hear you speak of moving past your childish misadventures. In your state I would rather think a doctor would order you to stop.'

'It has been said.'

'I suggest you listen. We both know the tide has turned on this revolution. Let it die, Mademoiselle du Bugue, and enjoy the time you have left.' His arm tightened around her waist so acutely it stole her breath. 'And if you do not, consider that I have two of your friends in my care.'

'Tell me,' said Camille, fighting to keep her voice steady. 'When you are done with whatever it is you are planning, will you let Guil go?'

The duc smiled again, a wry curl of his thin lip. 'I rather think that's up to you.' His grip loosened, and the dance drew them apart, cutting a twisting path between the other couples, then bringing them together again. The duc had lightened, moving so casually it was as though he hadn't been making threats a moment before. But Camille understood him all too clearly. Guil was his insurance policy.

They finished back near Al, Ada and Delacourt.

Camille closed her eyes, concentrated on one clear breath without a cough or hitch in her chest. The dance had been too much for her, the fear that strung her too tightly when she needed to stay calm to ease her muddy breath.

She and Al had come here on a mission. James and Comtois should have made it into the duc's palace by now. She had kept the duc occupied.

Camille's eyes snapped open. 'Where is Clémentine?' All heads turned to her. 'I mean, your sister, Monsieur le Duc, does she not join us tonight?'

Ada's eyes widened. Before she had kept herself at a distance, but now Camille thought she was trying to get her attention.

'My sister does not care for balls,' said the duc. 'She remains at home.'

Camille's stomach sank.

James and Comtois would not be alone.

Camille hadn't thought the plan through. She should have made sure all three were attending.

She was losing her grip.

Her mouth was open to say something but she had no idea what it was. The floor was unsteady, shifting beneath her feet, and she clung to Al as weak as gossamer. The candles snuffed out one by one, sinking the world into a narrow point of focus – or, no, it was her. She was being snuffed out.

There was an arm around her, holding her up and Al's voice coming from somewhere. 'Excuse us, all of this has taken a toll on her.'

The air grew cooler, there was a stone wall to lean

against. Something cold pressed against her temples. She meant to say she was fine but her breath came too short. She saw the ballroom, the bright gold of the candlelight and the black of the gowns and decorations.

And the duc, watching her. Witnessing her collapse. Triumphant.

10

The Duc's Palace

Clémentine, Guil and Olympe hurried through the palace, their way lit only by the lamp Clémentine carried, its shadows slicing the world into a burst of wall, a window, the tread of carpet, the face of a bust.

The palace was shut up for the night. Dark, silent, the sinister echo of being dragged through the corridors to Ada's experiments haunting their steps. Passing those rooms, they heard voices; on the wall, a flare of shadows from a candle. Clémentine pulled them around a corner and they waited as two workmen hurried past in hushed conversation. Guil caught a flash of a face, the familiar angle of a jaw. His brows furrowed, watching their passage along the corridor and down the stairs towards the kitchens. The taller man looked back – Guil's heart jolted.

James.

Clémentine and Olympe had already snuck away. They hadn't seen James.

Guil hung on the sharp blade of the moment, a

decision he knew would define him. He could imagine it: following James out, the night air on his skin, freedom.

Olympe left behind.

The decision was made as soon as he had the thought.

Olympe and Clémentine were only a few metres ahead. He caught them up easily. Olympe reached for his hand and he squeezed it in comfort.

Their path ended high up in the palace – not quite in the servants' area that would be too often traversed, but in a quiet set of rooms facing the formal gardens.

'This was my mother's apartment,' said Clémentine, unlocking the door. 'She died a short time after I was born. They were shut up then.'

The apartment was only two rooms connected by a joining door and decorated in the grand, heavy style of several generations before. The windows were tall and narrow and barred, shutters rusting where they were folded shut. A large bed was made up with fresh sheets. Through the connecting door, Guil could see a cot set up in what must have been the salon. It had the cold, stiff feeling of a home long lifeless.

He thought of his family's home in Marseille. His mother receiving visitors in her bedroom between various stages of dressing. An affectation of the rich, his father had called it, but his mother had enjoyed luxuriating in the money their business brought in. Their townhouse was always noisy with the sounds of the harbour a street away and the downstairs room where his father did business open to all comers, his sisters squabbling from room to room while Guil clerked in the back office. The noise of the ships, the people, the sun etched into his mind so strongly … if he closed his eyes he could smell the salt and sweat and stone.

Clémentine's mother's rooms struck him as unbearably sad. To live like this, with every luxury and yet not warmth at all.

'I think you should be safe here,' continued Clémentine. 'You'll have better food and it will be kept clean and warm.'

Guil went to the windows to touch the bars. It was a sheer drop to the terrace three storeys below.

'I'm afraid the doors will stay locked. The bars are… My mother, after she had me, wasn't well. So they put the bars on to keep her safe. To stop her doing anything stupid. Please don't do anything stupid. I'm trusting you.'

Guil frowned. 'Did they work?'

'I beg your pardon?'

'Did they keep her safe?'

Clémentine's expression hardened. 'They didn't need to in the end because she died of an infection of the blood. Sepsis. They had worried about the wrong danger.'

Olympe padded through the room barefoot and silent, touching the counterpane on the bed, the washstand that held water still steaming from the kettle.

'This was all my grandmother's?'

'Yes, darling. Come. Sit.' Clémentine drew a chair and sat Olympe down. A brush and towel sat on the washstand, and Guil realised just how prepared Clemetine was. How well she had planned this.

His opponent was clever and had a wealth of resources at her disposal.

As Clémentine cleaned Olympe's face and teased the knots from her hair, Guil quietly made an assessment of the room. It was comfortable, but sparse. No mirrors, no paintings, no busts or vases. Nothing sharp or heavy. A beautiful prison.

'I'll send a proper bath and fresh clothes tomorrow – for you both.'

Olympe kept reaching to her face to feel her bare skin. Guil wanted to stay close to her, but Clémentine had claimed the spot by her side.

Setting the cloth and brush down, Clémentine held both Olympe's hands in hers and looked at her earnestly. 'I am trusting you to understand this for what it is. Now I need you to show me you trust me.'

Olympe's face distorted in a scowl.

'Why?'

Why trust Clémentine – or why did she help imprison her in the first place, Guil didn't know.

Clémentine searched for words. Shook her head. 'I don't have a good answer. I'm so sorry. I went about protecting you in the wrong way, but you're here now, aren't you? Safe, and home with me? We can only get past this if we come to each other with open hearts. Here, I have given you all this. Will you give me something in return?'

Olympe snatched her hands back, but said nothing. Closed her eyes as exhaustion set in. She didn't resist when Clémentine drew her to the bed and tucked her in.

'Sleep, darling. We'll speak again tomorrow.'

Clémentine led Guil to the adjoining room and the space set up for him. He noted he had not been afforded fresh water or a washcloth, but the bed looked clean and warm.

She pushed the door half-closed and stepped closer to him to speak in a whisper.

'You understand what I am saying. This can only continue as long as there is no trouble. If he finds out, if there is trouble because of it … I don't know what he might do.'

Guil thought of the duc firing the pistol into Camille's hip back in England, and shivered. He understood too well.

'Where would I go? This palace is yours. And I would never leave Olympe.'

They returned to Olympe's room where Clémentine kissed her goodnight, touched her hand to her cheek, then left, locking the door behind her.

Guil approached Olympe but she rolled over, back to him.

'I'm tired,' she murmured. 'Please.'

Guil backed off. 'I am not far. If you need me…'

Olympe lay small and curled in the vast bed, stroking one finger over her cheek. The shadow of the mask that had trapped her too long.

Or – no. The ghost of her mother's touch.

11

Bal des Victimes

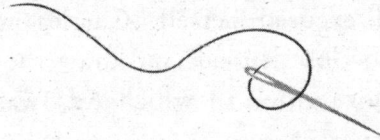

Ada held her coupe of champagne, eyes lingering on the balcony where Al had taken Camille. Her heart was racing. She hadn't seen Camille's chest so bad since … possibly ever. She had too many questions and not a single answer.

The duc was watching her thoughtfully, and Ada dragged her attention back to him.

Charles was speaking. 'It seems our experiment tonight has been a success. You have the confirmation of many guests, and we know they will show up for a spectacle.'

'Quite true,' agreed the duc. 'We must make our evening something not to be missed.'

Ada's eyes flicked back to the balcony where Camille and Ada had disappeared behind one of the heavy black drapes hung from the ceiling. 'Do you really think she's done?' she asked lightly. She didn't need to clarify who.

The duc thought about it. 'In such a revolution we have all tried to kill each other at least once. Perhaps

I can find it in myself to forgive her.' He gave Ada a satisfied smile. 'After all, she's right. I *have* won.'

She forced a smile to her lips and raised her glass. 'A toast. To sense prevailing.'

The duc and Charles lifted theirs, and echoed her words.

She set her empty coupe onto the tray of a passing footman and excused herself. Charles was more than happy to close her out and draw the duc into a political conversation of which Ada was not yet allowed to be part.

As she crossed the hall, her path drifted from the curtains with chamber pots set behind them, towards the balcony instead. With a final glance, she slipped behind the black cloth and out into the frigid night.

Camille was slumped against the wall, Al holding a wet cloth to her face. She rushed over in fear.

'What is it? What's the matter?'

Al looked at her in surprise, then something unbearably sad crossed his eyes.

Ada hesitated, frightened. 'What's going on?'

'I'm fine.' Camille spoke before Al could. Her voice was too light, too thin. 'It's hot. I haven't slept.'

A lie, but one Ada so desperately wanted to believe. She brought her hand to Camille's jaw, felt the flare of fever beneath her skin. Worry warred with her desire. She hadn't held Camille like this since England.

'Should you be here?' she asked softly.

Camille covered Ada's hand with her own, the tension between them pulled taut like a wire.

'I said I'm fine. Are you? Is it…' Camille trailed off.

Behind the curtain the noise of the ball whirled, so close the heat spilled out. And somewhere near, the duc. They were playing with fire.

Ada swallowed everything she wanted to say, and said instead, 'We don't have much time.'

'I know,' said Al. 'I'm keeping watch.'

'No. It's something else.'

As simply as she could she set out the duc's plan: the electrical demonstration, the guests, a coup. 'It will take place on the sixteenth.'

Camille's face dropped. 'But that's in four days.'

'I know. Do you have a plan?'

Camille licked her lips. 'Nearly.'

Another lie. Ada knew Camille too well to fall for it.

'You have to do something.'

'We're working on it,' said Camille with false bravado. 'Do you have the details of his plan?'

Shame closed her throat. She couldn't bear for Camille to know what she had helped create.

'Not yet.'

A beat of silence. Once, Ada would have known what Camille was thinking without having to ask. Ada had hoped talking to Camille would give her strength, but it only filled her with dread. She'd held onto the belief that beyond the duc's palace was a saviour with a plan. If she played her part, she would never have to do any worse than what she had already done.

That illusion was shattered. All that remained was the thought of a knife in her hand and the soft give of flesh.

The duc and Olympe. The two people without whom no massacre could be committed.

The curtain billowed inward, revealing snatches of dancing, music, all black and red and gold. Dripping in blood.

Ada drew a breath, and stroked Camille's face. 'Remember when we danced on the rooftop?'

Camille nodded. 'I would dance with you now if I could.'

Ada touched Camille's hair, the gentle wave that ran through it even cropped this short. Was this still the girl she knew? The girl she fell in love with? Or had they both changed too much to find each other again?

'What do you think?' asked Camille, a little bashful.

'Beautiful,' said Ada. 'I will always think you are beautiful.'

Perhaps they could find their way back from this.

Camille drew her close, their mouths a breath away.

Al interrupted them. 'Quick – he's looking for you!'

In a surge of panic, Ada drew back before Camille could kiss her. 'I have to—'

'I know. Go. Go.'

There was something unreadable in her expression and the unsettled feeling struck Ada again. There was some piece she was missing. But there was no time. The duc could not discover her here. With a final squeeze of Camille's and Al's hands, she slipped back inside, poised in the shadows. Al was right, the duc was advancing through the ballroom, scanning the crowd. She needed cover.

She spotted Marchand making his way towards the banquet table, and hastily slipped into his path.

'Deputy! Have you tried the venison? I am considering the menu for our own gathering and wanted the opinion of a man of taste.' She gave a syrupy smile. Marchand hesitated, then took the bait with gusto.

'I'd advise against venison, my dear, you will be thought unoriginal. Veal, however, makes a delightful addition to any meal...'

Ada manoeuvred them into the duc's sight, careful not to look in his direction. From the periphery of her eye, she registered him crossing the floor towards her – and Al and Camille leaving the balcony unnoticed.

A clock was ticking. Ada had told the battalion, but they had told her something too, without saying a word.

She was on her own.

If they were going to stop the duc, Ada would have to take matters into her own hands.

12

Rue de Charenton

Al held onto the leather strap as their carriage halted in the backstreets near Port Saint-Antoine. The door opened and James and Comtois hopped up. Al rapped his cane on the roof and they set off towards the Marais.

'So?' Camille was half in shadow, the lanterns flashing squares of light across her throat as they swung like pendulums with the motion of the horses. Al had wedged his body against hers to keep her upright. He could feel the feverishness of her skin even through their clothes.

When they had left the ball, she had turned to him and asked who the funeral had been for. He had laughed at her grim joke at first, then from the confusion in her eyes realised she was serious. He had explained what they had been doing – the Bal des Victimes, the duc – and Camille had slid back into herself with a flash of fear quickly tamped down, insisting she had made a joke after all. In the carriage she had given directions to Au Petit Suisse – Al had quietly corrected the driver out of earshot.

James took his hat off and smoothed his hair away from his face. His cheeks were pink from the cold.

'We found it,' he said.

Comtois reached into his jacket and pulled out a fold of paper. 'We couldn't take the schematics without raising suspicion, but I made a copy as best I could.'

He unfurled it and held it in the scrap of light.

'It's clever. Horribly clever. A chain of electricity like you see at any display, but it is the people themselves who complete the links.'

Al studied the mess of lines and angles. 'What does that mean?'

'Think of it like this: the duc aims to use Olympe to generate a current in the ceiling – like a storm cloud – and each person standing on that metal floor will be a lightning rod.'

'Four hundred lightning strikes at once,' said James. 'We don't have the power to create anything like that with a standard electrostatic generator, but Olympe could do it.'

Al thought of Olympe in the grounds of Henley House months ago, blazing blue and bright, bolts of power bursting from her in every direction. The duc had finally understood how to harness that ability, and direct it to a target.

'That is extremely messed up.'

'Can you stop it?' asked Camille.

'Give me time. I barely understand the plans yet.'

'You don't have time. You have four days. The duc plans to throw a party of his own.'

She explained what Ada had told them.

'It's a trap,' said James.

'It's a bloodbath,' said Al.

Comtois tapped his finger against the window. 'Clever again. A coup made as modern and efficient as the guillotine made execution. In one evening, all his opponents will be out of the way. He will be able to install whomever he likes on the throne, in the government.'

The colour drained from James's face. 'We have to stop it.'

'We can't be seen to do anything to get in the way of the duc's plans,' said Camille. 'Guil is still alive.'

Something unclenched in Al's chest at the news. They had hoped, but they had not known for sure.

'If we put a foot out of place, draw any suspicion onto ourselves at all…'

She didn't have to finish the sentence for them to understand. The duc had no mercy.

Camille sat forward, eyes glittering. 'What we do now means everything. Not just Guil's life, or Olympe's, or Ada's, or even ours. We must stop the duc, for the sake of everyone attending this event. For the sake of Paris – all of France. This is the end for the duc. We have to ensure it.'

It was the Camille Al had known when he had joined the battalion, intense and fervent in her determination. But doubt coloured the memory. How much of her fire had always been fever?

They had four days to stop the duc, or everything they had sacrificed would be for nothing.

Al only hoped Camille could last that long.

PART THREE

Drowning, Drowning, Drowned

13 October 1794

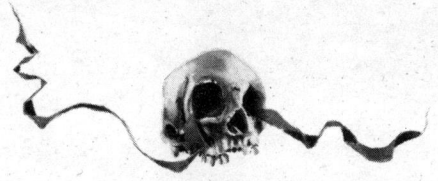

1

The Duc's Palace

Ada picked up the knife.

It was a delicate thing. A fine ivory handle, old and well used enough that it dipped and rounded in the shape of the human hand, dark lines scored through where the bone had become brittle. The blade itself was as slim as her finger, curved to finish at a wickedly sharp point. A skinning knife from the kit of a naturalist; one of the many objects that filled the duc's rooms like a cabinet of curiosities.

She had learned a well-balanced knife had its centre of gravity exactly where blade met handle. Neither too heavy nor too light, merely an extension of her hand that she could wield like a painter with a brush. The duc had made her art death. He had taken the beauty she had seen in the world and twisted it towards killing.

She had done so many unspeakable things.

Perhaps she could do one more.

Ada slipped the knife up her sleeve.

Opening her bedroom door, she found Clémentine standing outside, hand raised to knock. Both women stared at each other in surprise.

'I need you to come with me.' Clémentine spoke quickly, hushed, and closed a hand around Ada's wrist. The knife shifted against the skin of Ada's arm and she wondered if Clémentine felt the handle.

'What's going on?' Ada asked.

Clémentine didn't reply.

She led Ada through the palace, past the ballroom where the scaffolding was being dismantled, cleaners taking the place of workmen to ready the space for the event in three days, past the laboratory rooms and the office where she had spent months researching theories and writing up her work, Charles cherry-picking the best of it to present as his own, past the dining room where she had breakfasted with the duc for months, past the drawing room where she read and took tea and played cards.

In the upper reaches of the palace, they stopped outside a set of rooms Ada had not been to before. Clémentine drew a key from her pocket, face crumpled in indecision. For the moment Ada forgot about the knife and the plans she had for it, her curiosity piqued.

'Whatever it is, you can tell me,' she said softly. 'You trust me, don't you?'

Clémentine wavered, then nodded, fitting the key to the lock.

'I've done something. You cannot tell Philippe.'

The Dining Room, Hôtel de Landrieu

James sat down at the breakfast table, having assembled himself a sensible plate of cold ham, a few slices of cheese and a soft white roll from the selection of food on the sideboard. He had been up early, unable to sleep while his mind was full of the duc's strange creation, and sat with the stolen schematics trying to work his way through every wire, every join, every switch.

He wasn't sure Camille had slept at all. He had found her already up, sitting at her desk with a distant look. She had refused to let him examine her when they had returned from the ball, blaming her fainting fit on the noise and heat. The silent truth lay heavy between them.

Al was the last to arrive at breakfast, yawning theatrically and sprawling himself across a chair to lick butter from a knife in lieu of a meal. Camille had a stack of papers in front of her and a pot of coffee to herself and nothing to eat; Comtois was hastily shovelling down as much as he could manage. James thought of his months in hiding that had wasted the fat from his bones. They were all damaged. Each of them missing pieces of themselves.

James looked down at his own sensible breakfast and neat clothes and wondered what he had lost. It felt like nothing compared to Camille and Al, and yet everything. It wasn't that the Revolution had taken something from him. No, it was what he had done.

He had lost himself.

Comtois pulled out the schematics, making pencil marks across the diagram, his coffee cup leaving a ring in one corner.

'What's it all about, then?' asked Al. 'How doomed are we on a scale of one to ten?'

'If you have nothing more helpful to offer than a smart quip, I suggest you be quiet and allow me to focus on my work,' said Comtois without looking up.

'Er – Docteur, why don't we take the plans to the other room?' said James. 'We'll have more space to spread them out, away from –' James carefully ignored Al, who was twisting his face in a surprisingly good impression of Comtois's scowl of concentration – 'breakfast.'

Comtois obliged to be moved into the neighbouring drawing room they had turned into a makeshift laboratory. Without Ada, no one had thought about what they might need. James had his medical bag and some textbooks, but half the things Comtois talked about went entirely over his head. He should have been starting another term at the university hospital, but with Wickham dead he'd taken a few months out while a new tutor was found for him and the other students. The truth was, he couldn't imagine going back to that life now. Knowing Camille and the battalion were on the other side of the Channel fighting for something so much bigger than themselves, how could he have been content with the smallness of tutorials and lectures, exams and revision?

Not that he was any more use here.

Comtois had made a whole series of notes across

the plans that James couldn't begin to understand. The plans themselves brought to mind the illustrations of the network of veins and arteries in the human body, a complex network of interdependent pathways it took a lifetime to comprehend. He'd followed the elementary ideas around electricity enough to follow Wickham's experiments, but this was too far advanced. He appreciated why Camille wanted to bring Comtois into their group: without Ada, they were helpless to understand the duc's plans.

'Can I ask you something?' said James.

'If the answer is short.' Comtois spoke around the pencil clamped between his teeth.

James mustered the right words. 'Do you think we can do this? Work out how to stop this ... this machine in time?'

Comtois looked up for the first time, a fine eyebrow arched. In that moment he reminded James so strongly of Wickham it was like a blow. That wickedly sharp intellect, the derision for anyone too slow to keep up with his thinking. James felt himself back in the surgical theatre, Wickham scalpel in hand, looking at James with a sneer when he said something stupid. And Edward beside him, suppressing a laugh as James floundered for something to say.

Edward. Another knife in the chest. Maybe it wasn't Wickham he saw in Comtois, maybe it was Edward. Someone burning so brightly in their intellect and ambition, someone looking for a cause that would have them. Perhaps in different circumstances, he and Edward could have ended up in Comtois's place.

'You're asking me if I can comprehend and dismantle the product of a lifetime's work in a matter of days?'

James flushed. 'If I can help…'

'You can't.'

James didn't need a further hint. He shut the door quietly and rejoined Camille and Al.

'How does it look?' asked Camille. 'Is he close?'

James gave a weak smile. 'Give him time. It's complicated.'

'We don't have time. He needs to deliver his side of the bargain or I'm throwing him back where I found him. We're not a charity.'

'Any more,' said Al.

Camille glared but said nothing.

James poured himself another cup of coffee for something to do.

Camille flipped the page in her book and James saw a list of aristocratic names: a pre-Revolution directory of the French nobility. A list of the duc's potential targets.

'That's not going to end well either. Disaster, my constant mistress.' Al pulled his chair closer to James with a screech of wood on wood, and spoke sotto voce. 'Toss for it?'

'What?'

'Heads, you ask Camille what she's planning; tails, I run away so you still have to ask?' He pulled a coin from his pocket. 'Comtois is trying to solve a Gordian knot next door and if he doesn't complete his quest, we all fall into a nightmarish future ruled by the duc. Maybe we should have a plan B?'

'Fine, I'll ask.'

'Those who are about to die, we salute you.'

James turned to Camille, casually elbowing Al, and cleared his throat.

Camille looked up. 'Yes?'

'Not to rush you or anything, but – ah – the duc's event is in three days. What do we do if Comtois can't figure it out in time? Shouldn't we have a backup?'

He looked at her hopefully.

Camille stared him down. 'That sounds sensible, yes. What are you suggesting?'

'Oh. My plan?'

'Yes. I want to hear your plan. Surely it's not only me who has ideas?'

James wanted to sink into the earth. 'No. That's fair. I'll – we'll – think of something.'

He knew what his plan had to be.

If Comtois was in part responsible for the situation with the duc, then James was responsible for Olympe ending up in his clutches.

Comtois was cleaning up his mess.

James had to clean up his own.

He was saved further embarrassment by the arrival of a footman.

'Do you still require the carriage this morning, madame?'

Camille frowned. 'The carriage?'

Realisation struck James at once. 'The salon – Madame de Beauharnais's literary salon is this morning. We accepted the invitation a week ago.'

Al groaned. 'Do we have to go? I can't be held

115

responsible for what I'll do if someone tries to talk to me about poetry.'

'Perhaps now isn't the right time.'

Camille's frown deepened. 'We have to go. Beauharnaise was executed by the Jacobins, his wife is exactly the sort of anti-Revolutionary figure we should show ourselves to be associated with.'

'Are you sure?'

'You know what the duc said. Guil's life is at stake.' She slammed her book shut. 'We cannot let our façade drop for a moment.'

Al stretched and stood. 'In that case, I need to change. I can only be charming in green silk.'

James ordered the carriage ready. It took Camille a moment longer to get up, and she held onto the back of the chair as though a spell of dizziness were passing over her. James came to her side and cradled her arm in his.

'Are you all right?'

She shook him off. 'I'm fine.'

Her fire would take her through the day, and maybe the next, but they both knew there was only so long she could spend that coin before the debt would come due. James thought about saying something, then decided not to.

Perhaps it was kinder to let them live the lie a little longer.

2

The House of Madame
de Beauharnaise

James and Al flanked Camille as they entered the
salon.

The cult of the literary salon had been long
established in Paris when Revolutionary ideas
spread through its members. The shape of Camille's
childhood had been formed around her parents' daily
departures to attend the different salons around the
city, or the frantic hours of preparation when they
were to host their own. The advent of adulthood
was marked by her passage from listening from the
cracked door of her room, to hovering in the corner
of the drawing room filled with guests who spoke
over her. Slowly, she had found her feet – and found
Ada. Camille could not remember which room at
whose house it had been when she had first seen Ada,
but the moment itself: the golden play of candlelight
against her brown skin, the curls teased down to
frame her face, the bright, quick look in her eye as

she drank in the cleverness around her. Camille had been captivated at once.

Madame de Beauharnaise's salon was not one she remembered from before. It looked as they all did: the best room in the apartment thrown open to a mixture of students and politicians, writers and lawyers, artists and philosophers, gathered in the name of knowledge and the edification of man.

Only now, that light of hope had been firmly quashed and a tension lay thick in the air.

Five years of chaos, of utopian dreams turned bloody, had left few willing to trust. The political landscape shifted like a snowdrift, unstable and treacherous. One wrong move and an avalanche could swallow anyone whole.

Camille held James's arm tighter. They had to come, she was sure of it. The duc would be watching them, he had all but said as much. But the atmosphere was unpleasant, all whispered voices and darting glances. *Everyone* was watching *everyone.* Robespierre was gone; who would succeed him was an unsure bet. It would not be difficult for the duc's coup to triumph. Indeed, Camille suspected half the guests at the salon would thank him for bringing stability.

They took a turn around the room, assessing the crowd. Faces she recognised, quiet nods and tentative smiles in their direction growing more bold. There – a man who'd paid them enough money to rent their rooms over the Au Petite Suisse for a month in return for rescuing his son. And here, a woman whose husband owed his head to the battalion's quick thinking. Al greeted them all, as charismatic as he had ever been, accepting thanks graciously and making sure they were seen by everyone present.

Six months ago, they would never have acknowledged her in public. Now, Camille had her hand grasped, her cheek kissed. She was a saint among them. Just as the duc had said at the Bal des Victimes: she was the hero of the aristocracy her battalion had saved.

The thought was a galling one. Perhaps the duc had been right. This had all been the stupid, ill-conceived game of a child. None of the people she saved deserved to die; she had thought her parents would have been proud. What a foolish idea. The truth was she acted from anger and pain and some desperate attempt to rewrite the failures of her past. All she had done was contribute to the fall of their beloved Revolution.

Their hostess took the floor and called for quiet as chairs were brought forward by an army of servants. Al found them three towards the back where they drew together in a line of defence.

'Thank you for gathering with me today, to share this little moment of culture, this brief sojourn to the artistic imagination. I, as many of you, have lived so long beside grief, become its common companion. But in poetry only have I found some quarter...'

Al groaned quietly. 'Oh god, I just knew it was going to be poetry.'

Out of view from everyone but Camille, he tipped the clear contents of a flask into his tea. James, god love him, was earnestly trying to be interested in some truly excruciating lines of verse. Camille shut her eyes, allowed the drone of the reader's voice to wash over her. She felt tired all too easily these days. If only she could rest, just for a little while, she was sure she would be able to think more clearly, come up with a better plan than to trust the enemy who had nearly sent Al to his death. It ticked away at the back of her mind: Comtois and the duc, this electric machine everyone was so afraid of that made so little sense to her. She was so far out of her depth she couldn't let herself think about it for more than a moment. Turning to Comtois would have to be the right choice. He would solve the puzzle, there was no other option.

Solve the puzzle, stop the duc, save Olympe, Ada and Guil.

That list was getting too long.

She must have slept without realising for James was rousing her gently and all around the the crowd was standing, chattering a little more lightly than before. Groggily, she allowed herself to be lifted to her feet. That flame of determination still burned inside her, though it might be small and fragile. But there, she had done what she'd intended. They had come somewhere public, been visible as harmless socialites – no, better than that, antagonists to the Revolution. The duc could look on this as proof she had been telling the truth, and Guil would be safe a little longer.

The crowd parted, and a woman moved against the flow, coming towards Camille. Dressed plainly, she stood out in a way she clearly wished she didn't, and came to them quickly, surreptitiously.

'Camille Laroche?'

Camille exchanged glances with Al and James. She had gone by that name when they lived at the Au Petit Suisse. Now she went by her old name, du Bugue.

'Camille Laroche, of the Bataillon des Morts?' she asked again.

Several heads turned towards them. Camille stiffened. 'At one time, yes.'

The woman took her hands abruptly, pulling them close enough she could see her eyes bloodshot from worry and the deep line etched between her eyebrows.

'Please. You must help me. My husband is in the Saint Lazare prison. They say he is a supporter of Robespierre but all he ever did was attend a few Jacobin club meetings, like so many in this room. He is no devil. But they will not listen.' She gripped Camille's hands tighter. 'Please. I have nowhere else to turn.'

More eyes on them now, the centre of attention in the salon moving slowly towards them. A flare of panic shot along Camille's spine.

Sick to her stomach, she pulled her hands away and took a step back, schooling her expression into something cold and stony.

'We do not do such things any more, and certainly not for a Jacobin,' she spoke loudly enough for everyone to hear. If gossip were to reach the duc's ears, let it be of this moment. 'My advice to you is leave the city, put as much distance between you and your husband. That world is over now, and you must find a way to live in this new one.'

The words tasted bitter.

The woman crumpled, but nodded. Accepted her helplessness all too easily.

James found her hand but she shook it off. She couldn't accept comfort, not with this guilt on her head.

Al called the carriage around, and they joined the wave of departing guests. Their outing had been a success.

But all Camille could think was, no, her parents wouldn't be proud of her.

They wouldn't even know her.

Hôtel de Landrieu

Al had barely dismounted the carriage when Camille whipped through the entrance and into the hôtel like a streak of fire.

'Comtois!'

Her voice echoed off the marble floors and high ceilings.

'Comtois? Where the hell are you?'

Al and James hurried after her. Al wasn't sure whether she'd collapse before she found him.

In the end, he was where they had left him in his makeshift laboratory, bent over the plans of the duc's invention, his hair yanked this way and that, his shirt untucked.

'Well?' she snapped. 'Have you cracked it?'

He glared at her. 'Obviously not.'

'That's not bloody good enough.'

'It's complicated.'

'Oh, well, okay, then. I'll just send a message to the duc and ask him to hold off for a few weeks, shall I?' She slammed her palm on the table. 'I don't care if it's complicated. You're here to do one thing and so far you haven't done it.'

Comtois snapped. 'Then maybe you should have brought me in earlier so I actually had enough time to decode the life's work of a mad man! You think I am not trying hard enough? You force me to stake my life on solving an impossible task. I want this done more than anyone!'

They glowered at each other across the table.

Al leaned against the wall, and hid a yawn. His parents had fought all the time. It left him feeling suddenly exhausted, with the urge to hide from the world where he would be alone, but safe.

'I still think you should just blow the whole place up,' he said instead.

There was no point to hiding, he'd learned that. Nowhere was safe.

'Shut up, Al,' said Camille, but Comtois looked at him.

'Blow it up?'

Al shrugged. 'I don't have a clue how that contraption works, but I imagine it won't work well smashed to a thousand pieces.'

The corner of Comtois's mouth quirked. Then he burst into a peel of laugher and dropped down into a chair, head in his hands.

Camille scowled. 'What's so funny?'

'Because that's actually a good plan.'

Al blinked. 'Is it?'

'It's better than anything I've come up with.'

Camille hesitated, and Al didn't miss the way she held onto the edge of the table for stability.

'All right, then,' she conceded. 'Let's blow it up.'

'Hang on a moment,' said James. 'What about Olympe and Ada and Guil? They're inside the palace, we can't risk blowing them up too.'

Comtois shrugged. 'We'd only need a localised detonation, something to damage the controls. You'd give yourself some decent cover to get them out too, but I don't really care what you do about your friends.'

'Cam – I'm not saying you're wrong but—'

'Then don't say it.'

'It's too risky.'

'You want a risk-free plan? What's your plan, then?' asked Camille, turning on James. 'Go on, I'd like to hear it. You all wait for me to come up with something. You're all far too happy to let me take responsibility for everything. You can't always do that. What will you do when I'm—'

She pulled herself up short, the unspoken words loud.

'To be fair, I came up with the blow-it-up plan,' said Al to break the tension. Everyone ignored him.

James coloured, but stood his ground. 'We could try to get Olympe away from him again but that hasn't worked so well for us so far. And the duc will have them guarded... Or we could do something to the guests? Stop them coming – or get them away from the ballroom.'

'Good,' said Camille. 'Sort that out.'

James opened his mouth then shut it again. 'All right.'

'Fine.' A stalemate. Camille jerked her hand at Comtois. 'You do whatever it is you think is a risk-free plan. I'm going to get gunpowder.'

Camille slammed the dining room door behind her, plates rattling on the sideboard.

James and Al exchanged a look.

They were running out of time on too many fronts.

3

Olympe and Guil's Room

Guil snapped upright as the door opened and Ada stepped in.

She was blank with shock.

It had been too much to hope that Clémentine's gesture of moving them to better accommodation would mean a stop to the experiments. Guil positioned himself between Ada and Olympe. He would not let her out of his sight again.

Clémentine hovered behind her. 'It's better like this, don't you think? It's as secure as those horrible cellar rooms, and no one ever comes to this part of the house anyway so really it's about the same, when you think about it…'

Clémentine stopped, realising she was gabbling.

Ada shut the door behind her. 'I won't tell anyone.'

Olympe was resting in bed, black hair fanned out across the pillow. The storm cloud of her laid dormant, the light snuffed in her eyes.

She watched Ada.

'She's not strong enough for more experiments,' said Guil.

'I'm not planning any,' said Ada, but she wouldn't meet Guil's gaze.

What was Clémentine playing at?

'It's good to see you without the mask,' Ada continued, with a pathetic note of hope in her voice.

Olympe's mouth twisted in a sneer, and she rolled over, back to Ada.

Clémentine sat on the bed, stroking the hair from Olympe's cheek. 'See? We all want the best for you.' Olympe shrugged her mother's hand away.

Guil considered Ada. There was a strange tension emanating from her that he couldn't place. Perhaps she knew of further planned experiments that Clémentine did not. But some piece still seemed missing.

A thought caught in his mind: if Ada truly was the duc's ally, wouldn't she be angrier about this betrayal?

His rage got the better of him. So what if Ada was playing her own games? This was all her doing. He could allow himself no sympathy for her. If she felt ill at ease with her new bedfellows, that was her problem.

'This isn't a zoo,' said Guil. 'You can see for yourself Olympe needs peace.'

Clémentine smoothed the covers. 'You are a good friend to her.' She caught Guil's hand for a moment, squeezed it. 'My brother is nearly done with his silly scheming. It will be different then, I promise. This is nearly over.'

Over her shoulder, Guil caught Ada's reaction. She looked grey, as though she was going to be sick. Then Clémentine swept her out, arm hooked through hers and talking about the plans she had for the winter season.

The lock clicked and he and Olympe were alone.

She sat up, covers slithering down to her knees. Static already clouded her hair around her face, running across her skin like tears. Guil took a step back – but Olympe closed her eyes, balled her fists and drew all the electric current back inside herself like rainwater seeping into the earth. He had never seen her exert so much control.

Olympe opened her eyes. A constellation of stars filled each one so brightly they shone.

Guil swallowed. 'Olympe?'

Her fists twisted the silk of her nightdress taut, the warp and weft of the fabric straining.

Then it went slack. She shook her head. 'I'm fine. I'm fine.'

'Are you sure?' Tentatively he sat at the foot of her bed, choosing a different spot to Clémentine.

'Yes. It was – a shock.'

'As it was for me.'

Olympe looked at him properly, sliding from angered goddess to anguished girl in one motion. 'I can't believe it's her. Like a demon snuck in and stole my friend.'

'I sympathise with the sentiment, but we have to remember that is the person we knew. That is still Ada. Only a side we were not privy to before.'

'I still can't understand it. It's as though I have all the pieces but however I try to fit them together I can make no picture.'

'Sometimes people do things we don't understand.'

He thought of himself, nearly two years ago,

slipping away from the snuffling, snoring bodies of his sleeping comrades, stolen rations filling his pack as he melted into the night. His army friends had not understood his desertion. Meeting Jean-Baptiste with Ada had proven that to him.

'I should have known you cannot trust anyone,' said Olympe. 'If my mother could do what she's done to me, why not Ada?'

She was right, but the thought still hurt.

Olympe went quiet, drew her knees to her chest and wrapped her arms around her legs. She seemed somehow smaller, more fragile than she had when she was in the mask. Guil had not known what to expect after she was freed, but it had not been this.

Olympe spoke softly. 'I will not go back into that mask. That cell. Whatever it takes, I will do it.'

Guil went to his room to give Olympe privacy to change into the fresh clothes that were waiting on a chair by her washstand. When he came back he found her kneeling beside it, crouched over something on the floor. A flash of blue illuminated her face, the sharp look of concentration. There was a hum of static in the air.

Guil frowned. 'What are you doing?'

'I found a mouse,' she said without looking up.

He leaned over her shoulder to observe the tiny body of the mouse pressed against the skirting board. It had the withered, stiff appearance of something that had been dead for a while.

Olympe held her finger out to its grey body, and let another pulse of electricity spark blue. A whisker twitched.

'What are you doing to it?'

'In England I met a man called Edward,' she said.

Guil remembered the boy with skin mottled like a bruise, his frightening strength. 'I saw him. The experiment.'

'Edward,' Olympe corrected. 'He died, and they brought him back with electricity. Like me.'

'You were treated with electricity before you were born,' said Guil.

'The start of life, or the end of it – what difference is there? Electricity made us who we are.' She pulsed another spark into the mouse so its legs kicked. 'He tried to be who he was. He tried to be more than what he had been made for. They killed him for it.' She looked at Guil, eyes bright and unreadable.

She sent a final burst of current into the mouse and in a flash its whole body contorted, tiny claws curling, limbs pumping. Then it was up, eyes blazing blue, and skittering across the boards. It bumped into a chest of drawers where it sparked off a metal fitting, and scurried quickly underneath.

Olympe looked at the blue shimmer over her fingers thoughtfully.

'I wonder what they will do to me?'

4

Hôtel de Landrieu

Al drifted around the sprawling expanse of the house now meant to be his home. It had been his home for most of his life, in theory. It was where he had been born, in his mother's room between the carved oak posters of her marriage bed.

There had been some debate when he arrived whether this pink, squirming thing was her husband's or the product of one of her various lovers. It was the fashionable thing to take a mistress or paramour, and it wasn't always easy to be sure where a child had come from. The dates of her husband's travels had been examined, and it had been decided that on the balance of probabilities, Al was his.

Al felt like he had been living in that liminal space since.

Who was Léon to tell him he could never escape uncertainty? He knew that. He *knew* that, in the core of his being, it was written into the cord of his muscle and the snap of his bones. He existed in borrowed space, borrowed time. He had grown familiar with that uncertainty like the pain of a splinter buried too deep; a constant companion, pain as ever present as the air around him or winter that would sound the death of autumn.

If he didn't want to face more of it, then it was not because he was a fool.

He came to the blue room, unoriginally named by his mother, he assumed, because all the upholstery was blue. It was not his room, but as close as there had ever been. Between early childhood in the nursery and the school dormitories of Louis le Grand, he had never been assigned a room of his own.

Al crouched in front of an unused armoire. In his time it had held nothing more than mothballs and spare cleaning supplies.

And one more thing.

He pulled open each drawer in turn until, reaching to the very back, he found what he was looking for: a small bag of dried chestnuts. They were withered and smelled of camphor, but when he broke one open and chewed it, the taste was acceptable.

He flopped onto a sofa, legs swung over the arm and worked his way through the bag. It had been a long time since he had had to hide food around the hôtel. That life had been behind him. For a while, *life* had been behind him. The death warrant was a full stop waiting to happen. Before that, his parents throwing him out. So many full stops in a life he could only live in snatches, one eye on the clock, one eye waiting for time to be called and another door to close. In a life like that, figuring out what you wanted from it meant little. It was easier and safer simply not to want.

Something hard was wedged between the seat and back of the sofa, small and cylindrical. He dug it out and held the laudanum bottle up to the light. More than a dribble left at the bottom. Desire and guilt bloomed together.

Léon wasn't wrong. Al did run away. He ran away to the bottom of a glass or the sticky drip of bitter drugs. He'd been running long before the battalion, before England and living with the shock and trauma of his parents' deaths. Grief had been like a cold wave crashing over him. He'd wanted to leave all of it. Stop existing. But he did know, he *did* know, that wasn't an option. Because, for all that it made no sense, fate had traded his parents' lives for his. So he'd come back to Paris. Found a reason to keep going, because suddenly everything he did mattered. Everything he chose would be something he would have to live with for the rest of his life. That was why he cared.

Camille had found out she was going to die. He had discovered he was going to *live*.

He didn't know which sentence was worse.

Al looked at the laudanum.

The horror of the vast, unknowable future reared up before him. He pulled the stopper out of the bottle and let a skin of laudanum stretch over his tongue, deep, familiar self-loathing settling heavy on his chest.

'Debauched party for one?' James swung into the room, hands in his pockets.

Al corked the bottle smoothly and slipped it into his pocket, along with his vulnerability.

'Of course, dear boy. I'll make the end days of Rome look like a nunnery.'

James pulled up a chair. 'I've been thinking.'

'My condolences.'

'We can't stop the guests attending. There's not enough time, and how could we reach everyone? So we'll have to do something at the event itself. Stop them gathering in that deathtrap.'

The bitter taste lingered in Al's mouth, his head fuzzy and soft. Everything that hurt felt so far away.

'Drug them.' His voice sounded alien. 'That's what I would do. Spike the drinks. No one asks twice what's going round on a tray.'

James's eyebrow raised. 'Are you suggesting we give a whole party the runs?'

Al smiled at the ceiling. 'It'll clear the dance floor.'

'Right. Well. I can think of something to make everyone ill. We just need to work out how to spike the drinks. Before it's delivered would be easiest to spike the whole batch, but there are too many variables. We'll need access to the kitchens at the duc's palace. We could get hired as staff for the event. That would give us a lot of access.'

'You want to try the same trick twice? You don't think they'll recognise you as the pretend workman?'

'It's a risk.' James clenched his jaw. 'If Camille gets the explosives, we'll have a way in to set them up. But we can't rely on her to see this one through. We're on our own.'

'Dying makes things tricky like that.'

'It's not something to be glib about,' snapped James.

Al rolled onto his side, eyes slipping in and out of focus. 'I'm not glib. You're right. We have to do this one for her.'

'We have to give her a last win.' James looked away in pain. 'So we let her hunt for explosives. But this job is ours.'

5

Clémentine's Laboratory

Ada walked in mute shock from the room at the top of the palace all the way through the unending corridors and staircases to a small cabinet to one side of their private apartments. Clémentine led and she followed without thinking. Ada couldn't understand what had just happened. Clémentine had acted against the duc in such a daring way. All the rules that had seemed so fixed the day before had gone.

If Clémentine was capable of this, what else might she do?

The cabinet was Clémentine's own laboratory; less than half the size of the laboratory Ada used for the duc's projects, and kitted out in scraps the duc had discarded. Clémentine's withdrawal from the duc's research had been gradual. As their experiments had grown more visceral, more bloody, Clémentine had turned her face from it.

Ada had thought her unwilling to see what they did to her daughter, what consequences her choices had wrought.

Now Ada understood she must have been forming her own plans all along. Clémentine had always been a creature of survival, shifting and adapting to the walls closing in around her. Why would that stop now? Ada knew that all too well. Clémentine had betrayed her confidence when it suited her.

It would not do to underestimate her.

Clémentine had slumped behind her desk, head in her hands.

Ada came over, touched a finger to the stained wooden corner. 'You moved them,' she said.

'Yes.'

She searched for the right words and could only come up with one. 'Why?'

Clémentine looked up, a fire in her eyes. 'You saw how they kept her.'

Ah. There it was.

Ada hadn't.

She had never ventured into the cells, only summoned Olympe when she was needed. Clémentine hadn't been the only one unwilling to confront what she had done. There was only so much Ada could acknowledge before she would break; if she'd known all of it, it would have been impossible to go on.

So instead she hid herself in the other truth: it was a risk she could not take. Her place in the duc's trust was tenuous. His political star was rising and Charles vied for the duc's attention, it was all she could do to keep up with them both. She was no use as a sleeper agent if she lost her footing and the duc slipped out of reach. If she'd shown any interest in Olympe and

Guil beyond what was needed for their research it could raise the duc's suspicions. And if she saw them privately she didn't know if she would be able to resist the temptation to tell them the truth – and that was the last thing she would be able to do. So it was easier never to see them.

Ada swallowed around the thickness in her throat.

'It was monstrous,' she said. A safe guess.

Clémentine brooded at her desk. 'I have let Phillipe have too much control.'

Clémentine had felt able to let the duc use Olympe before, but maybe her time apart, her time in prison herself, had changed her.

Suddenly, Clémentine went to a workbench and pulled back the sackcloth covering it. Beneath was a glass tube, wiring, something that looked like a battery and a length of carbon. Ada crossed to the bench, studying the apparatus.

'Let me show you something,' said Clémentine.

She closed the shutters, sending them into darkness. Then she moved the wires to do something Ada couldn't make out, and within the briefest of moments the carbon began to glow, at first red, then orange, into yellow and finally white hot, as bright as a candle flame. Clémentine took the glass jar, which Ada saw now was the chimney of an oil lamp, and placed it over the carbon. The light was diffused, a soft warm light that illuminated the room as well – better even – than a candelabra.

They stood in silence for a moment, observing the miracle of the creation of light.

'Beautiful, isn't it?'

Ada held her hand near the glass, feeling the heat. 'Astonishing.'

'I always said Olympe was a miracle, not a monster. Look at what her gifts could lead to. A burst of current into a battery could create how many of these? How many households without the money for candles given reprieve, how easy to light our streets? How many women going blind sewing in the dark? It is a revolution of its own.'

'Has the duc seen this?'

Clémentine's expression closed off. 'He has. He called it frivolous.'

Ada was incredulous. 'Frivolous?'

'A toy,' sneered Clémentine.

'Surely he can see the potential?'

Clémentine yanked the wire out and the glow faded. 'Let me tell you the truth about my brother. He thinks the only power worth having is that which creates the powerless. Society makes him powerful, which makes me powerless. You're his pet right now, but don't you see how easy it was for Charles Delacourt to slide into place at his side? The duc will only ever see us as powerless. As tools for him to use as he wants, and I'm a fool for having forgotten it.'

Ada thought, then, of her own father. Another man who courted the power society would grant him, who thought any action he made justified because he was so convinced of his own cause. How her life with him had been comfortable but cold; how Clémentine must have spent most of her life in the same way. An unmarried mother at the mercy of the men around her. Easier to acquiesce to the order of the world than fight for something different.

But Clémentine was older now, hardened. She understood her own power.

Ada thought of the glowing carbon. The invention as revolutionary as anything the duc had achieved.

The puzzle pieces shifted again.

6

A Village Outside Paris

J ames elbowed his way through the crowded tap room, cap pulled low and feet chafing in the worn boots he had used when sneaking into the duc's palace the night before. Al was right, trying the same trick twice was dangerous, but he pushed the thought from his mind. There would be lots of unfamiliar staff brought in to run an event this big, he'd be just another face among hundreds. He couldn't let his courage fail him now.

Camille needed him.

He owed her this.

Together in the blue room he and Al had split the job down into its parts: James would get hired into the kitchens to spike the drinks, Al would wrangle an invite to circulate among the guests and persuade them all to drink. James didn't need anything complicated: a little vitriol of copper was as effective an emetic as anything else he could obtain from a pharmacy, and his medical bag was well stocked with the staple. The plan was simple; the difficulty was in the execution.

It had brought him to a tavern in the nearest village to the duc's palace, a scrap of crossroads and cottages serving the tenant farms on the duc's land and travellers on their way to Paris. He couldn't approach the kitchens directly and risk the cook recognising him. But they had been watching the duc's movements for months to come up with a plan of attack, and he knew that most of the servants came to this tavern if they got a moment.

His target leaned against the bar, nursing a beer: the head footman of the duc's household was tall and handsome, as footmen were required to be, and was angling for the position as under-butler when the moment arose. He drank with his fellow servants, but never to excess, and considered himself a wise judge of character.

James took up a spot near the head footman at the bar and ignored him. The barman poured James a half-measure from the tapped keg and held his hand out for payment. James made a show of pulling out a scant handful of clipped slivers of coins and carefully counting them out to make exact change. The barman showed no interest in James's downcast expression or the meagre scraps returned to his pocket. James took a sip of the beer, angling his head to show his clean profile, the strong set of his jaw.

'More clip than coin, there,' said the head footman, easing along the bar.

James glanced at him, a tentative smile at his lips. 'Happens when payday doesn't come that often.'

'A truth we all know. What is it they pay you for?'

'Lately? Anything as will pay enough for bed and food. Before, I was in service. Started off as a boot boy when I could hold the polish and worked my way up. Hard to find places needing someone who knows how to serve at table and care for the silverware. Seems like the world doesn't want us for anything.' James gave a false laugh and drank. 'Not that I need to be bothering you with my worries.'

The head footman held out a hand. 'Henri.'

'Louis.' James took his hand. He nodded at Henri's large tankard. 'Looks like someone pays you all right.'

'They do that.' For a moment James didn't think he'd take the bait, then Henri said, 'I'm same as you. Footman come up from boot boy. Nothing wrong with it. Honest work and you're better fed than working the fields like my father and his father.'

'Salut to that.' James knocked his glass against Henri's and they drank.

The trick wasn't to seem too eager. Better the offer than the ask.

'You're not from round here,' said Henri, and James faltered for only a second.

'I suppose you'd recognise me if I was,' he said smoothly.

'That, and there's something in your accent.'

Inwardly, James cursed. He had thought his French perfect.

'You spotted it.'

Henri shifted, propping both elbows on the bar. 'Let me guess.'

James held himself with false lightness, waiting.

'Belgium. Wallonia.'

The tension melted away. 'Guilty as charged.'

'I knew it. Something flat and Germanic in those vowels.' Henri drained his tankard. 'I'm going to offer you a job, Louis.'

James's eyebrows shot up.

'Not a permanent one, mind. We've got a big production going on at the house. We need as many extra footmen as I can get my hands on. Can't guarantee it'll lead to anything permanent but if you're half the worker you make yourself out to be I'd be surprised if it doesn't. Consider this a trial. How does that sound?'

'When do I show up?'

'Are you doing anything now?'

Abbaye de Saint-Germain-des-Prés

Camille leaned against the wall at the corner of the rue des Ciseaux and the rue Sainte-Marguerite. The autumn evening was short, and already the lamps were being lit. Opposite, through a break in the rows of shops and townhouses, was the recently dissolved monastery. The Revolutionary government had sold off some church property for the national good, and kept some for itself to be used as billets for soldiers, warehouses and stores. Right now, the abbey was put to use as a factory producing salpêtre. The key ingredient in gunpowder.

The metal gate to the abbey side-entrance had been

reinforced and two guards stood watch. Comtois was next to her in a battered felt hat pulled down to cover much of his face.

'Is it really necessary to drag me along?'

'Yes. You're the only one who can tell me if what I've picked up is worthless. I need you.'

He sank further into himself, as though he could will himself into invisibility.

They had been there for an hour, observing from various positions around the abbey and the buildings that clustered close to it. The guards hadn't changed. There was no sign of exactly where the salpêtre was being stored, but she'd noticed a dray cart loaded with barrels exiting a service yard to the rear earlier on. The abbey estate was sprawling, with hundreds of windows and doors and alleys. It was unguardable.

'Getting in won't be the problem,' she said. 'Getting out with a useful quantity will be the hard part.'

She felt a desperate pang of longing for Guil in that moment. With his soldier's uniform and training, he would have been invaluable.

And she missed her friend, the one who could tell her what side of the edge of madness she walked on. Now she was only careening forward, unable to see whether a cliff edge loomed in the mist.

Her head throbbed. It hurt so constantly it was part of her. A too-lightness that made her thoughts scatter, slipping between her fingers.

'You're not going to keel over on me, are you?'

She hated the look of genuine concern on his face. It made her feel small and helpless and out of control.

Camille grabbed his arm and marched them away in a surge of energy.

'Hey! Let go. Where are we going?'

'To break in.'

'Oh. I suppose it's that easy.'

She led them through the warren of alleys threading through the stables and laundries and tenements butting up against the abbey. It was hard to trace the line between the abbey itself and the flotsam washed up against its bulk, but then Camille turned down another alley and the solidity of the stone was unmistakable.

As were the series of windows hastily stripped of stained glass and boarded over.

Camille looked up at the thin boards, held in place by a single nail at each end.

'Yes. I think it might be that easy.'

The Duc's Palace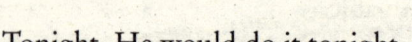

Tonight. He would do it tonight.

Guil paced before the door, a makeshift lock pick in hand. They needed to balance leaving it late enough for the palace to have gone to bed, with early enough they'd have as long a stretch as possible in the dark to get away. The moon was waning; tonight it would be a new moon. The longest stretch of darkness they would be afforded for another month.

Following Clémentine's visit, Olympe had asked to be on her own. He'd been confused, and a little hurt.

After so much time in that cell solitude was the last thing he thought she would want. But she'd rolled deeper into her covers and shut her eyes, so he had taken her at her word and gone to his room. He understood sorrow and the strange things it demanded.

So he'd stripped his room for anything he could use to get them out. Behind a dresser no one had thought to move, he'd found it: a hat pin, dropped countless years ago in a moment of haste and never retrieved. The strain of the last few days was catching up with him and he must have slept, because when he'd woken, the connecting door was locked, and he had heard Clémentine's voice murmuring to Olympe who was crying softly.

That had left him more ill at ease than anything else.

First, he opened the door to the corridor. It was silent, only the tread of Clémentine's and Ada's feet marking the pile of the rugs.

He took his shoes off and tied them together by the laces to hang around his neck: they must move as silently as possible.

He kneeled at the connecting door between his room and Olympe's.

He had done his best to memorise the route Clémentine had led them through, and had replayed their route to the outside countless times in his mind. Along the corridor to the main staircase – the servants' staircase was far more likely to be in use so exposed as it was, the grand staircase was their best bet. Then down to the ground floor and the first open room with windows they could reach. His shirt around his hand to break the glass, and then out into the perfect, crisp autumn air.

Then it was several hours' walk to Paris. They could be disappearing into the crowd by sunrise.

The hat pin clicked against the last tumbler. The door swung inwards, revealing Olympe's room, silent and dark. Guil padded to her bedside, rested his hand on her shoulder.

'Olympe. We must go.'

She woke, confused. He drew her from her bed.

'Guil? What are you doing?'

'They are all abed, this is our best chance.'

She fumbled into her slippers and followed him out into the corridor.

'Wait—'

'If we are fast, we can get to the outskirts of Paris before anyone notices.'

Olympe stopped and Guil was pulled up short. She wrenched her arm from his hand.

'Stop. Guil—'

'What? Is something wrong?'

In the darkness, Olympe was nothing but shadow and the pinpricks of light in her eyes.

'I'm not going with you.'

Hôtel de Landrieu

A collection of glasses filled the baize table in front of Al, each one drained to the dregs. Beside them a bottle of brandy was knocked on its side. He knew this was not good. There was a memory, hazy and indistinct, of arriving at the club already unsteady on his feet and ogling anyone with a pulse. Fortunately, it was the sort of club where that behaviour made you an automatic member.

Somewhere above the colonnades of the Palais Royal, a vigorous night-time economy of sex work, gambling tables and druggeries welcomed nightfall. Al had brushed away the advances of all three and settled in for a session of industrial strength drinking. He was there to obtain an invitation to the duc's electrical demonstration, but he'd already found his target – a sandy-haired youth who held his drink as well as a bucket with a leak – and was watching him from a dark corner table as far away from the atrocious musicians as possible.

It was nothing more than going through the motions at this point. Work out a job, acquire a target, execute the plan. He could do it with his eyes shut – or so drunk the floor was wobbling, as it may be.

Was this really a life? Was this really what he wanted to do with the one that had unexpectedly dropped in his lap?

It was better than some ways he could spend it and worse than others. He was no Camille, he didn't live for the thrill of a daring plan pulled off. He had no intellectual curiosity like Ada, or guilt like Guil. He had nothing. He was nothing.

Al glanced back over at his quarry and found him missing. Searching the crowd of heads he spotted him near the door.

With a curse, he staggered up and grabbed his jacket and cane.

The man didn't get far.

After shuffling out of the Palais Royal, he turned into an alleyway and leaned against the wall as the tinkle of water rang out. Al wrinkled his nose. Paris already smelled terrible, it didn't need every passing pissant adding to it.

It should have been an easy move. Brush past, and a little light fingerwork to lift out the invite Al had seen him wave around the card table in pride. But perhaps the seventh brandy had been a bad idea, because somehow Al's legs disobeyed him and he ended up knocking the man into the wall.

He turned, more cross than Al expected, a line of urine splattered down his trousers. Al opened his mouth with the full intention of apologising, but instead found himself laughing hysterically. The man grew furious and grabbed for Al's lapel.

This was all becoming rather tedious. He didn't want to be out in some stupid stinking alleyway in the middle of the night with angry drunks. He wanted to be cosy and drunk at home with a soft bed waiting and a warm Léon. This was all Camille's fault. If only she didn't have to be dying, Al wouldn't have to do selfless things like smack this man over the head with his cane.

It only took one hit. Al swung it at the side of his head with a healthy crack and the man dropped to the floor, where there was more than just urine to stain his trousers.

'What a shocking display of violence,' said Al to nobody. 'What is Paris coming to?'

He bent down to riffle through the man's pockets to take the invite, and also his money for good measure, before enduring a short fight with gravity to get back upright.

The money came in handy to pay a passing sedan chair to take him back to his hôtel, where he stumbled into the battalion's apartments on the wrong side of sobering up and smelling of someone else's piss.

The place was empty.

Al drifted through the countless rooms. Camille's study – empty. James's bedroom – empty. Even the hastily outfitted room they had put Comtois in – empty. The stoves burned warm, candles were lit waiting for the household to return. But no one had.

He was all alone.

The feeling hit him like a wall. Maybe it was the drink. Maybe it was everything that had happened in the past few days, but suddenly he was crawling onto the nearest couch and curling up in a ball to sob, deep and long like he had as a child when he had still held hope, before he had learned crying meant nothing, before he had learned to bury himself in drink and music and other people's bodies.

The sofa was stiff horsehair and smelled of years of smoke and sweat. When he stopped crying, the silence slipped in around him and as he lay he began to pick out the texture of it; the tock of the carriage clock, the crackle of a low quality candle flame, the hush of his own breath against silk upholstery.

He could go back out now. Smother himself so it was impossible to think, to feel anything at all. But he had spent half the night doing that already and he had sunk deeper and deeper into the void that had cracked open inside him.

He had done the only thing he knew to do to make the feeling go away and it was not working.

The darkness had wormed deep inside him now and he could not escape it.

If this was how life was always going to be, he wasn't sure he wanted the future he'd been granted.

The memory came to him then of Ada finding him at the Bal en Crystal, picking a fight with Léon, lashing out at Ada the closer she tried to get to him. He didn't deserve the people around him. He pushed them away like it was a sport. Against all odds, there were those who still loved him, but he didn't know how to be around them without trying to destroy it.

His mother and father had never loved him. He had grown up in the barren spaces where love should have been.

But they were dead now. That was over.

All he had now was the battalion, Léon.

But for how much longer?

8

Abbaye de Saint-
Germain-des-Prés

Ada stepped out of the carriage on the rue Sainte-Marguerite, avoiding the slop running through the gutters, and on the other side Charles and the duc dismounted. The abbey loomed in a mass of shadows too tall to be lit by the lamps strung over the streets; a metal gate opened and they were ushered into the silent stone corridors and courtyards beyond.

She had been so distracted all day she had completely forgotten about the duc's planned trip that evening. He'd refused to explain why they were visiting a salpêtre factory, only smiling at his own coy mystery. Charles seemed less pleased that Ada was being brought into whatever secret he and the duc had been discussing behind closed doors for months.

At this time of night, the factory was quiet, production shut down for the day. Signs of its new use marred the walls in smoke dirtying the paint, chips in the whitewashed murals. Ada caught glimpses of manufacture in the nave as they passed through the cloisters, a flash of machinery, workbenches. A strange collision of grand industrial scale mapped against medieval gothic.

They were delivered to a back room, one of several off a long corridor that snaked the length of the nave. Inside it was whitewashed, with plain furniture as simple as the abbey was grand. It had the feel of a room that had been clerical at its inception and would go on being unremarkable until its destruction.

The most striking thing was the bed, and the boy sitting on it. He was pale and slender, perhaps fifteen, and dressed as plainly as the room was. But there was something in his poise, the assured disregard for anything but his own wants and comforts.

Ada looked to the duc but before she could say anything a different man rose to greet him. Of an age with the duc, they could have been brothers if not for the overt differences, short where the duc was tall, stocky where he was lithe.

'My dear duc. How good to see you. When you said you had news that couldn't be put in writing, I knew at once what it must be.'

The duc smiled, clasped his arm. 'François, I knew you would. The cause is grateful for your loyalty. The Master of Armaments is an important ally.'

'I may only have this factory right now, but whatever you need I will turn it to your service.'

The duc went to the boy, kneeled before him and kissed his hand. 'Monseigneur le Dauphin.'

Ada's eyes flew open.

There was no way this boy was the Dauphin.

Louis Charles, the only surviving son of the king and queen was just nine, and secured in the Temple prison, though rumoured to be dead.

So who was he?

Charles copied the duc then moved to one side, radiating displeasure.

The duc summoned her forward. 'Let me introduce my protégée, Ada Rousset.'

She curtseyed, staring fixedly at the floor.

'My pleasure.'

The boy stretched his legs. 'Tell me, how much longer am I to stay holed up in here?'

'That is the good news I have come with. I expect all obstacles to be cleared in a matter of days. Then you will be restored to your grateful public.'

François brought a jug and glasses. 'A toast?' He poured five cups of claret. 'To the Bourbon restoration!'

Ada echoed it and drank, unfeeling.

'I don't mean to be rude,' she began, 'but who...' There were not enough questions.

François laughed. 'I'll let you field this one, Phillipe.'

'Ah, Ada, do not trouble yourself too much. The noble house of Bourbon is scattered far and wide. Monseigneur le Dauphin might be from a cadet branch of the family, but we have been assured by genealogists of his claim.'

'But the Dauphin – I mean, the king in the Temple?'

The duc and Charles exchanged looks. 'After everything he has been through, he is not in a state to rule,' said the duc diplomatically.

'I heard they've walled him in and he's not spoken a word since his deposition against his mother,' said the Dauphin.

The duc closed his eyes, pained. 'There are many such rumours, yes.'

'So this is…' His replacement, Ada wanted to say.

'France's future,' supplied the duc.

'I am ready to serve,' said the boy earnestly. 'I watched what happened to my family from Vienna; I could not do anything to help then, so I will do whatever it takes now.'

Ada felt a flash of sympathy for this boy. What story had he been told to winkle him out of his safe home over the mountains? Young and malleable and willing to obey the duc's every command.

She saw it now. A king like this would need a regent.

Her thoughts were interrupted by yelling in the corridor.

Ada recognised that voice.

The Duc's Palace

'I'm not going with you.'

The world lurched sideways. Guil stared at Olympe, uncomprehending.

'What do you mean? Of course you are.'

'No, Guil. I'm not.'

'We can escape. This is why I manoeuvred us from those cells.'

'And I'm grateful, I truly am. But I cannot leave.'

'Why? What will you do here?'

He heard his voice grow louder, loud enough to echo off the walls and carry through the palace.

He reached for her arm and she stepped back.

Her patience broke. 'No. Guil. It's over. It's *over*. Can't you see that? They've won.'

'That's not true. Camille—'

'—is nowhere to be seen. Even Ada saw the truth. There is no meaning in fighting.'

'No *meaning*?'

'You think I can run for the rest of my life? It was always coming to this.'

'Olympe—'

But his voice had carried too far.

They had been heard.

Footsteps drew near, candlelight bobbing on the wall. Guil looked at the approaching shadows in panic. This was their one chance.

Olympe took another step back. Mouthed the word, *Go*.

He hesitated, the knife edge of indecision cutting him to the quick. The terms of his choice lay stark before him. To survive, to stand any chance of helping the battalion stop the duc, he must desert again.

Or he could stay, powerless but loyal.

The blade would cut him however he held it.

He made his choice, holding the pain close.

He bolted, sick to his stomach, and left Olympe alone in the dark.

9

Abbaye de Saint-Germain-des-Prés

I t was the muffled work of a few minutes to pry the boards off the windows of the abbey, hoist themselves through the window, and into the cool, musty interior. Camille crouched on the floor where she dropped, gathering her breath that would not come.

She waited for the noise of discovery, angry voices, footsteps, muskets.

Comtois scrambled over the ledge and landed beside her.

'Now what?'

Bracing herself on her legs, she forced herself upright. 'We're close to the service yard. They must store the gunpowder nearby ready for transport.' She went to the door, and finding it locked, took out her picks. 'We search the place until we find what we came for. Then … then I'll work out what comes next.'

The picks slipped in her sweaty fingers, her concentration scattered. Behind her came scuffling noises from Comtois moving around, but she ignored him.

One thing at a time. Unlock the door. Find the gunpowder. Get it out.

'And you're looking for…'

'Barrels prepared for transport. They mix it here and take it directly to the garrisons.'

The last tumbler clicked and the door opened.

'Like this?' Comtois was standing next to an unsealed barrel. He had dipped a scoop inside and was examining the coarse black powder.

Camille was glad the dim lighting hid her flush. Her stupidest mistake yet. She hadn't even bothered to search the room they had broken into.

'Yes. Exactly.' She dusted her hands off on her knees. 'Well, then. Is it enough? How much do we need to get rid of that – that machine?'

She felt stupid not knowing what to call the duc's creation. Ada would have explained it so she felt special, drawn into Ada's mind, given a place laid with love and patience.

Instead, all she had was the horrified reactions of a man she barely trusted, and a man she had only just learned to trust again.

Comtois eyed the contents. 'It will do. Even if we only damage the control panel, that will stop its use.' He fell silent for a moment in thought. 'I am sure you have considered that now the machine has been created, it can be created again.'

She had not.

'I know.'

'You are only buying yourself time.'

'I know.'

Time she didn't have.

She changed the subject. 'We can't move a whole barrel. We'll have to bag it up or... Or something...'

'This is gunpowder, not a barrel of flour. You can't just—'

But Camille was already kicking around the room, finding old sacks, boxes, rags and cups and anything else they could use to move it. She felt a frenzy building in her. There were so many things she couldn't think about, landmines that threatened to crack her open if she brushed against them. She pushed aside a crate to reveal a trapdoor.

'Look, there's a cellar. Maybe there's a route to the street. Or something we can use.' She grasped the ring and heaved, but it was leaden – or was it just that she was too weak? 'Help me.'

'Camille. Stop it.'

She had never heard him say her first name.

Things must be getting desperate.

She pulled again, head swimming. 'This is it. It'll be in here—'

Comtois bumped against her, fighting her grip on the ring. 'Stop it. You shouldn't be doing this in your—'

'My what?' She flung her weight into it, every fragile bird-bone set on this one task.

'Your *health*. My god, they should never have let you out.'

'*Let* me out?' Her voice was too loud. They were

shouting. Some faint, rational part of herself had a growing feeling of dread.

Something gave way; the trapdoor lurched open and the two of them collapsed into the gunpowder, spilling it over the floor.

The wind was knocked out of her. Camille lay wheezing, breath snatched.

This wasn't how she had planned this.

The door swung open to reveal the duc looking down at her. Smiling.

Abbaye de Saint-Germain-des-Prés

Ada felt sick with horror. This could not be happening.

She had done too much for it to end like this.

Camille sprawled on the floor, dusty with grey powder at the duc's feet. Alone. Helpless.

They weren't even close to the end.

This wasn't it.

This would *not* be it.

The duc observed Camille – small and squalid – and Comtois, with a sneer. 'Lost your taste for the hunt, was it?' he said. 'My, my. Lies upon lies.'

Ada raced through every option, and there were none. She should have done something at the ball. Camille wasn't up to this job. She should have told Al to stand her down.

She should have acted already.

Why hadn't she?

Months alone, close to the duc. It would have been the work of a few moments. One swift move of a knife and this wouldn't be happening.

She had been weak.

She thought, when it came to it, she would be fast. Sharp. She would make the decisions that needed to be made.

Instead, she stood dumbfounded. Useless.

Useless and helpless. They were quite the couple.

The duc lifted his oil lamp, throwing shadows across the scene, and raised his voice to summon the guards.

But Comtois was already up and charging into him. Ada didn't understand why he was here – or why he was with Camille – but he moved fast, a bullet striking the duc who crumpled, dropping the lamp. The guards were thundering along the corridor. Charles made a grab for Comtois, but he shot past, darting left as the guards went right.

'Get that man!' hissed the duc. Charles helped him up and they ran after the docteur.

It all happened in a heartbeat.

Ada was frozen.

The lamp smashed on the flagstones where gunpowder was spilled across the floor.

The flame caught.

A crackle, the lick of fire springing up.

Ada saw the barrels packed into the room. The boarded windows. The black void in the floor.

Camille on her back, eyes wide and face pale.

Ada dived, snagging an arm around Camille to pull

her slithering through the trapdoor as the fire reached the barrel and the gunpowder storeroom of the abbey ignited.

A flare of light so bright she saw it through the filigree skin of her eyelids, the empty swoop of the fall, weightless and stomach swell. The memory of another explosion: Al and Guil and the churn and boil of river water like thunder.

Then the impact.

A thousand blows rained down over her body; she curled around Camille as they fell, smacked into floor and stone and wood, noise like pain, like the burst of her own heart. Tangled together, they slammed onto the cellar floor, the weight of a building collapsing on top of them.

Something cracked, gave way.

She was falling, falling, down through the dark, through the underland, and the sense that all around her were the bones of Paris's other misfortunate dead.

PART FOUR

Descent

13 October 1794

1

The Catacombs

Consciousness came with the sharp taste of blood in her mouth.

Ada opened her eyes to darkness.

A weight lay across her back, jagged and needling. Beneath her hot and cold, rough and soft. She couldn't make sense of it. This was not her bed.

For an unshackled moment she thought of her mother's funeral. The dark, dank hole they had lowered her into, dirt and stone and prickling things. Ten-year-old Ada had wanted to climb down with her, and in her confusion, Ada thought she must be back there. Climbed down into the grave with her mother and two metres of earth holding her in place.

In the end the truth was both more prosaic and more terrifying.

The explosion in the abbey came to her in a rush of noise and fear and heat. The lantern dropping as Comtois collided with the duc. Flame racing along the scattered line of gunpowder, death waiting at the end of its path. An opening in the floor – she hadn't thought consciously of it but acted on instinct, an arm around Camille's waist as she pulled them both through.

The warmth below her was Camille, still cradled in her arms.

Bruised and winded, but alive.

Ada shifted, shucking plaster and floorboards and twisted bits of metal and barrel. And bones. Bones littered the floor, buried into the walls.

Were they sheltered in the old abbey crypt? Had the explosion snapped and wedged bone like shrapnel?

But no – she remembered hitting the floor then falling again. The space around her was too narrow, a long corridor buried in the earth.

She knew where this was.

The duc had first taken her into the network of old mining tunnels running beneath Paris like veins, shown her his hidden laboratory, his hidden sister. The subterranean world that had sheltered him while the Revolution had raged above. He had shared it with the thousands of bodies that had been moved from Paris's overflowing cemeteries. The disposable dead. Forgotten and inconvenient.

Ada lifted herself up and looked at Camille. Her skull was too clear beneath her skin, the ring of eye socket and sharp line of jaw. She could see the corpse she would become.

It was as though a door had been softly opened, an understanding she had resisted for too long.

A howl swelled inside her, hot and urgent and broken – but there was not time for that now. She could not let herself break.

Camille was here, for now.

And waking – a flutter of eye moving beneath lid, warmth bright in her skin. Ada brushed the earth and plaster dust from Camille's face as she opened her eyes – too glassy, too bright.

'What happened?' she croaked. 'Ada?'

'Yes. It's me. Here – sit up slowly.'

Camille righted herself, wincing, and touched the smear of blood in her hair.

'The explosion damaged the abbey foundations. I think we're in the tunnels below.' She explained the old mining network, the second city.

Camille blinked, adjusting to the gloom. A little light filtered from above, but a mound of rubble filled the tunnel, blocking the way they had fallen through.

'We're buried alive,' said Camille in a whisper.

Her hand reached for Ada's and for the first time in too long, they held onto each other in the face of horror.

'I suppose we're not getting out that way.' Dark humour tugged at Camille's mouth and Ada laughed louder than she was expecting to.

'No, I don't think we are.'

They stood, and took in their situation. There was only one direction to go, though the light died just a few metres ahead.

'I think I might be able to find a way through.'

'I trust you.'

Camille was barely more than shadows. Euridice, waiting in the underworld. Ada poised to lead her out, if only she could hold her nerve. If only she didn't look back.

Hand in hand, they walked into the darkness.

In the dark there was nothing but each other to cleave to. The cold earth pressed in on them, formless and unyeilding; Ada keeping one hand to the wall, the other knotted around Camille's. Her eyes strained wide, trying to adjust to the lightlessness. Time collapsed into one continual moment: the hot rush of her breath, the cautious shuffle of her feet over scattered bones, the echo of Camille a pace behind her.

She had promised Camille she could find a way through. The city was not so vast, the tunnels would be finite. But the longer they walked, the more she remembered what she had heard: streets swallowed into collapsing tunnels, shafts blocked off for safety, mine heads kilometres outside the city.

To go forward took belief that had no foundation. But what else was there? To stop would be to accept their own helplessness.

Ada squeezed Camille's hand harder.

The light was a shock when it came. First, a shape in shapelessness, a sense of volume, depth. Then, texture in the walls, variations of brown and grey. Ada could no longer assign it to hopeful hallucination. There was light.

There was escape.

A few fumbling metres further it broke through in

white shafts, geometric fractures making a maze of dust motes in the air. Ada reached up to trace their shape and felt cold flagstone. Their ceiling was someone's floor.

Camille and Ada fell into a practised union, Ada making a stirrup of her hands for Camille to climb. The flags were badly grouted in places; Camille ran her fingers over them, feeling for weakness. Her thigh pressed against Ada's cheek and Ada let herself take comfort in their closeness.

'Got it.'

Camille pushed the loose flag out of place and grey light washed into the tunnel. Ada boosted Camille up through the gap and waited as she moved round to pull Ada up after her. They collapsed onto the fragile floor, rolling quickly to one side as another flagstone gave way.

They were in a crypt.

Ada sat up, blinking in confusion.

She *knew* this crypt.

Camille wrestled a trunk out from a niche, opening it to reveal Ada's old crossbow wrapped in oilcloth.

Ada started laughing, unravelling from exhaustion and shock and tension. It was too much.

Camille whistled. 'I knew you were good, I didn't know you were *this* good.'

It made sense. The Saints-Innocents charnel house was not so far from the abbey. Paris's underground mirror city was just as complex and vast as the world above.

Camille sat beside her and they fell into silence. Ada didn't know what else there was to say. Too much and at once nothing. She wanted to talk to Camille for ever, to extend this reunion for as long as she could, but there were no words for what she felt.

She interlaced her fingers with Camille's. 'I'm sorry.'

'For what?'

'For hurting you.' Ada closed her eyes. 'For everything I've had to do.'

Camille didn't speak and Ada was glad of it. She knew Camille had asked her to do this; there was no absolution she could offer. But still, she was sorry it had meant hurting her. She was sorry they had spent Camille's precious time apart.

'What were you doing in the abbey?' she asked eventually.

'Getting gunpowder. Our plan is – was – well, it's gone now.' Camille hid her face in her hands. 'I think I'm messing this all up.'

'Tell me. Maybe I can help, like old times.'

So Camille did. She explained the plan to destroy the duc's machine, the backup James and Al were working on to drive the guests from the ballroom.

'I don't know what to do about Olympe,' said Camille. 'I've tried and failed to help her so many times.'

Ada's brow furrowed at the thought. Things had become so complex. She had been shocked by Clémentine's secret conversations with Olympe – though she shouldn't have been, Olympe was her daughter after all. For all their recent time together, Clémentine knew her far better, was far closer to her.

'The duc will be guarding Olympe diligently in the run-up to the event,' she said instead.

'I know. He'll expect us to go for her – I need to play on that somehow. Misdirect. You need to help James and Al.' Camille stopped, muddled in her words.

The fear that Ada had been nursing grew further. Camille was not okay. She had been waiting for Camille to tell her the next plan, to bring it all together. But it was clear: Camille couldn't solve this one.

The battalion was finished.

Camille, Al, Ada, Guil. Each stood alone in their own darkness. They each had to find their own way through.

'I just need time to think,' continued Camille. 'I'll find something.'

Ada took a breath. Took Camille's hand. Looked away.

'I'll take care of it. Just listen. If – if things don't work out like you meant, I can do it. The duc and I are alone a lot. If I'm quick, I can do it before he realises.'

Camille's eyes widened. 'I can't ask that of you.'

'You're not. I'm telling you. If that's where things end, so be it.'

They sat in silence again. Above they could hear the market in full swing, the harsh sound of horseshoes on cobbles. Ada dug through the supplies stashed in their old safe house and found a skin of water, a few hard tack biscuits and withered apples. Taking a knife, she sat and forced Camille to eat. A smear of blood marred her temple, and her short hair haloed around her head. Ada wet a cloth and washed the blood from her face, cleaned the cut by her eyebrow where a shard of stone had nicked her skin.

'Cam—'

Camille touched her finger to Ada's lips, quieting her. 'No more words. I'm tired of words. I just want to be with you, while I can.'

Ada hesitated. 'While you can?'

Camille didn't stumble. 'You know we can't hide here for ever.'

Ada saw the lie in it. The hundred secret, awful things beneath the surface, but right now she would let the fantasy live. Hold the pain off for another moment.

The corner of her mouth curled. 'Can't we? Shame.' She hooked an arm around Camille's waist and pulled her close enough to feel her breath. 'I guess we'll have to find something else to do while we're here.'

Camille kissed her, long and slow and sweet.

Ada didn't want sweet right now. Sweet would kill her.

She knotted her hands in Camille's shirt, held her closer, nipped her bottom lip.

Right now Ada wanted to know Camille was alive and in her arms. She *needed* it.

Camille shuddered against her, then responded in turn, digging her nails into Ada's arms, deepening the kiss.

Maybe that was what Camille needed too.

The two of them, complicit in a lie; existing only in the slender gap between truths. Weeds among the cracks. Something living. Something that endured.

While it could.

2

The Duc's Palace

When Henri had said *start now* James hadn't realised how literal that suggestion had been. He'd followed the other man on the short walk to the duc's palace, glad to hasten through the busyness in the kitchen to avoid the cook, and had landed straight into carrying an army of ornate furniture into the ballroom. The scaffolding he had seen before had all been taken down, and the copper floor was covered by sackcloth to protect it as they repopulated the room for the big event.

Servants were working around the clock to ready everything in two days' time. It was easy enough for James to pass unnoticed so long as he was quiet and helpful and ready to lift, push, carry or mop anything in his path. There was much to learn from eavesdropping: the party would be big, the guest list was long and prestigious, the duc was anxious it came off well.

He had said nothing to Al, but he had volunteered himself to infiltrate the palace because he had another mission.

Somewhere in this building was Olympe.

James was the reason Olympe was here. James was the reason she was locked up again, caged like the monster she worried she was.

It was his responsibility to break her free.

Carrying a mop and bucket, he traced the shape of the house, the grand upper rooms, the hidden staircases into the kitchens and storerooms, the stables, the scullery. In the last, he found a route down to a deeper cellar. A store for things to keep out of sight, vegetables or junk, he thought.

Or people.

It smelled musty and damp, moss-slick stone and the loamy smell of roots. The light from the room above only reached so far; James left the mop and bucket by the steps, and edged along, pushing at each door. Potatoes, broken bits of furniture, kegs of beer – he noted this for the night of the event – then two final doors. The light was barely anything, a glint on metal, a spill of water.

Both unlocked; the rooms empty.

James frowned. The air smelled different. The tang of bodies lingered, of urine and breath and fear. Around the cells, the dirt scuffed: a struggle.

Someone had been held here, but no longer.

In frustration, James collected his mop and bucket and returned to the scullery. It made no sense. The rest of the palace was too well traversed. Surely the duc would have kept Olympe somewhere dark, somewhere secret.

And Guil. If Guil was still alive.

The duc needed Olympe. He didn't need Guil. That unspoken fear had hung between the battalion in the months since they left England. Only one thought comforted him: if the duc wanted Guil dead, he wouldn't have taken him from England alive.

'Where have you been hiding that mop? We've been begging for them in the orangery.'

James startled to find a maid advancing on him, hands red from scrubbing and mob cap hanging limply over her brown hair.

'Er – sorry.'

He offered it to her but she didn't take it.

'Not me, you dimwit. Get over there. Honestly, taking on you extras is more bother than it's worth.'

James took his opportunity to escape, and hurried in the direction he remembered seeing something like a greenhouse. After a few wrong turns he stepped into the humidity of the glass structure tacked onto the side of the palace. Metal ribs arched over palm trees that brushed the first floor windows, a few unhappy orange trees struggling to thrive in the coldness of autumn and a mess of ferns spilling over the bed borders, browning and curled on the tiled paths. A sheen of wet showed it had already been mopped, but James took his out and pushed it around as he thought.

Working here would give him plenty of time to hunt for Olympe, but a bigger problem presented itself from the conversation he'd picked up: the party would serve champagne to start. He couldn't tamper with those bottles before they were opened, so he'd have to spike each glass in turn, which would be ferociously difficult. But if they were to serve a toast with the champagne it would be the best opportunity to ensure all the guests drank.

The doors slamming open and the duc and Clémentine swept in.

James ducked sideways into the greenery and held his breath.

It was late into the night, and Clémentine was in a housedress, hair hanging loose around her shoulders. The duc had been dressed for a visit outside, but it was almost hard to tell underneath the dust and blood and rips.

'Philippe – slow down – tell me: what exactly happened?' Clémentine hesitated to touch her brother's arm, as he held it stiffly.

'The damn place blew, what more do you need to know? That infuriating girl was there, and that rat Comtois. Found them scrubbing around in a powder store. She played me for a fool with her stories of penitence and reformation. She is the same little weasel she was from the first day I met her.'

James's heart stuttered. Camille – an explosion.

The duc peeled off his ruined jacket and continued, 'We had the girl cornered, so I chased Comtois when he bolted. The rat and the weasel. Vermin, vermin everywhere. I don't know which idiot made the next mistake because the whole abbey went up like a tinderbox. I'd say I'd have expected them to take more precautions but these fool Revolutionaries couldn't organise a pi—' He broke off, coughing.

'Sit down, Philippe, please. Oh – Marie, thank you.' A maid brought a jug of water and a glass.

Clémentine steered her brother into a rattan chair and poured him a drink. 'Where is Ada?'

The duc waved her off, and drained the cup.

'Well? Where is she?'

'Not a damn clue.'

Clémentine went grey. 'What do you mean?'

'I mean it was chaos. She's able to look after herself. I had to get the Dauphin out—'

'He's *not* the Dauphin,' snapped Clémentine. 'He's just some offshoot you're using as a puppet. Philippe. Are you telling me you *left* Ada there?'

He glared. 'What did you want me to do? Run *towards* the explosion?'

Clémentine fell back with a yelp of horror. 'My god, that poor girl. We must send a search party at once.'

'There are men working already. If she's dead there's nothing we can do. If she's not, she'll be taken to a hospital and we can find her tomorrow.'

The noise of the slap cracked through the glass and tile of the orangery.

Clémentine held her hand before her in shock.

'I would say I'm sorry but I'm not. You are inhumanly callous.'

The duc sat still in incredulity, the red mark on his cheek clear where it had lifted the plaster dust.

'How dare you,' he hissed.

Clémentine was shaking in anger. 'How dare *you*. You speak so much on loyalty but you know *nothing* of it.'

Clémentine bolted, tears threatening, and after a moment the duc followed, cradling his injured arm.

James crawled out of the vegetation, reeling. An explosion that Ada and Camille had both been caught up in. It was too awful to imagine. He was an idiot, he should never have let Camille go with Comtois. He should have gone himself, or told her it was too dangerous. Or done *something*.

Just as bad: the duc knew about them now. It was a terrible risk for him to be here – and Guil, oh god, Guil. The duc had said his life was forfeit if the battalion worked against him. How long before the duc acted on his threat?

He turned tail and raced through the palace with only one thought: find Guil. Then find Camille and Ada. There were too many people to save and only one of him but he had to try, however hopeless it may feel. What else was the use of him, if he didn't try?

He seemed so incapable of doing the right thing.

James swung into the servants' staircase, and came face to face with someone racing down.

Colliding with him, eyes wide in shock, was Guil. The two of them crashed to the steps, the world lurching as they fell.

Saints-Innocents Crypt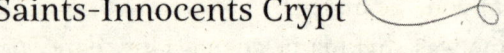

Camille pulled her shirt over her head. Her shoulders hurt. And her ribs. The blast had left her mottled with bruises that were beginning to show, green and black and purple, rising like rot on milk. Ada had covered the map of her skin with her mouth, tasting her weakness and damage with her tongue, finding the truth of her.

'You have to gō back to the duc.'

Ada kneeled in her shift, holding the limp form of her dress.

'I don't want to leave you again. Maybe if I stay with you, I can help.'

Camille kneeled with her, helped her into her dress, laces and buttons and ties. 'Ada.'

'*Please*, Cam.'

Camille hated the way her face crumpled, how every feeling shone through like sunlight through stained glass. Ada was suffering, and Camille had to hold her in it.

'Why didn't you tell me in England?'

Camille fastened the buttons at the nape of her neck, fingers brushing delicate skin.

'It's your chest, isn't it? I told you, I kept telling you to go to a doctor.' Ada's voice broke.

'There's nothing any of them could have done,' said Camille softly.

'Couldn't they have bought you time?'

'At what cost? If I'd left Paris, abandoned the battalion—'

'Damn the battalion! I would pay any of it for you to live.'

Now the words were spoken out loud it was too awful. The bald truth, raw and unbearable to behold, became more real than it ever had done when James said it, or when her own body clamoured at her to pay attention.

A sob broke free. Something in Camille split open and she bawled, shaking and gasping for gulping, too-shallow breaths. Ada wrapped her arms around her as she unravelled.

'I'm going to die.' The words mumbled into Ada's shoulder, mouthful of cloth and sweat. 'I'm going to die.'

Ada stroked her hair, rocked her like a child.

'Okay. Okay. You're not alone.'

They stayed like that, tangled in a different way to how they had been before, but just as intimate, just as essential.

When she quieted, Ada drew back, held her face.

'All right. I'll go back to him. Let me fix this. It's going to be okay, I promise.' Ada kissed her again and Camille wondered if she was savouring it a little longer than before. 'I'm going to make this okay. Just hold on.'

They emerged from the underworld of the crypt, Ada leading the way to the charnel house. At the top of the stairs, she paused, checking to make sure Camille was following her. A look of distress crossed her face, a thought Camille couldn't read.

'I'm sorry.' Ada turned abruptly, and went into the market.

Camille stood halfway down the steps, unable to proceed, but unwilling to go back.

She was lost to the world of the living.

But not yet ready to enter the world of the dead.

3

Salon, Hôtel de Landrieu

An empty bottle of brandy lay on its side next to a spray of smashed glass and torn labels. The fumes still hung in the air, sweet and burning.

Al had stared at the bottle for half an hour, his knuckles clenched white with tension, then threw open the window and upturned first the brandy, then the port, the sherry, the gin, the wine, scouring out every drink that littered his rooms and pouring them all onto the patio far below. Then, with a shout, he had swept his arm across the table of empty bottles, sending them crashing to the floor in bursts of coloured glass.

Now he sat alone in the middle of the carnage, in his shirtsleeves, playing Patience and drinking tea.

Tonight was not a night for sleep.

The door opened but he didn't look up. The teapot was cold and he was expecting a refresh of hot water.

But the sounds were wrong, the scrape of shoes against the parquet, someone panting.

He dropped his cards at the sight of Guil, hollow

and gaunt and shaking with the exertion of holding himself up.

They stared at each other in shock.

'Well, that's unexpected,' said Al.

Guil dropped onto a sofa and buried his face in his hands.

James appeared at the same moment, covered head to toe in dust and looking as shell-shocked as Guil.

'I suppose we'll need more tea, then,' said Al, and rang the bell on the console table.

A footman came in and took instructions for hot tea, towels, water and something sweet.

'Is one of you going to tell me what happened or are we going to get through this whole conversation with interpretive mime?'

James spoke. 'I found Guil in the duc's palace, and helped him escape.'

'That is both extremely obvious and tells me nothing, congratulations.' Al looked between their devastated faces. 'It also sounds like good news. Why don't you have good news faces?'

James scrubbed a hand over his face. 'Because I overheard something else.'

'Yes?'

'It's Camille and Ada. The abbey Camille went to with Comtois to get explosives … it blew up.'

Al sank down onto a chair. 'Oh.'

'Ada and the duc had gone there for another reason I didn't catch – something to do with the Dauphin? A new Dauphin? And only the duc came home.'

Al picked at his nails with twitching fingers. 'But

they'll be all right, won't they?' he said lightly. 'It's Ada and Camille. Buildings blow up on them every day.' His eyes searched their faces, refusing to see the grief there. 'They'll be all right.'

James closed his eyes. 'We came back past the wreckage. It was all rubble. The whole thing. Mounds and mounds of rubble. It's a miracle the duc got out at all.'

Al shook his head. 'There's no way that scrote got out and they didn't.'

'Al—'

'No. Stop it. They wouldn't give up on us so easily. I'm not giving up on them.'

James looked as though he was about to say something else but thought better of it.

Al rose, pacing past the smashed remains of his drinks cabinet. God, he should have waited another night to do that. He wasn't ready. He needed it still.

No – damn – that was exactly why he had to do it.

Clenching and unclenching his fingers, he went to Camille's desk, looked at the scatter of notes and letters and papers in the hope it would resolve itself into some sort of plan.

'We need to think what to do next. You got Guil away from them – that's a point for us.'

Images pushed their way into his mind of Camille and Ada, snapped like dolls in the rubble of the abbey. Some part of him had always thought it would end up like this. Alone and grieving and unloved.

Was this what Léon feared too?

'You got into the palace.' Al forced himself to keep

speaking. 'Good. I've got an invite. So that plan can still go ahead.'

'Al,' James tried again. He looked so unutterably exhausted. 'Stop. Please.'

Al lingered by the desk. If he stopped all the awful thoughts would flood through him and he didn't know if he could take it. James hopeless, Guil broken from months of imprisonment.

Al landed on a new thought. 'What about Olympe? Did you see her when you found Guil?'

James shook his head. 'Guil escaped. Olympe—'

'Do not think to look for her,' said Guil quietly. It was the first thing he had said.

Al frowned. 'Do you mean they took her out of the palace? Hid her somewhere else?'

'No. She is there. But it's too late.'

'She's not dead—'

'She is perfectly well. She is in a comfortable room, attended by her mother.'

'I don't understand.'

'Then hear this.' Guil lifted his head from his hands, anger and guilt flashing together across his face. 'Olympe will not be rescued. She has chosen her side. It is not us.'

4

Rue Saint-Honoré

14 October 1794

The hospitals were hopeless. When dawn came, James had walked the city, searching the beds for Camille or Ada, but they weren't there. Relief warred with dread.

If they weren't injured but alive, next he had to turn to the rows of bodies laid out in the grounds of the abbey. He paced outside the grounds for half an hour, desperate for answers but unable to face what could be waiting; until he went inside he could hold onto the fantasy that things were not what they seemed.

When he finally went in and found neither of them it was more painful than he expected. He was desperately glad not to see their corpses, but the not knowing was overwhelming. Were they trapped in the rubble? Had they fled somewhere? The image of the duc returning, covered head to toe in chalky white dust like a ghost in some cheap theatre production, kept forming in his mind. The duc had left them there. Even Clémentine had thought it inhuman of him.

James had left Guil at the hôtel with Al. He was shell-shocked from his escape, barely able to speak about what had happened to them in captivity. James still didn't understand why Olympe hadn't come with him. Guil had said something about Clémentine, about Olympe turning back to her, but James couldn't recognise the girl he knew in Guil's descriptions.

His feet had taken him south to the darkened windows of the prison at the Luxembourg Palace, and the Au Petit Suisse café facing it. One window had been smashed and was covered by boards already papered with playbills and advertisements. He hadn't been here in months, unconsciously avoiding it when he travelled around the Left Bank. Now his thoughts had brought him back to where it had all started. When he had come to Paris half a year ago, he had been so clear of his purpose and confident in his ability to right every wrong. His father's approval would be won over, and finally he could thrive in a future of his own creation.

Instead, all he had done was hurt so many people he cared for – Camille, Edward, Olympe – for nothing. His father's opinion of him was his father's problem. He couldn't change it, because whatever James did, his father would never consider it good enough for the simple reason that James was the one doing it.

It had been a freeing thought when he'd finally come to it. Heartbreaking, but a weight of hope had lifted from his shoulders. There was no one to do anything for, but himself. He could only live by his own idea of good enough.

The door to the rooms over the café was locked, and he didn't have the key. He'd wondered if Camille might have come here, but there were weeds growing undisturbed around the door frame so he assumed not.

Another memory struck him. Another doorway in Paris that was far more familiar than this.

He cut through the series of townhouses on the rue du Cloître-Saint-Benoît, behind the Sorbonne. The ground-floor shops were all tentatively open for business, but few seemed well stocked. Halfway along he stopped at a door painted green; it had been propped open with a bucket to reveal a passageway and courtyard beyond, and a woman mopping.

He had come to Camille's parents' apartment so many times before the Revolution. Before his mother had been too sick to travel. After her parents' executions, all their possessions had been seized by the state and sold. Camille had been left with nothing.

He found her sitting on the steps near the first floor. Distracted, hair pale with dust, a smear of blood along her cheek. James fell to his knees before her.

'Camille. Oh god, Camille, where have you been? Are you all right?'

She looked up in confusion, unable to slot together the pieces of the life she found herself in. 'James?'

'Yes. It's me, I'm here. We heard about the explosion. What happened? You got out – what about Ada? And Comtois?'

There were too many questions, too many uncertain things. She shook her head.

'I don't know. I don't know.'

'It's okay. We'll figure it out.' He didn't know what he was promising, but it felt important to take this burden from her. He took her hands, stroked his thumb over her skin that felt too hot, too thin, too delicate.

'Ada said the same thing.'

'You saw Ada?'

Camille nodded. 'She saved me. I had to send her back to the duc.' She looked at him properly for the first time. 'What are we going to do? The duc will lead his coup tomorrow. I only had this plan and it's gone…'

James explained that he and Al had had better luck with their plan.

She rested her head against his shoulder. 'I want to go home.'

'We can do that. Can you walk? I can get a cab.'

She shook her head. 'I'm not sure where home is any more. Maybe home doesn't mean anything.'

James said nothing, but stroked her hair, savoured feeling her alive and close.

'Maybe there's only now. Only ourselves. Nothing more.'

He held her and they sat together, each thinking of home. Thinking of what they would do for those they owed.

5

Backstage at the
Théâtre Patriotique

Fire had left its mark on the Théâtre Patriotique. In the six months since Olympe had set the place ablaze, the backstage area had been cleared of char and debris, leaving a void the height of the building that was half-open to the sky. No performance had been held since, the windows boarded over, and leaves and rain had warped and smothered the stage.

It had caught Al's eye as he searched for Camille and Ada. Leaving Guil at the hôtel to recover, Al and James had split up to cover as much ground as possible, but it seemed hopeless. He had gone north towards the Temple, and the memory came to him of the last time the battalion had truly been together and something like happy: attending a matinée billing at the Théâtre Patriotique soon after rescuing Olympe. It had only been short respite, the four of them and Olympe, sharing something as simple and pleasurable as a variety show. James had not become one of them yet, nor Olympe. And the show had descended into hell as fire ripped through the performance, leading to the death of tens of people, crushed in the foyer or from smoke inhalation.

What did it mean that their only happiness was tied so inexorably with death and pain?

Maybe there was no other way.

They were the Battalion of the Dead.

The curse was in their name.

Léon was in his old dressing room that had survived the fire almost untouched. Smoke had blackened the ceiling and wall where it had rolled in around the door. Al waited on the threshold, black marks flaring across the floorboards from his feet, for Léon to look up from the drawers he was digging through. He was in shirtsleeves despite the cold, his embroidered waistcoat hanging open.

Al swallowed. Knocked.

Léon startled, smacked his head on an open drawer, and turned to Al, cursing.

He didn't stop when he saw Al.

'Hello to you too,' said Al, and regretted it; he didn't mean to start that way.

'Don't tell me, you need my help to infiltrate an elite gang of criminal tailors? No, you're playing the high tables on a riverboat gambling den? Or maybe you just want a quick—'

'I came here to apologise.'

Léon leaned against his old dressing table and folded his arms. 'Oh? A modern-day miracle.'

Al bit the inside of his mouth. He deserved that.

'You were right. I'm a coward and I don't treat you the way you deserve.'

Surprise registered on Léon's face, but he schooled his expression into cool indifference. 'Correct.'

Al remembered the last time he had been in this room with Léon, at the start of the Olympe job, when he and Camille had come to Léon for intelligence on the duc. It had all been a game to him, a chaotic, dangerous game, like dancing on the edge of a cliff, like drinking to the point of oblivion with strangers he couldn't trust not to mean him harm. Everything Al had done had been a gamble, his life the stakes. Because it was an empty bet, spending borrowed money. Part of him wanted to be back there, in the easy, casual way he would reach for affection from Léon, and drop it when it made him uncomfortable, the consequence-free world he had moved shallowly around.

Death would have been easy.

Living was so much harder.

'I don't think we should see each other any more.'

Al exhaled, the weight of the words slipping from him. Léon deserved better. Al had to own up to what he had done, and make things right.

Léon didn't react.

'No.'

Al blinked. 'What do you mean, no?'

'We're not breaking up.'

'Excuse me?'

'Go away and figure out whatever it is you need to figure out in this existential crisis you're having, then come back to me. I'm not letting you destroy what we have because you hate yourself too much.'

Al stared at him in shock. 'I... You... What?'

Léon returned to the drawer he had been searching through, and pulled out a signet ring. 'What do you think – worth a few sou? The pawn shops all scam you these days, but I think I can pass this off as a family heirloom.'

'If you need money...'

'Absolutely not from you.'

Léon slipped the ring on and found his jacket; as he moved past Al, he kissed him on the cheek. 'Sort yourself out. Come and find me when you have.'

Al stood in the doorway, one hand at the warmth Léon had left on his cheek until the memory of his kiss faded and Al was alone in the ash and ruins.

6

The Duc's Palace

Paris was poisoned.

Ada couldn't see it any other way. It was long walk back to the duc's palace from the abandoned safe house at the Saints-Innocents charnel house. Tricolor flags hung limp and unsure from windows jammed tightly shut against the cold. Dawn had come at some point during their time trapped in the tunnels and the day was foggy and shallow. Another day of rising prices, unrest, uncertainty that made life like skimming lightly over a deep, dark pool. Crossing the Place de Grève three bodies in phrygian caps hung from the old gallows the guillotine in the Place de la Révolution had replaced. Another riot must have happened after the explosion, or perhaps at the same time. Violence in Paris erupted from nothing, then slipped back beneath the surface until another score came to be settled.

The memory of bones and dirt in her mouth crowded Ada's mind. She would have given anything to stay with Camille, to stretch their moment together and forget the world needed something of them. Bruised and grieving, she wasn't sure what she had left to give, but she had seen what the consequences of her failure would bring. Smelled the burning flesh and imagined it a hundred times over: the duc's ballroom thronged with what government Paris had left burning where they stood.

She wondered if the rest of the battalion had any idea just how much carnage lay in wait. They had seen the duc's cruelty first-hand but they had not spent months with him. Months watching the Revolution dwindle and die, smothered like a flame with no air to burn, seen the streets turn from sans-culottes control, to the Royalists hunting down the same men who had hunted them. Something worse than the Terror was coming, and it would be the people who suffered.

In the darkest moments, Ada wondered about letting the duc go ahead with his coup. There would be death and horrors unimaginable. Though perhaps he would bring stability with him in the reinstating of the old order. Maybe people would prefer that, after five years of chaos.

But blood would be on her hands. And worse – on Olympe's too. What the duc wanted to use her for, Ada could not allow it. Even if Olympe had formed some sort of trust with Clémentine again, Ada could not let the duc turn Olympe into a mass murderer.

The sun was moving towards the horizon again by the time Ada reached the duc's palace. She was dizzy with headache and hunger, her throat raw and body a knot of pain. And cold, she was so, bitterly cold.

The servants didn't recognise her at first, ignoring the filthy, strange scarecrow of a girl who moved through the grounds, but Ada would not slink. She would not slip politely through the back entrance. She walked up the steps to the front door and hammered on it until the butler answered in confusion and distaste.

'Where is he?'

'I beg your pardon, mademoiselle?' The butler knew her and could not shut her out, as much as he looked like he wanted to.

'You know who I mean.'

The butler nodded towards the salon and Ada limped through the bright corridors smelling of polish and paint. The duc was hunched over his desk, scribbling a letter with furious strokes of his quill, Charles was beside him waiting in his riding coat. Clémentine stood up like a bolt when she saw Ada, hands covering a shriek.

'Ada!'

Standing in the threshold, she thought she might faint.

'Good god.' The duc dropped his paper. 'You're alive.'

Clémentine burst into tears and pulled her into an embrace that shocked Ada.

'We sent people to search the hospitals for you but had no word,' she said. 'What happened to you?'

Clémentine held Ada in front of her and looked over her cuts and torn clothing. Ada didn't know what to do with her mothering. Clémentine sat her in a chair and brought her water, a cloth to clean her face, something to drink.

Stumbling, Ada explained an edited version of the truth: the explosion had buried her in the tunnels below the abbey but she had found a way out. She knew what question about Camille the duc was about to ask, so she struck first.

'Did you catch Comtois? What was he doing there?'

The duc didn't miss a beat. 'We lost him. I assumed him dead, but it seems miraculous survival is possible.'

'And the Dauphin?'

'Safe, thank God,' said Charles, crossing himself. 'He is upstairs, resting at our hospitality.' He turned the questioning round to her. 'What of the Laroche girl?'

She didn't like the way he looked as though he could see every thought in her head.

Ada had considered what to tell the duc on her long walk back: perhaps that she had seen Camille dead in the wreckage – but that was too easily proven false. And, desperate, stupid hope though it may be, she couldn't wish Camille dead, even in service of stopping the duc.

Ada shrugged. 'Last I saw she was in that room. I don't know what happened after that.'

Charles's eyes narrowed. 'Convenient she knew about the powder store.'

Ada scoffed, her scorn not hard to fake. 'Everyone knows what they do at the abbey. She is clever, for all your man François's security, it wouldn't be impossible to find a way in.'

'Perhaps you told her, hmm?' Charles pressed, sensing his opportunity to evict her from the duc's trust.

'Perhaps she asked for your help and you couldn't turn her down, not after all you'd been through together?'

Ada met his eye dead. 'I've never been to the abbey before last night. You never told me about the Dauphin. How on earth would I have managed this little conspiracy you have concocted?'

She had never spoken so brazenly to him, but Clémentine's words stayed with her. The duc cared about power. To seem weak was a death sentence.

Ada risked saying a little more. 'I know you think the duc indulgent for involving me in your work. That I am a vanity project.' She glanced at the duc, affecting the cruel sneer both men habitually wore. 'Maybe Charles has been planting these ideas in your head, monsieur.'

The duc bristled. 'Charles has no more ability to influence my thoughts than you do.'

'Then I hope you trust me when I say I knew nothing of this.' Ada knocked back the brandy Clémentine had given her. 'Camille is a law unto herself.'

The duc was easily distracted by his hatred. 'Not clever enough to know what's good for her. Pretending to have given up her futile fight, then sneaking about directly under my nose. Conspiring with my enemies. She made a fool out of me, and I will not have it.' Anger rippled through his voice.

'Oh, stop it, Philippe,' said Clémentine. 'You don't know why they were there. Perhaps it has nothing to do with you.'

'For all I know Comtois approached her with some scheme and she decided to try it. I said she was clever,

I didn't say she had good sense,' said Ada. It was a precarious game, not giving away too much about Camille while directing suspicion from herself.

'Whatever she was planning, it is over for her now. Charles is to take a party of men to pry her out of that hôtel she occupies. I told her if she crossed me there would be consequences. We have space in the cells,' he said with a cruel smile. 'I will house her next to her soldier friend. I told her the price of her meddling was his life. Now she can see the consequences of her actions for herself.'

Ada's heart skipped a beat. Camille – now Guil – it was all falling apart.

If the duc looked in those cells, he would find them empty. He would know Clémentine had betrayed him.

From the opposite settle, she could see fear grip Clémentine too.

Ada made a show of yawning, bored of the conversation. 'Do as you wish, but we cannot be distracted from the demonstration tomorrow. There is much still to prepare. Don't let Camille draw your attention away. She's not worth it. Let them both rot while we finish our work.'

The duc laughed. 'A little harsh on your old friends.'

Ada felt the weight of the past twenty-four hours lie heavy on her.

'I've made my choice. I'm here, aren't I?'

'That's enough, both of you.' Clémentine rang the bell for the servants with a trembling hand, and pushed the duc away from Ada. 'She has been through too much already. Stop being so paranoid.'

Ada let herself be ushered into a bath, her skin scrubbed raw of blood and plaster dust.

She could run now, try to warn Camille, but what good would it do except to give away her true allegiances?

She had come too far now to turn back.

Camille had to fend for herself.

And if she fell, then Ada would have to be ready to stop the duc herself.

Whatever bloodshed it cost her.

7

Hôtel de Landrieu

The first hôtel particulier Camille had ever set foot in had been following her parents to a political salon at the start of the Revolution. Their carriage swept through the gates and into the cour d'honneur, the cobbled courtyard flanked by high, carved walls and shimmering nine-pane windows and a grey slate roof brilliant in the spring light. Footmen lined the steps and the hall inside; in the salon, a table of patisserie and fruit laid out for the men and women who filled the room, strolling arm in arm, laughing with bright eyes and wild gestures. Camille had sat unspeaking in a corner of the room, listening and looking with unbridled joy. She saw the future like a vast, unspoiled plain on which utopia could be built.

She had thought she would be a part of it.

Five years and so many deaths later, the future had turned out to be something very different. Her home was a hôtel more grand than she could have ever imagined, and the future was something she would have no part in at all.

Rain slicked the tiles of the Hôtel de Landrieu, running along stone gutters and sluicing into the drains; weeds grew along one corner of the courtyard, moss like fur growing over the flagstones where water pooled. The sedan chair was set down at the top of the entrance steps and Camille climbed out unsteadily. James had hired the chair and ran alongside it in the rain; his golden hair had gone dark, a curl clinging to his temple. He held his jacket over her head to shelter as they went inside.

They found Guil alone. A ceramic stove radiated heat that didn't reach far and he'd pulled a chair up close. Tears prickled Camille's eyes. James had told her Guil was safe but it was something else to be with him. It had been so long since she had seen his face, the brush of his lashes against his cheek, the poise with which he held himself. He stood abruptly, the jacket he'd pulled over himself as a blanket slipping to the floor, and they met in a hug so strong it crushed the air from her chest. She buried her face in his shoulder, smelling his familiar scent, the warmth of his arms, and the cord of his muscle.

'I missed you,' she said.

'I missed you too.'

'Camille?' Al stood at the door, holding an umbrella that dripped water onto the parquet. 'Oh god, Cam, you're okay.'

She let herself be passed between Guil and Al, from one embrace to the next.

'I'm sorry I scared you.'

'As you bloody well should be. You're lucky lack of sleep looks so good on me.'

They sat around the stove as rain streamed down the windows. Al, Guil and James all in the same place. Her boys. The battalion a little closer to being whole.

A little closer to the end.

'What happened at the abbey?' asked James.

Camille explained how she and Comtois had broken in and found the gunpowder but an unexpected run-in with Ada and the duc had led to disaster.

'What happened to Comtois?' asked Al. 'I always said blowing things up wasn't the way forward.'

'I don't know,' said Camille. 'Maybe the duc caught him?'

James shook his head. 'I was there when the duc got back to the palace. No one knows what happened to Comtois.'

'Perhaps he ran,' said Guil. 'He saw the duc and panicked.'

'Er, but don't we need him to disable the duc's machine?' asked Al. 'No offence, James, but he was much smarter than you.'

'I won't argue.' James had gone pale.

Camille closed her eyes. She was failing. She couldn't see a way through this.

The memory of Ada came to her, offering to take matters into her own hands. She had looked so determined. So troubled.

Camille couldn't let her do what she was suggesting.

Ada still had a future; Camille couldn't let it be stained by blood.

They all had a future: Olympe, James, Al, Guil.

All of them would have to live with whatever choices they made.

Only Camille had the freedom of her actions having no consequences.

She opened her eyes.

A path forward had come clear.

No fate. No destiny. Everything was a choice.

She knew what she had to do next.

Guil's broad hand closed over hers and squeezed, a gesture of solidarity and comfort he had offered her so many times before. Her heart clenched at the idea she had him back again.

Her eyes snapped open.

He didn't know.

All this time captive with the duc and he didn't know.

Camille withdrew her hand, and Guil's expression darkened at her own solemn look.

'What is the matter?'

'There's something I need to tell you about Ada.'

The Duc's Palace

Ada paced outside the door. In one hand she had a key. In the other, a knife.

Still damp from her bath at the nape of her neck and between her breasts, she had been scrubbed clean and slipped into a silk housedress.

She was overcome by the desperate desire that none of this had ever begun. She couldn't pinpoint where it had all gone wrong. Should she have realised the Olympe job wasn't what it seemed? Should they never have started rescuing people? Should she not have left her father to join the battalion? Or had it all gone wrong when she first met Camille? At every other point she couldn't imagine herself having made a different choice, having turned away from someone who needed help to save her own skin.

There was only that first meeting with Camille at the salon her father had taken her to. They had been so young. So naive. The Revolution had still been in its golden days of nascent possibility. The king had been alive. Camille was still well. Change seemed good and needed and pure. Decisions had felt easy.

She had met Camille and she had been beautiful and the most interesting person Ada had ever met and kissing her hadn't been anything complicated at all.

That was the moment that had led her here.

Frightened. Alone. Clutching a knife.

She couldn't undo everything that had happened, but she could stop it now, stop the oncoming horror with the quick slice of a blade.

What was one more life on her hands, after everything she had done?

Ada opened the door.

Olympe sat in the middle of her bed, shrouded in white silk and the curtain of her dark hair. Softly, Ada came inside and padded across the rug, satin slippers making no sound as she closed the distance between them.

When she came closer, a sound stopped her.

Olympe was crying.

Ada slid the knife away, her conviction of a moment ago gone between one breath and the next.

'Olympe?'

She startled, looking up at Ada in shock. Her face was dark and roiling, the shadows on her skin rippling like a storm rolling in.

'Ada.' Fury crossed her face, betrayal and sadness. Then exhaustion.

Ada sat on the end of the bed. 'I know you must hate me.'

Olympe scrubbed at her tears with her sleeve. 'Hate doesn't begin to cover it.'

It was the first time she had been alone with Olympe since before England. She had been a coward, hiding behind the duc and Guil and the experiments to keep her distance from the girl she had unforgivably hurt.

Until that moment some part of Ada had hoped it could be forgivable.

'I'm sorry.'

It was pitifully insufficient, but it was all Ada could think to say.

'You're sorry. My mother is sorry. Guil's sorry. Everyone's so sorry but they still do exactly what they want to and I pay the price.'

Guilt soured in Ada's mouth and the knife felt so heavy in her pocket. That she had ever thought of turning it on Olympe sickened her. The duc had made her into a monster.

The weight of her secrets was a burden she could no longer bear.

'I need to tell you something,' said Ada. 'Both of you. Where is Guil?'

At that Olympe started crying again, angry, bitter tears.

Oh god, had the duc already wrought his revenge for Camille's actions?

Ada rushed to his open door.

'Don't—' Olympe's voice stopped Ada in the threshold, but she could already see the truth: Guil was gone.

The bottom vanished from her stomach. No. No. Please, no. Visions filled her mind's eye of Guil slumped among the corpses of her experiment subjects, a neat bullet hole in his temple. His throat slit, a sharp red smile soaking her hands in blood.

'Where is he?' she whispered.

'He left.'

'Left where? Did someone come for him?'

'He escaped. My mother was trusting enough to think she could put us somewhere like this and he wouldn't break out. She doesn't know the battalion like I do.'

A rush of relief flooded through her. If Guil had already gone, then that was one less life she held in her hands.

She went back to Olympe in confusion. 'If he escaped, why are you still here?'

Olympe looked so small in the bed, in the grand, cold room.

The sense of foreboding grew.

Olympe wiped her tears away again then looked

at her hands, the black nails and streaks of blue and purple winding along her fingers.

'I don't know. He tried to take me with him but I kept thinking, where would I go? What would I do? I don't know what I could do with my life that I would ever be safe. My future always ends up here.'

Ada felt sick. 'You chose to stay?'

Olympe nodded, a new desperate light in her eyes. 'You understand, don't you? You chose this. Here, him. So did my mother. It is not so bad a choice, is it?'

The horror of it was dawning on Ada. She knew she would hurt Olympe in carrying out Camille's plan, but she hadn't realised just how much damage she had done.

She chose her words carefully. She had thought to reveal the truth of her role with the duc, but now she was unsure if there was anyone left in the palace she could trust at all.

'What if there was a way to guarantee a different future for you? A safe one?'

Olympe shrugged. 'I can't see beyond the end of today. There's just nothing.'

Ada couldn't speak. She couldn't think. All she'd had left was the thought of getting Olympe away from the duc, stopping her being a sick weapon in his coup attempt. That would have made all the dark things she'd done worth it.

But she had never thought Olympe wouldn't want to leave.

That Olympe would look to *her* as a reason not to.

Every path forward led to more hurt, more betrayal. There was no absolution waiting for her.

'You're crying,' said Olympe.

Ada touched her face and found it wet.

Olympe looked unsure. 'What's wrong?'

Ada covered her face with her hands and sobbed.

'Everything. Oh, everything.'

Hôtel de Landrieu

Guil stared at the faces of his friends and found strangers looking back at him.

All he had thought about for the months and months of his bitter captivity was the life waiting for him with the battalion if only he could return to them. But in his absence they had changed and left him behind.

No, if what Camille had told him about Ada was true, Camille had closed him out a long time before.

'You made Ada into a sleeper agent.' It wasn't a question. He was testing the idea out, holding it up against his memory of Ada and the month in Paris where there had only been the two of them against the duc. Every word, every look was cast in a new light. He had known she was keeping things from him and they had fought about it. Her betrayal in England had fed his most paranoid thoughts – but apparently even those hadn't begun to touch what had really been going on.

'Yes,' said Camille. 'It was the only way I could see.'

And he saw it too. That was the worst thing, he saw it all perfectly.

Camille had been playing so many moves ahead of everyone; it had been obvious from the start they were outmanned, outgunned. There was no way for them to win in a fair fight. So Camille had sown a seed as early and as quietly as she could, which had bloomed into the nightmare they were living now.

The nightmare that would give them a chance against the duc.

A traitor stood by his side.

A knife was waiting at his back.

Before he could say anything more, Comtois appeared, wrestling with a job lot of rubber that was fractionally too big for him to carry.

Al stared. 'Good god. The dead are risen. Quick, someone write to the Pope.'

Comtois set down the rubber and smoothed his jacket. 'Rumours of my death have been much exaggerated.'

The rubber flopped across the parquet like a strange sea creature washed up among them.

Guil cleared his throat and nodded towards Comtois. 'Is this another part of the plan you need to fill me in on?'

'Oh, she kept that from all of us,' said Al. 'Short version is without Ada we're all too stupid to figure out what the duc is planning to do with Olympe.'

The ill ease grew in Guil's stomach. Another plan of Camille's he could understand. Another plan he had been excluded from.

'Do you have a problem with it?' asked Camille and he knew the question beneath it: are you still with me? Oh, how many times had she asked him the same thing before some hare-brained scheme, a daring light in her eye? That fire still burned in her, but now it burned cold and ruthless.

The gap between himself and the battalion grew a little wider. He didn't know where he fit in with them any more.

'No, I have no problem with it,' he said. 'I'm with you.

For now.

Pulling her shawl tighter around her, Camille went to inspect the rubber. 'Where have you been? And what is this?' She nudged a toe against it.

'I will admit, when I saw Philippe I panicked. I ran into the backstreets before he could find me – the explosion was well-timed. No one was looking for another person fleeing the abbey.'

'That explosion gave you freedom,' said Camille. 'The duc could assume you dead. Why not run all the way?'

Comtois drew himself up to his full height, shoulders uncurling after months mired in fear and shame. 'I thought about it. But seeing Philippe again made me think something else too. Even in those scant minutes I saw all of him, his arrogance, his cruelty. And I realised: he is my responsibility. I did his work for years. I took Olympe. This is my mess.'

The battalion exchanged glances.

'Well, I won't argue with you on that one,' said Al.

'So you've come back for one last stand? Go out in a blaze of glory sort of thing, to ease the conscience?'

Comtois looked at him coldly. 'No. I intend to live to a happy old age. In fact, I intend for all of us to.'

Guil's gaze went to the rubber again.

Comtois smiled. 'I have a different plan.'

A footman arrived empty handed and breathless, interrupting the battalion before Comtois could explain.

'I'm sorry, monsieurs, mademoiselle, I tried to stop them – there are men here, they say they act under the Duc de l'Aubespine's name, they demand to see Mademoiselle du Bugue.'

As one, they froze.

It took Guil a moment for the words to pull together into something like sense. A great wall of noise lay behind them, a memory of the long deep dark of months in a cell, a darkness so total that only his breath, the scrabble of his fingers against his skin, made any meaning.

'I can't go back to the cells,' Guil said, voice half-swallowed in terror. 'They cannot find me here.'

'They absolutely cannot,' said Camille, snapping to attention. 'He's coming for me. I'm the one he saw at the abbey, I'm the one he knows will come back here. Guil, Comtois, we have to hide.'

The sound of footsteps and shouts came from the corridor outside.

'*Now.*'

9

Hôtel de Landrieu

Al stood alone in the centre of the drawing room.

To keep his hands from trembling, he shoved them in his pocket. His heart thrummed like the fragile wings of a bird beating against the cage of his ribs.

The door to the servants' passage swung shut behind the rest of the battalion carrying the rubber, falling flush with the wall so it became invisible.

What was he doing? Al couldn't face the duc's men alone. This was a farce.

The sound of doors being kicked in ricocheted down the corridor, growing closer.

No, he had to do this. He had to be brave. He owed his friends so much more than his bravery, but right now it was all he could offer. It was imperative that Camille and the others escaped.

The more time Al could buy them the better chance they had. Their lives were at stake. He knew the duc made no empty threats.

God, he had picked a terrible time to stop drinking.

The voices and booted feet arrived at his door. It was too soon. They would still be in the building – perhaps a few floors down now. Maybe they could get out through the kitchens – or the gardens—

The door slammed open so hard it cracked against the wall, gouging a fist-sized chunk from the plaster. Al bit the side of his tongue. A pack of men rumbled in, spreading out at once to search every corner. Each was twice the size of him, holding weapons, knives, blackjacks, cudgels. Al felt suddenly frail, a paper doll among lead soldiers.

A man broke off from the pack, nondescript in an expensive suit and a condescending expression. Al felt a twinge of recognition. Someone he had seen with the duc – ah, the Bal des Victimes. Charles Delacourt.

'Where is she?' The man spoke as though he were at a tailors' ordering a few yards of silk made up into jacket linings. As though Camille was nothing but a task on a list to complete.

Al leaned against the back of a settle, hands in his pockets, and looked him up and down with all the moneyed indolence he could summon.

'Of whom do you speak?'

Delacourt sniffed. 'I promise you, she is not worth defending. Don't make this any more troublesome than it needs to be.'

'You burst into my home with no warning, demanding I hand over a person with no name, and you accuse *me* of being troublesome?'

'If you protect her, then I must assume you are working with her.'

Al yawned. 'If I thought you knew the first thing about me I'd be terribly offended you could ever think I *work*.'

Al took his snuff box from his pocket, but before he could take any, one of the men grabbed his arm and twisted it behind his back.

Delacourt took a step closer.

'Where. Is she.'

Al smiled. 'Dans ton cul.'

The man wrenched his arm further so Al's shoulder screamed. Then came the cold kiss of a blade against his throat.

His smile faltered.

'I don't believe I asked for a shave,' he said, feeling his Adam's apple bob against the delicate edge. 'Tell your friend to put away his razor.'

Delacourt regarded him, a lack of light behind his eyes. The glassy, dead look of a man who saw the world as a series of calculations, where blood and honey were only two costs on a balance sheet.

'What are you willing to pay for this girl? Your soft skin? Your home?' The knife dug in deeper. 'Your life?'

Al lifted his chin and held Delacourt's gaze.

That question of his life. What was it worth?

He knew the answer now.

'Go ahead. Kill me. The world would thank you.' He didn't smirk, or joke. Merely let authority enter his voice, let his certainty control the room. 'But perhaps the duc wouldn't, when you bring a murder investigation to his door. It's one thing to plot a political coup, it's another to come into a man's home and slit his throat. People rather frown on that sort of thing. Could happen to them.'

The silence stretched between them. Al waited for the slice of metal against flesh, for his bluff to be called.

And he knew then, at the darkest moment, he knew he would not falter. He would not fall.

He knew who he was now, and what mattered.

'Monsieur!' someone shouted from the window. 'I see them – they're running for the delivery entrace.'

Delacourt turned with a hiss. 'Get after them.'

Al found himself dropped on the floor like a sack of refuse.

Delacourt gave him a final cold glance, and the duc's men swept out, leaving Al alone. He lay there, chasing his flighty breath, the ghost of the knife against his throat.

A knife that was now pursuing Camille.

He had done all he could. At least he could say he tried.

10

The Hôtel Kitchens

Their flight was too quick for thought. A frantic patter of feet descending the cramped stairs floor after floor to the kitchens, where they stalled. There were several ways out of Al's hôtel. The main gate could only be reached through the front doors and the cour d'honneur, but was, of course, already blocked by the duc's men. A servants' entrance led from the kitchens into a side street to facilitate deliveries of food and other supplies without bothering the tranquility of the hôtel. But from the bubble of tension radiating through the passage, it was clear that had been occupied too.

The remaining option was the garden gate across the carefully cultivated grounds. Near the greenhouses was a break in the wall that surrounded Al's compound, another delivery entrance for the gardeners and other heavy items like slates to repair the roof or new timbers for rotting floors. If that was guarded too, they would only find out after a fifteen-minute walk across open ground.

James, Camille, Guil and Comtois crushed themselves into a disused storeroom barely big enough for the four of them.

'Well?' said Camille. 'Who is for the garden? I will not force anyone to go if they think it too much a risk.'

'Is there no place to hide?'

The search party couldn't be heard from down here, but it was only a matter of time before they were found. As big as this place was, hiding was too dangerous a game.

James shook his head. 'You have to go. It's the only way to shake them for sure.'

'I have an idea,' said Comtois.

'Another one?' Camille arched her brow. 'You've certainly found your muse.'

Comtois gave her a withering look. 'It's called trying to save our sorry lives. Listen to me. There's a network of tunnels under the city – old mines that are no longer used. They go everywhere.'

'The catacombs,' breathed Camille. Her face had gone pale. 'But the only entrance I know of is in the crypt of the Saints-Innocents charnel house. That's too far to run with the rubber.'

'I know somewhere nearer,' said Comtois.

'I don't think we have another choice,' said James.

'Okay. We'll try it.' Camille peered round the door frame towards the kitchen. 'The garden gate is a risk but maybe with enough of us we could win a fight if we have to.'

James looked at the thronging servants with a frown. 'No. You need to walk out of the front. It's the shortest way to the catacombs entrance and the last place the duc's men will be looking.'

'Apart from all the men out there currently?' sneered Comtois.

'What are you thinking?' asked Camille.

'Just be ready,' he said. 'I don't know how long you'll have.'

Before he could lose his nerve, James left the storeroom and snatched two cloaks from a peg. The kitchens were busy with servants preparing a dinner they would not eat, the sinks and tables lined with young women. James moved among them until he found one around Camille's height and colouring.

'I'll give you an obscene amount of money if you come with me right now, do everything I say and ask no questions.'

He felt himself blushing as he said it, made worse by the way she looked him up and down, the corner of her mouth lifting.

'I'd go with you for nothing but if you're offering...'

'Marie-Jeanette!' exclaimed the cook. 'This is the last time I will tell you not to flirt with— Oh, excuse me, monsieur.' She broke off as she recognised James.

There was no time to explain. He put the cloak around the girl's shoulders to cover her kitchen uniform, and took her hand, leading her from the servants' quarters and up through the palace.

'You must run quickly. Do not let go,' he said as they approached the front doors. Two men stood blocking their way. He took a step inside the entrance hall, moving loudly enough to draw their attention, then yanked the girl away and turned tail towards the back of the house.

For a beat he thought they might not have seen him, but then he heard shouts and the slapping of feet against the marble floors. A grim smile crossed his lips.

Now the hard part.

At the back door, he paused to light two lamps, giving one to the servant girl.

'Do you want to do it outdoors, monsieur? Only it's quite cold and I've never known a gentleman to be at his best in the cold.'

James was thankful that the hood of his cloak hid his burning cheeks. 'Just hold this and follow me.'

They ran slowly across the manicured grounds, the lamps swaying and bobbing, sending arcs of light across the topiary. Someone in the house should spot them. He needed to draw them all out, like pus from a wound, leaving Camille and the others a clear path to freedom.

The men from the front door were at least following them still. He could track them as the sounds of their footsteps changed from the smack of leather soles on flagstone, then the crunch of gravel, and finally the soft pad of grass. James barely remembered where the garden gate was; somewhere to the right and halfway down the boundary wall. Finally, he saw the flash of his lantern reflected in glass and they were there. The gate was just beyond, and as he'd worried, this one was guarded as well. He pulled the kitchen maid further along and boosted her over the wall before scrambling over himself, ripping half the buttons from his jacket and smearing moss along the silk of his stockings.

Dropping onto the street, the men at the gate spotted them – as he'd hoped – and they set off at a faster lick down the rue des Quatre-Fils, away from the front of the hôtel. Looking back, he saw a mass of bodies pounding the cobbles in their wake, before darting around a dray cart.

He kept going down rue Michel le Comte, cloak flaring behind him as he ran, until they hit a knot of traffic that slowed their pace.

The duc's gang were closing the gap.

On the other side, James turned into rue Beaubourg, but it was blocked by an abandoned barricade from a riot.

A heavy hand landed on his shoulder, and James and the maid were yanked into a mass of men, their hoods ripped away. The maid had gone pink with embarrassment and shock, and James glared at them with as much ire as he could muster.

'What on earth are you doing?'

Charles Delacourt emerged at their centre. The man James had seen with the duc at his palace. A more respectable replacement for his old thug, Dorval.

'Why were you fleeing the hôtel?' he asked.

James let embarrassment show on his face, held the maid closer.

'Since when is it a crime for a gentleman to enjoy the staff?'

He hated the words as he said them, but they were too easy to believe. Delacourt certainly did. A flicker of anger crossed his expression. He turned to the man from the front door.

'I thought you said you had seen the girl and the docteur?'

'I – I did. I swear. They looked just like them,' he stuttered.

Delacourt smacked him across the face with the head of his cane, leaving a weal on the man's cheek.

'You have cost us vital time. Camille du Bugue will be running free and laughing at us as we speak.' He turned back to the others. 'Go! Find her. The duc gave you an order. Go!'

They scattered.

James could only hope Delacourt was right.

He had bought Camille an exit.

He prayed Comtois could find her a refuge.

PART FIVE

Bataillon des Morts

14 October 1794

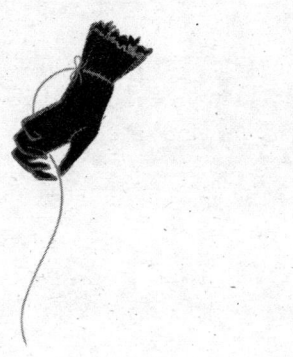

1

Olympe's Room

Ada splashed water from Olympe's washstand on her face. Her skin felt too hot from crying, salt crusting in her eyes already and the collar of her dress tacky and damp. Olympe had fallen asleep, curled around a pillow, her face hidden in its fabric. As silently as she had entered, Ada let herself out of the room only to find Clémentine coming along the corridor.

Ada shut the door behind her quickly, and stood in front of it. Clémentine stopped, one eyebrow arching in curiosity.

'I didn't know you were up here,' she said.

'I wasn't expecting you either,' said Ada as calmly as she could. Her mind was racing, tracing out different paths forward. Clémentine would go into the room no matter what she did now. It was only a matter of time before she discovered Guil had run. Ada needed to move first, and keep control.

'Guil's escaped,' said Ada before her confidence failed her.

Clémentine's expression fell. 'What? How?'

'I don't know. He's clever, he found a way. But Olympe stayed.'

Ada hated the way Clémentine smiled, the genuine bright joy she felt at her daughter's choice – then hated herself for begrudging a mother the love of her daughter.

'What will you tell Philippe?' said Ada.

This was not Ada's problem. She hadn't been the one to take Olympe and Guil out of the cells. She could see Clémentine's mind working through the same courses of action as she had done only minutes before.

'Nothing. We tell him nothing.'

'Guil will go back to Camille.'

'So what? Let them do what they want. The demonstration is the day after tomorrow, Philippe is distracted. As long as Olympe is here he doesn't need to know anything about it.'

The secret shared between them grew, changed shape and slid its fingers into the cracks between Clémentine and the duc.

Ada squeezed her arm. 'You're right. No one else needs to know.'

Clémentine squeezed back. 'Just a little longer, and this will all be over.'

The knife tucked up Ada's sleeve grazed the skin of her arm.

Clémentine was right.

One way or another, it would be over.

No fate. No destiny.

Everything was a choice.

Underneath Paris

For the second time in as many days, Camille descended into the world of the dead.

Comtois was true to his word. The catacombs were barely half a minute's walk from Al's front door, through a storm drain and a boarded-up mine entrance.

This time, at least, she had light. Camille held the storm lamp she had brought from the kitchens close as they descended through the dark passages. Being buried alive in these tunnels with Ada only the day before, she had sworn she would never go underground again until her body met its final rest.

She was to meet that day all too soon, it seemed.

For what felt like hours, they followed a twisting path that only Comtois knew. Here and there, old posts and struts from the mine survived. In other places, rockfall blocked off branching tunnels. Camille shivered. This was not a safe place for the living.

Eventually, Comtois stopped them. The tunnel widened out into a chamber about the size of their parlour back in the old battalion rooms above the Au Petit Suisse. It had been kitted out with a table, a cot, and into the walls were dug a series of alcoves to serve as shelves. Bones were stacked everywhere, walls of rib bones nestled like lovers, vertebrae scattered like dice.

'We're roughly under the Bastille. There are passages up into the remains of the castle all over the city. Leftover siege defences and routes to move prisoners in secret,' explained Comtois.

Camille frowned. On the shelves were items she recognised from Comtois's laboratory in the hôtel. A dusty sulphur globe, lengths of wire, and tools she couldn't name.

'What is this place?'

'One of the duc's old hidden laboratories.'

Camille spun on her heel. 'You've brought us to the duc's territory?'

'Abandoned.'

'How can you be so sure?'

'Because for five years of revolution I hunted him. I knew what he was working on and I knew he had to be stopped. But every time we found another one of his underground lairs and raided it, we were too late. He had moved on. Sometimes I think that man would survive the end of the world.'

Guil sat down in the cot. 'I don't think we have a choice, Camille.'

She folded her arms, but she was too tired to fight. 'I know. I know.'

However hard she struggled the earth pulled her back down. Her grave calling.

Everything Guil had sacrificed to stop the duc, everything Ada and Olympe had done. What all of them had given. They fought so hard.

But it was all slipping through her fingers and into dust.

230

15 October 1794
James's Bedroom, Hôtel de Landrieu

The human body was split open on paper.

Muscle and artery traced through flesh like veins in a fallen leaf, and thin inked letters denoted scapula, tendon, gut. James turned the page in his anatomy book to the well-studied diagram of the human lung. Bronchioles like tree roots, blooming ink and watercolour. Pink and healthy on one page, shrunken and cloudy on the facing one. He thought of Camille's cough. The wet noise and blood in her handkerchief.

Olympe had copied that page, lying on the floor of the garret room in London. A sketch was still tucked between the pages of the book, but he hadn't been able to bring himself to look at it. His guilt was too alive, too sickening. Camille's body was failing her, but for Olympe it was the people around her who'd failed her. Her future had been taken away by those who were meant to give her one. First her mother and her uncle had treated her like an experiment. Then he had lied to her, gained her trust and kidnapped her. No wonder she hadn't gone with Guil. Why would she ever trust anyone again?

She had never had a chance at a life of her own.

He closed the book and slipped it back onto the shelf.

It had been a sleepless night in the hôtel.

James had returned with the kitchen maid, who had been put out to find herself deposited back downstairs thoroughly unravished, though with the money promised. Al had been waiting in the salon, chewing the quick of his nails, and James hurriedly explained what had come to pass. What had happened after Camille, Guil and Comtois fled, neither of them knew for sure, but they could only hope that their friends had found sanctuary in the catacombs. They would wait for morning when their movements would be less suspicious to try to reunite. They would need to take the rubber to Comtois, and the duc would have men watching them.

As dawn turned the sky from navy to grey, James made a decision.

Al could go to the catacombs.

James had somewhere else to be.

Only Ada stood between Olympe and the duc. Olympe might not trust James any more, but he would see her have one more chance. He was due to go to the palace on the day of the demonstration, but he would go now. He would not abandon Olympe any longer.

In a bag he packed his clothes as Louis, and a bottle of vitriol of copper to spike the drinks. It was quiet in the hôtel when he passed through the hallways.

He paused at Camille's desk and wrote a brief note; he owed her that much.

'Coffee. Who's keeping the coffee hostage and can I kill you.' Al appeared, slumped dramatically against the door frame, wrapped in a silk banyan and looking like an extra from a play about the Black Death.

James scrubbed the tears from his eyes. 'This is early.'

'I know. Sobriety is terrible. Why has nobody warned me.'

The smashed and emptied bottles hadn't been lost on James, though he knew it wasn't the right time to go into it. Once they got through the duc's demonstration – if they all got through – then maybe it would be time. He would go back to England, maybe persuade Camille and Ada to come with him so he could spend his mother's last days alongside Camille's. There would be so much pain to come, but he could make the time count.

'Give this to Camille.' James held out the note.

'Give it to her yourself, I'm not your messenger.'

James slung his bag over his shoulder. 'I'm going to the palace.'

'Oh.'

'I have to. What Guil said about Olympe … I have to believe it isn't true. I have to give her another chance.'

'I understand.'

James left with the dawn rush of Paris waking up. He pulled his hat low and started walking south.

This was his business. He was responsible for Olympe being where she was now.

He had to set this right.

2

The Catacombs

Guil woke before dawn after a few fitful hours of dozing and rose to stretch his muscles.

It had been too long since he had slept in a proper bed for Guil to be bothered by the ungiving floor of the catacombs. Indeed, he suspected he would have found the finery of Al's hôtel particulier harder to rest in. Still, he didn't sleep. He couldn't. When he closed his eyes he was back in the cell beneath the duc's palace, listening to Olympe sobbing behind her mask.

He had escaped the dark for barely a day and here he was again. Any hope he had fostered had frozen over, as brittle and delicate as the first frost over a deep, cold lake.

Wakefulness offered no respite.

For the first time in months, Olympe was nowhere near. He had left her in the duc's palace.

He was a deserter again.

Guil splashed a little water from his canteen, welcoming the cold sting of it against his face and neck. Paris began to rouse with muted church bells tolling somewhere above the catacombs. Through a sewer grate, he watched a wintery dawn bring the sky from black to grey; colour leeched away like a ghostly sketch of a bright world now dead.

He couldn't see a way through this. Returning to the batallion should have been a triumph. An enfolding in the safe embrace of the familiar, the trusted.

But there was nothing safe or familiar to find; James was preoccupied, unsure; Al in the grip of something transformational; Camille a fragile shadow of the girl he'd fallen for. No one had told him the truth of her illness yet, but the contrast was stark. He knew death when he saw it. Her strength and fire and pig-headedness remained, but the outer softness of her had sloughed off, leaving only the wavering flame, burning bright and pure and easily snuffed.

And Ada. The pulled-tooth gap she left among them, as painful in her absence as Camille was in her presence.

Now he knew the truth of Ada's mission, he was torn between renewed fury at her for keeping it from him, and fear for the frightening line she walked. The last time he had seen her, he had turned his back on her. Refused to see any doubt in her eyes. Guil thought of all the things he had witnessed her do, the dark, monstrous depths she had plumbed with the duc to keep his trust.

When she escaped – if she escaped – he wasn't sure what kind of girl would walk out the other side.

A little later, Al arrived with an arm full of rubber and a note.

They met him amid the rubble of the destroyed Bastille fortress where the underground tunnels reached the surface, and swallowed him down. Guil and Comtois helped carry the rubber to the laboratory.

'Can you work here?' Guil asked Comtois. 'The plan you spoke of before.'

Comtois nodded. 'It'll be rough work, but this will do.'

Al handed Camille the note with a look of pity.

The rubber left a tacky echo on Guil's fingers as it warmed between his hands. Sap cut from trees thousands of kilometres away and brought to Paris through networks of colonial trade and exploitation, to become erasers and adhesives in factories. A scientific curiosity still subject to curious study in order to determine how it could be best used. An amount this size would have cost Comtois a fortune. All he would say was that he had used up the last of his political capital, so this had to work.

If it didn't, it wouldn't matter anyway.

They wouldn't survive the duc.

After Al left, Guil set about helping Comtois prepare the rubber.

Comtois wiped his hands on a cloth. 'The duc is not our only problem.'

When Camile didn't respond he spoke again.

'He has the Dauphin.'

'He has someone he's calling the Dauphin,' dismissed Camille.

'Which is still a problem.'

'Your problem. I don't want any distractions when

we get to the palace. We stop the duc, we stop all of this.'

Comtois lost his patience. 'A figurehead will give the Royalists someone to rally around, even if you get rid of the duc.'

'So what?' Anger flashed in Camille's eyes. 'You propose hunting down anyone even tangentially related to the royal family? How is that going to work? Stop being the monster the world believes the Revolutionaries to be,' she spat.

'Sometimes death is necessary.'

Camille ignored him, turning over the note Al had delivered absentmindedly. Comtois tracked her with his eyes.

'The duc has to die. You know that.'

'I do.'

'And yet you will not get your hands dirty. Is that why you brought me onboard? To do the things you are not prepared to?'

Camille looked at him sharply. 'You have no idea what I am prepared to do.'

'I think you are the soft girl who still does things because she thinks they are right and good, but does not have the first understanding of reality. I am not your ally, I do not trust you. I am not blinded by love and faith, and I will not choose the safety of your friends over stopping the duc. Can you say the same? All I ask you is, are they worth it?'

She was thin as a rail but as strong and unbending. 'They are my family.'

'Do they mean more than those four hundred lives

you hope to save? More than Paris? More than the future hundreds of thousands of lives who will toil in bondage if the duc reigns?'

Camille only gave him a look of disgust, then stalked into another passageway, worrying at the notepaper.

Silently Guil returned to his task and Comtois clattered around the laboratory, taking out his anger on the tools and workbench.

Then his attention turned to Guil.

'Surely you sense the importance of what I am saying. You were a soldier, you know that harsh reality forces harsh decisions. You must have faced that when you deserted.'

Guil bristled. 'Do not speak on things you do not understand. Keep your words to yourself.'

Six months ago, Guil might have listened to him.

But those principles had been eroded. Proven meaningless. The Revolution he had put his faith in had died around him.

Now, he wasn't sure he cared what happened.

The Catacombs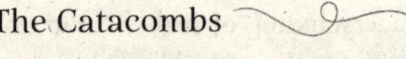

Camille knew what the note would say before she opened it.

She took herself somewhere private. There was nowhere to rest that was not already home to bones or the macabre tools of the duc and Comtois's trade.

James hadn't come with Al.

A scrap of paper, the ink badly blotted so a scatter of letters had bled together, but it was enough for her to understand what had happened.

James had left her without saying goodbye.

Camille folded onto the floor, back against a stack of femurs, and shut her eyes. The note, she kept hold of, a tie to the boy she had loved that had not yet been broken. Oh, she understood his play. The cold, mechanical part of her could tally the risk and benefits. He went to save Olympe – a gambit she wasn't willing to risk, but if James spiked the drinks first it didn't matter what he did after. If he interfered with the duc's plans in any way it could only play to their advantage.

The Camille who had led the Bataillon des Morts, who had climbed the scaffold and swam the Seine, was dying. She had lost her physical vitality; now there was only her mind, burning bright and frantic. All the girls she had ever been were crowding into her at once as the iron grip of Camille of the battalion slipped away.

The carefree child who had slipped between two sides of the channel, sheltered by money and plentiful family.

The young girl seduced by the romance of revolution, naive and hopeful and far too trusting.

The broken thing Ada had rescued after both her parents had been executed. All the money and family she had begun with had been worth nothing in the end, and Ada had been the only rock in a roiling ocean.

She was all of them, all of their thoughts and wants and ideas pressing in together, a clamour of the drowning pulling each other under.

If she couldn't orchestrate her battalion in an elegant plan, at least she could sow chaos.

Guil was right: there were a hundred ways a plan could go wrong, and a hundred ways it could go right, so let her plant a hundred seeds and find out which would rot and which would bloom.

Camille pushed the heels of her hands into her eyes. Her head felt so impossibly heavy. Each breath dragged through her like a knife.

No, Ada had not been the only anchor holding her steady. She had been angry and frightened when James had arrived in the battalion's rooms above the Au Petit Suisse bringing her past with him, but it hadn't taken too long for her to tangle herself in him again. She didn't know what they were to each other any more, but she could not deny she needed him. The foolish, foolish boy she had loved too hard, and too long.

Now he was gone, and she might die before she saw him again.

3

A Café on the Rue Saint-Honoré

Sobriety was awful. Everything was too bright and sharp and demanding. Al didn't know how the rest of the battalion did it. Their lives were miserable, he knew it, full of loss and loneliness and fear, and yet they all walked around sober and earnest like they were so much better than him—

No, stop. That was the bad thinking. The bitter, frightened thinking that led to his worst choices. He had finally made a choice he felt proud of, and he wanted to ease that out a little longer.

It didn't make this gritty coffee taste any better. With a grimace, Al knocked back the cup of what frankly should only be sold under the more accurate name of dirt water, and tossed it to the stall holder. October had turned bitter, a storm threatening in sullen grey clouds lying heavy over the rooftops.

That was the other thing he hadn't expected. Sobriety was *cold*. Paris without a blanket of wine was bone cold and finger numbing.

A necessary awful, he reminded himself as he set off towards the Pont Neuf, like lancing a boil or pulling a rotten tooth. Pain that would become salvation.

He hadn't been able to bear closing himself off in the catacombs so he had returned to his hôtel to help keep up an appearance of normal life. He hadn't spotted anyone tailing him, but the more he kept the duc's men distracted watching him, the better.

The Théâtre de l'Égalité stood a few streets away from the Palais du Luxembourg. Al swung around the back to the stage door and slipped in past men and women carrying rolls of canvass painted with backdrops, bundles of costumes, a spray of wigs in someone's arm, the lolling tongue of a pair of stockings dangling from a basket. There was still an hour before the matinée performance, and the actors were in their dressing rooms.

Léon had a starring role and a room to himself at the end of a corridor.

Al didn't knock.

Léon was sitting at his dressing table applying a powdery cake of make-up to his cheeks. He caught sight of Al in the mirror but didn't pause.

'Have you come to break up with me again?'

Al shook his head.

Wordlessly he crossed the small space, pulled Léon round by his shoulders and kissed him deeply. He tasted of grease paint and smoke and the lemon from his tea.

'I came to tell you I'm over it. All my stupidity, all my hang-ups. I'm over it. I'm all in. With you.'

The flicker of a smile curled Léon's lip, but he schooled his features into neutrality.

'Is that so?'

'You don't have to believe me yet, but I'm going to spend every day for the rest of my life proving it to you. If you'll have me.'

This time the smile broke through. Léon dropped the brush and flung his arms around Al's neck. Their kiss was deep and long and tender and Al wondered if this was what it would always be like, to kiss Léon in all his open-hearted vulnerability. If it would always feel so fragile, and so perfect.

When Léon drew back his face fell.

'What's wrong? What did I do?'

'Oh my *god*, I cannot believe you've gone and made a grand romantic gesture when I'm wearing a wig cap and half my make-up.'

Al cracked into a laugh as Léon took a cloth and scrubbed at the greasepaint smeared across Al's chin.

'I'd have done it even if you were stood neck deep in a pile of rotting fish guts outside Les Halles market.'

'Stop being soppy.'

'Make me.'

Léon threw down the cloth and hooked his fingers into Al's collar, drawing him onto his lap to kiss him again. Al pulled the wig cap off to run his fingers through the soft locks of Léon's hair, pulled his shirt from his waistband to spread his hands over the count of his ribs. Their heartbeats thrummed urgent together, a heat building in the spaces between their bodies.

'I have to go onstage,' murmured Léon.

Al pressed his mouth along the line of his jaw to his ear. 'They'll wait for you.'

Léon groaned another protest, but Al's hand slipped between them, moving downwards.

Neither of them spoke for a long while.

After, with the sounds of the theatre coming to life, Al turned to Léon, peeling the flush skin of his cheek from Léon's bare chest so he could meet his eye with the first earnest look he thought he had ever given him.

'Move in with me.'

'Oh?'

'We'll try to make it work. And if it doesn't, then what the hell, at least we can die trying.'

Léon kissed his temple. 'I have no intention of dying.'

It was a moment of clarity, a moment of true feeling. For the first time, Al could answer honestly, openly, buoyed by hope.

'Neither do I.'

4

The Duc's Palace

The rat catcher had been at work. Ada stood at her bedroom window watching him load his cart with sacks of dead rodents, his terrier yapping around his heels. She thought of the clutch of tiny bodies she had buried in the garden of the duc's old house when she'd first helped him kill. It had horrified her then, but months of horror had blunted the blade of her shock. The part of herself that felt shame and disgust and outrage, she had hidden safely for so long.

She thought she had plumbed the depth of the darkness she was in.

The knife lay on a pillow on the bed. The knife she had carried around for days, telling herself she was already in this deep, one more act of violence would throw her no further from herself.

A knock came at the door. Quickly, she slipped it up her sleeve, nicking the same sore scrape of skin, and Clémentine appeared.

'Well?' asked Ada. 'What is the order of business?'

At dawn, Charles had returned, rumpled and seething. Camille had evaded him; Ada gave silent thanks. The duc had sent Charles back out in fury, demanding he find Camille or not return at all.

Now, their attentions turned to their event tomorrow.

'It is all prepared,' said Clémentine. 'Philippe only wishes to conduct a dress rehearsal.'

'I have already tested the wiring with an electrostatic generator—'

'No, he means a true rehearsal.'

Oh. Olympe.

The net closing around her made her heart feel like a caged bird, battering at the bars. The duc had summoned Olympe, and he would see her unmasked. From the tension with which Clémentine held herself, Ada knew she was thinking the same thing.

There – a lever she could use to ease the gap between Clémentine and her brother further apart.

'We cannot ask her to wear that mask again,' Ada said. 'It is unconscionable. But what will the duc think? We have betrayed him—'

Clémentine interrupted. 'The mask is destroyed. Leave Philippe to me.'

Together they mounted the stairs to the highest floor and came to Olympe's rooms. A stack of books had been brought for her, and Olympe sat on the floor tucked into a defensible corner, leafing through a copy of Voltaire. Ada recognised the mark of her father's publishing house, a strange jolt of familiarity that left her disorientated.

The door to Guil's room remained open, empty.

Olympe started at their arrival, an instinct to protect herself bringing tension to her shoulders, eyes flicking wary between the exits. Then she seemed to remember the choice she had made and the new relationship she stood within.

'I told Clémentine about Guil,' said Ada, before the issue arose. 'She understands what happened.'

Olympe held her book like a talisman. 'Perhaps I am a fool.'

Clémentine enclosed her in an embrace. 'Never that. I am so grateful you are still here. I am honoured you trust me.'

When she drew back, Ada could see the hope in Olympe's eyes, the need for her choice to have been the right one. The need for her mother to make sense of a world too dark and cruel. She couldn't pretend she didn't understand.

'We must go,' she said softly. 'The duc is waiting.'

'Go where?' asked Olympe.

Clémentine stroked Olympe's face, the wild grey storm of her skin and the point of her chin and the curl of her black hair. 'Your uncle has asked for you. He wants only this one last thing, it is so nearly done. Then we will be free to leave and make a new life. Perhaps we can go to the country again. Somewhere with sky and distant horizons and peace. Would you like that?'

Olympe nodded, tears of exhaustion pricking her eyes.

Clémentine took her hand.

'Then follow me.'

'Louis! Where have you been?' James had barely stepped into the stable yard of the duc's palace before Henri materialised from the kitchens and spotted him in an instant. 'I had hoped you a reliable man.'

James smiled obliviously. 'I had to attend to my mother in Paris. The event is tomorrow, yes? I thought you expected me then.' He had decided to go with disarming confidence. Henri faltered at James's overbearing pleasantness.

'I had need of you yesterday, but according to everyone I asked you disappeared in the night and never returned.'

James let a note of confusion slip into his smile. 'Yes, monsieur, as we agreed, I could not expect lodgings to be provided, so I returned to Paris to stay with my mother.'

'Well. Yes. But I had not dismissed you until the event.'

'I am sorry, a misunderstanding. If I am no longer needed I can—'

'No.' A look of concern crossed Henri's face. 'Certainly not.' He seemed to accept James as genuine, and as before in the tavern, saw what he wanted in James, as so many people did. Henri was in need of a competent, clean-cut footman to ensure the smooth running of a high-pressured event. He would overlook anything that got in the way of that need. Sometimes James wondered what it said about him that people could project onto him exactly what they wanted. Camille in turns needed a saviour and a villain, his murderous tutor Wickham had needed a blindly devoted follower, his father needed a failure to feel superior to. Was he so empty that these visions found nothing solid to show their lie?

James smiled again, a mask, and his only face. 'Then I will do my best for you.'

Henri nodded, and directed James to the palace.

The door to the duc's kitchen opened, and James was swallowed up inside.

It was no difficult thing to find a silver serving tray and a discarded news-sheet; he folded the paper, arranging it neatly on the tray, and his cover was complete. A footman delivering a paper could go anywhere, and would be noticed by no one. Guil had described Olympe's location only in the most general terms; he had spent too much time locked in the cellar to know the layout of the house well. James had searched before as best he could, but had not found her. All he had to go on was the staircase where he had collided with Guil, and the narrative of Guil's frantic escape to trace in reverse.

He avoided the ballroom where the preparations were centred and took himself through quieter passages towards the wing of the house where he had found Guil.

His luck was almost too good.

James came out of a concealed door on an upper corridor and a few moments later, saw Olympe at the other end. She seemed so much smaller than before, like a sketch of herself, vague and smudged and quick to erase. He had done this to her, in part, and shame burned fierce.

Then Clémentine stepped out of a room and took her arm, Ada following behind. In an instant he went from relief to panic. He was an insect pinned under the lens of a microscope. Nothing stood between him and them. He had only met Clémentine for one hellish day, but that had been enough to sear her face into his nightmares. He had to assume she would recognise him just as quickly. And if Guil was right about Olympe's change of loyalties, perhaps he should fear Olympe's recognition too.

That had always been the risk of the plan, putting him so close to people who could blow his cover; it relied on the anonymity of the serving class to men like the duc, to be one in a mass of faces that were never noticed. And so far, it had worked. But in open ground like this, there was no hiding.

Could he make it back to the concealed door? Maybe. But if Clémentine hadn't noticed him yet, it would be drawing attention to himself for a footman to turn tail and run all of a sudden.

Ada caught sight of him first. Panic flashed across her face, and then she was smiling, sweeping round in front of Clémentine and Olympe to block him from view. He could hear their animated conversation, but James didn't wait another beat. Turning the handle of the nearest door, he slipped inside.

'Is that for me?'

James spun around, back against the door.

The room he had escaped to was sparsely furnished

but the same gilded skeleton of the rest of the palace, the high ceilings and parquet floor that was out of reach to all but France's wealthiest.

In a chair near the stove was a man – a boy – younger than James, with the hair and clothes that marked him as from the Holy Roman Empire.

'Is that for me?' he asked again, nodding towards the tray James carried.

James was dumbstruck. Guil hadn't mentioned anyone else being held up here, though how could he have known? The door had been unlocked, so the boy was no captive, but the space was bare and cold enough – it wasn't the room of a valued guest.

'I am the Dauphin, if that letter is for me, then hand it over,' demanded the boy.

Dauphin? James's mind raced. This was not the Dauphin, he was sure of that: the Dauphin was a boy far younger than this, and rumoured to be dead. So this was someone who thought himself the Dauphin, in the duc's palace, a day before the duc planned a coup.

It wasn't hard to put together.

'I apologise, I believe I have the wrong room,' he said. The charm he had used on Henri wasn't appropriate here; he wasn't a person to this boy. He was a tool to be used.

The Dauphin slumped back in his chair. 'Of course you have. Find me some cards or something, will you? And tell Monsieur le Duc I tire of being treated like a piece of furniture put into storage. I should be out at every assembly and ball, showing France how the tide has turned, how safety and stability are returning.'

On the other side of the door, James couldn't hear anything. Ada must have moved them on.

'Yes, Monsieur le Dauphin.'

'Go away.'

James fumbled with the doorknob and let himself out.

That was one blessing he could be glad of. To a boy like that, the strangeness of James bursting into his room didn't register, because James didn't register. A servant was nothing of interest. James knew this, because this was how he had behaved too many times.

The number of his sins was high.

Atonement would not come easy.

5

The Catacombs

Guil found Camille folded up in a passage beyond the laboratory, looking blankly at the void of the eye socket of a skull. Guil sat beside her.

She took his hand.

'You're here.'

He stroked his thumb over her fingers. 'I am.'

'I'm sorry we couldn't get you sooner.'

'Do not apologise. We all had to make sacrifices.'

At that she shut her eyes, sockets hollow and purple. 'How is she?'

Guil knew who she meant. What could he say of Ada?

Not the truth. It was too cruel.

'Brilliant. Brave. She is the best of us.'

Camille nodded. 'I wish I didn't have to ask it of her. Now she might be our only saviour.'

Guil thought of the duc's experiments, the sharp, violent death that smelled like smoke and roasting flesh. The cage the duc had built, disguised as a ballroom.

'If we fail, Ada said she would… She can get close to him. He trusts her. She could…'

Camille couldn't voice the words but Guil understood.

She shook her head. 'It can't come to that. I cannot allow Ada to have blood on her hands.'

'Then we will not fail.'

'Without Comtois, I have no confidence we could disable the duc's trap. We barely even have time to try. And if we failed, it would be too late.'

'Then can we not rely on James and Al?'

'Another risk. What if James can't get to the drinks? What if the dose is wrong? And even if we stop the duc now, won't he just try again? How many times before we slip and fail? Then all of it was for nothing. Sometimes I think: why stop him at all? What is the future but fear and downfall and we all suffer and die in the end so what does any of it matter?'

She stopped to suck in a trembling breath. Guil clasped her shoulders, brought her to look at him.

'Stop. Every plan has a hundred ways it can go wrong. We know this. But we cannot wait for a foolproof one to present itself. We must do the best with what we have. Remember, the duc's plan has a hundred ways to fail as well. He cannot risk using his device without everyone present and in place. He only has one shot – once he makes his attempt his hand is played.'

Camille crumpled and Guil pulled the two of them together.

'I've missed you,' she said. 'I've missed you so much.'

'And I you.'

Though his romantic feelings for Camille had long subsided, his love for her as his friend was as bright and sharp as it had ever been. She had been carrying too much for too long; he wanted to take her load from her.

Camille drew back and her face changed. A dark worry stirred in him.

'What is it? Camille, you do not look well.'

At that her face crumpled and she burst into tears.

'Oh, Guil. I am so sorry. Has no one told you?'

That dread climbing higher, threatening to overwhelm his defences. 'Tell me what? Is there yet more you have concealed from me?'

Then she told him.

The world broke into pieces.

'How long?' Guil's voice was thick with unspent tears.

'We don't know. James won't give me a specific prognosis. But not long.'

He didn't have words to put to the shock and grief he felt.

Under it was a strange flatness. Like he was a spectator viewing the action on a stage. Once the battalion had been his home, his family. A place he felt needed. A place to belong. He didn't recognise any of them any more. Ada a sleeper agent. Camille allying with Comtois. He had done everything he could for Olympe in that hell, and even she had harboured a secret. She had turned from him, as Ada had.

One vast, monstrous secret after another.

It was all so confused. Lies on secrets on lies.

He didn't know why he was there any more. He had left Marseille and his family with a vision of fighting for a new world, of putting his life on the line for his principles. He had told his father his conscience had demanded it.

What of his principles were left? What was he fighting for?

It had been too long since he had seen his blood family. Tasted salt on the air and kissed his mother's cheek.

He looked at Camille, the bones of her skull stark under her luminous skin.

He would stay until she passed from this world.

And then he was going home.

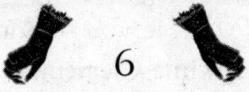

6

The Duc's Palace

Ada's heart rate had barely returned to normal when they reached the anteroom of the ballroom. What had James been doing there? Was Camille's plan in motion already? A murmur of guilty relief: perhaps she wouldn't have to use the knife after all. She needed to give their plan time to work – if she showed her hand too soon her advantage would be lost.

Beyond the open doors the copper gleamed like firelight, the infinite reflection bounding between floor and ceiling until it made her dizzy. The duc and his team of researchers were gathered around the panel in the wall outside where the eletrostatic generator was embedded. Two copper cuffs dangled from wires. Ada looked at the gaggle of men in their fine coats and powdered wigs, relics of a pre-Revolutionary world washing up against the demands of the new one. Men who observed death like a mechanical exercise.

The duc was in bright conversation, holding back the velvet curtain to expose the innovations at work. Then he caught sight of Olympe, unmasked, unchained, and his face fell as quick as a gunshot.

'Gentlemen, I will see you tomorrow.' He hastily dismissed the men while Clémentine held Olympe in the shadows. Olympe was looking into the ballroom in curiosity, at the panel in the wall: the machine that had been built around her as intimately as a corset for its one wearer. A machine she had yet to see the effects of. Blind in her mask, all she had known were the muffled sounds of pain and the smell of burning.

Once the men were gone the duc rounded on them in shock and fury.

'What is the meaning of this? Where is her mask?'

Clémentine put herself between Olympe and the duc. 'I had it removed. It was inhumane.'

'When? Why did you not consult me?'

'She is my daughter. It is my decision to make.'

It should be *Olympe's* decision, thought Ada, but this was a breakthrough.

The duc's fury crashed against the wall of Clémentine's determination, and for the first time, he faltered.

'Take more care that no one sees her,' was all he said before gathering himself together, smoothing away any sign that his authority had been challenged. 'We must be assured of the efficacy of our set-up ahead of the demonstration tomorrow. Prepare the test.'

Ada took Olympe to the operations panel. 'Will you agree to put these on?' she asked.

'Do I have a choice?' said Olympe.

Ada's stomach twisted. 'No.' It was the simple truth.

'Then don't pretend to offer me one.'

Olympe held her wrists out and Ada rolled her sleeves up to snap the cuffs in place. They fit snug to the skin, finely beaten copper bands that quickly grew warm beneath her fingers.

The duc checked the panel and the connections between the wires, then gave the signal. Olympe glanced towards Clémentine, who gave a nod of reassurance, and a blue sheen rose across the bare skin of Olympe's hands and face, shimmering and jumping with energy. When it was so thick Ada couldn't make out her features, it rushed downwards and into the cuffs. Ada had never seen Olympe exhibit so much control.

In less than a second, the current shot through the wiring to the ceiling, where it burst like a bolt of lightning to the floor, creating a flash so bright and loud Ada was flung back.

Silence fell. The ballroom returned to its serene appearance and Olympe stood in the cuffs, just a girl who held the world within herself.

The duc clapped his hands together in delight. 'Marvellous.'

'Take the cuffs off,' said Ada, shaking. 'You've done your part; you can go now.'

The duc stopped her. 'But we've only just started.'

'The machine worked, what more do you want?' Ada's mouth was running away from her; she needed to watch her words more closely.

The duc was too caught up to notice. 'We must repeat the test with a subject. We must know with complete certainty that our plan will be effective.'

Ada thought of another animal being corralled into place, another creature tortured and killed, and felt nauseous. She remembered the promise she had made Camille, that she would take the blood onto her own hands to save them all. What good was that promise if she let Olympe do this?

The duc rang a bell and a chambermaid arrived with a curtsey. She was a petite woman a little older than Ada, who she had seen around the palace dusting and polishing and carrying pales of coal. Dread bloomed hot and urgent.

'Go into the middle of the ballroom and stand still,' instructed the duc.

'Monsieur?'

'Is there a problem?'

'No, monsieur.'

Trembling, Ada stepped forward. Damn the consequences, she could not let this happen.

Clémentine got there first.

'Philippe! Enough.' Without hesitating, Clémentine strode after the maid, the heels of her shoes clicking on the polished metal. Ada imagined the effect if Olympe let off another burst of power, the electricity that would arc through Clémentine's and the maid's bodies as it reached for the copper floor. Death, horrific and inescapable.

'Clémentine, get back here at once,' ordered the duc. 'Do not interfere in what you do not understand.'

She reached the maid, took her arm and led her gently, but insistently, out of the ballroom.

'Don't be patronising. I understand your intentions

perfectly well and I am telling you I do not agree to be party to this.'

The thundercloud returned to the duc's face. 'How dare you tell me what to do. First you go behind my back, now you deign to thwart me in the very plan we have both worked towards.'

Ada saw her opportunity, and slipped forward between the warring siblings.

'Perhaps Madame de l'Aubespine is correct,' she said softly.

'You join this rebellion too?' snarled the duc.

'Attend me a moment. Consider the consequences of this test.' She lowered her voice further. 'We cannot ask Olympe to do this more than once. If she understands what she is to do tomorrow she will protest and it could cause disruption. Draw attention that something is … afoot.'

She knew Olympe could hear her, but the duc relented. He saw sense in what she said. Ada felt dirty, like the last months had left her smothered in some film of evil that would never leave her.

'Very well.' He threw his hands up in frustration. 'Have your way. But this is your contraption, Ada Rousset. If this does not work tomorrow then I will hold you personally responsible.'

'It will work.'

Before he could change his mind, she took the cuffs off Olympe and with Clémentine, led her away from the ballroom.

'What was it?' asked Olympe. 'What was I meant to do?'

'You don't want to know.'

Her voice shook, adrenaline working through her. She didn't know if she was going to throw up or cry, but whatever it was she needed to get away from Clémentine and her watchful eyes and the arc of her brow so similar to her brother's.

Clémentine touched a hand to Ada's arm and it was too gentle, too like a mother's touch, that Ada felt near hysterical. 'Take some time. I'll see Olympe back safely.'

Ada swallowed hard, nodded. 'Thank you.'

Clémentine embraced her so suddenly it was a shock.

'No, thank *you*. You are brave, Ada Rousset. A rare thing. I am glad you are here with us.'

7

The Duc's Palace

James traced Olympe and Ada to the ballroom below, his cover of the letter on the silver platter growing thin as he passed the same servants he had before. He was wandering, lost, a few corridors away when a crack of thunder echoed off the high ceilings.

Olympe.

He reached the anteroom and tucked himself into an alcove. An argument was going on, raised voices and a hissed exchange he couldn't follow. Then Ada, Olympe and Clémentine were sweeping past. Clémentine and Olympe went upstairs and Ada went down. He caught sight of her red eyes and distraught look.

James hesitated.

Olympe, and the mission he had given himself, was disappearing around the turns of the staircase.

Ada, the girl who had taken Camille from him, lay in the other direction, reduced to tears.

He should go after Olympe. He had made his plan.

But something had happened outside the ballroom. He could hazard a guess – some experiment involving

Olympe – though it felt deeper than that, as if tectonic plates were shifting deep below the surface.

An earthquake was coming, and he needed to know where to stand.

James hurried down the stairs after Ada in time to hear her summon a carriage. Where was she going? He couldn't let her vanish.

In the kitchens he discarded his tray and slid through the army of cooks, and out into the stable yard. Two grey mares were being harnessed to the carriage. Before anyone could say anything, James hopped up onto the footplate at the back, and affected a bored expression, inspecting minute flecks of dirt on his white stockings. The driver checked the horses' tack, wiped down his seat and didn't take another look at James as he geed them into motion. They drew round to the front of the house where Ada was waiting, face hidden by a mauve bonnet and a stole around her throat against the cold wind.

She gave the driver an address in the Marais district of Paris, and they set off through the fields long stripped of their harvest. The day was dark, as though the sun had lost its battle against the weight of oncoming winter, and slunk along the horizon in defeat. The road grew dense with traffic as they reached Port Saint-Antoine; in the city, they crawled through narrow, rutted streets, raw with hunger and unrest, and into the Marais.

They stopped at the end of a row of townhouses. Not as fine as Al's hôtel by any stretch, but prosperous and clean. Ada descended from the carriage, and spoke with someone at the door before returning and they drove off, heading west towards the Rue Saint-Honoré.

Rain needling the back of his neck, they drew up outside a printer's with a name that seemed familiar to James. Above the window, faded gold lettering read:

L'Ami d'Égalité

Printer's, L'Ami d'Égalité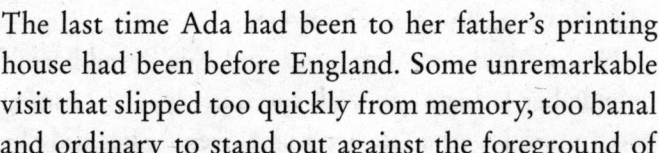

The last time Ada had been to her father's printing house had been before England. Some unremarkable visit that slipped too quickly from memory, too banal and ordinary to stand out against the foreground of fear and paranoia that had haunted her early days of working for the duc.

Returning now was like a return to a childhood schoolroom, at once deeply familiar, yet the angles and shapes somehow distorted, a wrongness twisted among the feelings of home.

Noëlle wasn't at her desk in the office downstairs. The room was half-cleared out of the usual mess of papers and books and folios and prints. The sign still hung above the door, but like most of Paris, her father was keeping his head down as he waited for the political waters to shift again. Ada thought of the duc closing the door in the room full of his political allies, that small, smug smile on his face.

Upstairs, only half the presses were in use. The room was cold enough that the printers wore gloves and scarves despite the physical nature of their work. At the wall of moveable type, the setters sat bundled up to their ears, hands flying over the upper and lower cases to assemble a manuscript in reverse. Ada picked up a sheet from a fresh pile of pamphlets and skimmed its conservative contents, nose wrinkling. Her father had shifted his colours so quickly she was surprised he wasn't outside on a stepladder himself, painting over the word égalité. But she couldn't judge him too harshly. He was a survivor, she understood that, and he told himself whatever lies he needed to believe his new course a choice, not a retreat.

No one paid her much mind, and Ada found herself outside her father's office all too quickly. She knotted her fingers together in her kid gloves. What did she think she was doing? What could she hope to gain from hurting herself like this?

The truth was so simple she couldn't deny it: she was a scared child, and she wanted her father to tell her everything was going to be okay. It didn't matter that he was singularly incapable of comfort. After what she'd just seen, she was desperate, and had acted without thinking.

As Ada made up her mind to leave, the door opened. A middle-aged white man appeared, a greatcoat thrown over fine breeches and a slightly out-of-date frock coat. He stilled, mouth an 'oh' of shock.

'Ada!'

'Father.'

He looked more tired than she remembered, more drained, like an illustration left too long in the light that had begun to fade.

He embraced her, then took his coat off and they sat down in his office.

'My daughter, I have missed you so very much. It is a relief to see you looking so well.'

Well? Ada felt like she hadn't slept in half a year and the worry line between her brows had become a fixed feature.

'I'm sorry I haven't written recently.'

His expression softened. 'You remind me so much of your mother, these days.'

An unexpected blow. Ada felt tears well in her eyes. She brushed them away but it was no good, everything she had swallowed down for so long was flooding out.

'Oh, my girl, whatever is the matter?' Her father came to her side. 'Don't cry, you'll spoil your beautiful face.'

But she couldn't stop. The duc's final experiment had been the bursting of a dam. She couldn't hide from the horror any longer. She felt the blood on her hands, smelled burning flesh in her nostrils. She had done that. She had created a killing machine for the duc.

She couldn't pretend she was above doing what needed to be done next.

She had to kill the duc.

Ada wiped her eyes with the handkerchief her father proffered.

'Papa, do you think I'm a good person?'

He smiled at her in confusion. 'What sort of question is that? Of course you are. You are principled, and good and loyal and I do not know anyone who could call you otherwise.'

She searched his eyes, looking for some doubt. He couldn't say that if he knew what she had done, but she wanted to hear the lie.

'If I did something that made me a bad person, would you still love me?'

He frowned. 'Did you do something?'

'Please, tell me you would still love me.'

'I will always love you. You are my daughter.' He took her hands. 'Ada, you're worrying me. Has something happened?'

She closed her eyes against another wave of tears. 'Oh, Papa, things are happening and they frighten me. I want to run away but I know I cannot. I must stay and follow the path set before me and that frightens me even more.'

He thought for a moment.

'What is right is often frightening.'

She wanted to laugh. He could say such wise things and yet would never act on them. God, she still loved him, even after everything he had done. It was impossible not to harbour love for a parent, however badly they hurt. The child part of her only wanted there to be someone older and wiser in control, someone she could cling to.

But the adult part saw his cowardice and cruelty for what it was. What did he know about doing the right thing? Where had all this wisdom been before when she needed it?

The thought came to her: maybe he could only do it now she had left. Now she no longer needed him as a father in the way she had before. Because she didn't need him. She might want a relationship with him, but she had survived without him through some of the worst months of her life. She had been so frightened for so long that she wouldn't be able to cope. That leaving would cut her off totally from her past, her memories of family and home.

But she was not the same girl who had sat in this office begging money and scraps of love. She'd faced more than he could ever understand. She was a harder, sharper person now, willing to do what was necessary to get things done.

She pitied him in his cowardice.

Ada pulled her hands from his and cleaned her face with the handkerchief. 'I must go.'

'You've only just arrived.'

'I know. I'll come again soon.'

If she were free. If she were able.

If she were alive.

'If I don't, will you promise me one thing?'

He was ill at ease, looking at her deep in thought. But he nodded.

'I know you do not think highly of Camille, but promise me you will look after her if she needs it? She has no family, and she is … not well.'

Her father looked like he wanted to say something else, but instead said, 'I promise.'

She kissed his cheeks and repinned her hat as she left.

She had come for comfort and she'd found it, in an unexpected way.

All she could do was make the best decision she could, and live with the consequences.

Everything was a choice. No fate. No destiny.

She thought of the knife, and the electric cage.

Her choice had already been made.

Ada finally emerged, tear-stained and stumbling for the carriage door. After a pause, she thumped on the carriage ceiling, giving the driver a new address James couldn't hear. They turned south, crossing the river again and threading past the Cordeliers and Odéon. It came to James as they waited in the snarl of traffic by the Palais du Luxembourg, how he knew the name of the printer's. It was Ada's father's press.

The carriage drew up to the pavement; the door opened and Ada stepped out.

A restaurant took up a corner plot opposite the Luxembourg prison, its windows fogged with condensation and a red and gold painted board proclaimed its name above.

They had returned to the Au Petit Suisse.

8

Théâtre de l'Égalité

The matinée let out into early autumn dusk. Al slid out with the crowds, the brim of his felt hat tipped up and his coat hanging open. For too long, the shadow of the death warrant had made him pull his hat low, slink through the shadows and hope no one noticed his existence.

He was done with that now.

He had stayed to see Léon in the play. Perhaps it had been a poor use of his time the day before the battalion's confrontation with the duc, but he didn't care if Camille berated him. He wasn't leaving the battalion like he'd threatened in London, but that didn't mean he couldn't build a life for himself too. He'd taken a box for all of Paris to see. This city was his home. He would make it have a space for him.

The theatre crowds clamoured at the line of cabs waiting in Place de la Comédie-Française, so Al turned south down rue Corneille to rue de Vaugirard where there was less competition. The street door to the battalion's old headquarters caused a pang of nostalgia. They had been difficult times, but it was the first place that had ever felt like home. Where the word family had meant something.

At the corner of rue de la Liberté, Al passed the steamed-up window of the Au Petit Suisse – and stopped. A familiar figure sat in the corner seat, curled in on herself like a puppet with its strings cut. Al let himself into the restaurant, paying no attention to the smart carriage outside.

There were a few patrons from the theatre taking seats near the door, and a scatter of students and lawyers filling the rest. Ada was at the table in the back that the battalion had occupied the night they had rescued Olympe.

He sat down opposite her forlorn shape.

'Hello, old thing.'

Ada looked up sharply, then her face crumpled with tears.

Al took her hand. 'That bad?'

Ada shook her head, unable to speak. Al had seen her upset before, angry, frightened, in all manner of dire circumstances, but she had never looked so unutterably lost.

He ordered wine from the waiter, and when he brought two glasses, Al waved one away. Pouring a large measure, he folded her fingers around the stem.

Ada drained the glass and returned it to the table, hands trembling.

'How did you find me?'

'Find you? My dear, you're at the same table we sat at for a year or more. It seems to me that you were looking to be found.'

The door opened, letting in a flurry of rain and three finely dressed young men. There was no space left, so they found a sans-culottes nursing a mug of beer.

'Move,' said the leader of the group.

The sans-culottes squinted up at them, a stubborn expression settled onto his face. 'Why should I?'

The men scoffed, and the leader winked; as the sans-culottes drank, the leader put his finger to the base of the tankard and tipped it up. Beer sloshed over his face and he leaped to his feet, wiping liquid from his eyes and spluttering. The men burst out laughing, and surrounded the table, capturing its chairs for themselves. Seeing he had been bested, the sans-culottes stormed out.

Al's fingers twitched for a drink. Anxiety lay thick through the room like the fug of pipe smoke; a few months ago that scene would have played out very differently. But Paris had turned on a knife edge. Robespierre's terror was over, and a new one was brewing. Al pulled a bag of pistachios from his pocket and directed his nerves into picking the shells apart.

'Does the duc know you're here?'

'No. At least, I don't think so.'

'Do you want to tell me why you are?'

Ada sank her head in her arms. 'No.'

'Fair enough.'

Al let the silence lie, the shape of it familiar between them. He knew her. She needed time to talk to herself before she could talk to anyone else.

'I'm frightened,' she said, after a while.

'I'm glad.'

Her head poked up. 'Excuse me?'

'I'd be more worried if you weren't.'

'Are you going to tell me something about fear keeping me sharp?'

'Looks like I don't need to.'

Ada poured herself another glass of wine. 'I don't like this role reversal.'

'Strange, isn't it? Tell me, what should I be drinking? Tea? Cordial? Lemon sherbet?'

'Don't mock me.'

'No, please, teach me your sensible and prim ways.'

'And now you're trying to distract me with light-hearted bullying.'

'My only skill.'

The waiter came again, setting lit candles on tables, as dusk fell into night. If it weren't for the detritus from a minor riot the day before littering the street outside, Al would have almost called their setting cosy.

'Shall I tell you why I'm actually glad you're frightened?'

'Go on. Enlighten me.'

Al rested his elbows on the table, leaning forward to hold Ada's gaze in a moment of rare sincerity.

'I am glad, because if you are frightened of what the duc is doing and what you must do to stay close to him, it means the Ada I know is still alive. Whatever you have had to do, whatever you have to do next, you will survive it. Your soul is still intact.'

Quite abruptly, Ada burst into tears. Loud, messy tears that drew looks from the other patrons momentarily distracted from their drinking and dinner.

Al shot them the evil eye, and scooted round to sit beside Ada, wrapping his arms around her.

'If I'd known you'd cry this much, I'd have told you your soul was fed to the devil long ago and we were all living in hell. Is that any cheerier?'

'You're so stupid,' she sobbed into his chest. 'I hate you so much.'

'And you.' He patted her head.

The door opened and a footman came in. He took off his wig in the fug of the crowded restaurant and transformed into James. Al frowned over the top of Ada's head.

'Oh, no. Is this going to turn into some tearful reunion scene?'

Ada sniffled and unpeeled herself from Al's side. 'James!'

'Er. The carriage driver wondered if you'd come to some sort of accident,' said James, pulling out a chair and removing his jacket. 'Sorry, I followed you.'

Ada pulled a purse of money from her pocket. 'I think this should be enough to keep him quiet. Perhaps he can think we are having an affair.'

James turned red. 'It's a good thing I have no reputation or it would be in tatters.'

'Dear boy, a reputation is like a fur coat in the desert: something to be shed as soon as possible.'

Ada snorted. 'I thought you'd turned a corner?'

'Who said which street I've turned onto? Perhaps I will find an exciting new vice to cultivate. Like only wearing pink cravats or swimming in lakes under the full moon.'

James took the money and left. He didn't return at once and Al poured Ada another glass of wine. The restaurant was nearly full now; the mixture of pipe smoke and sweat, the fiddle player starting up by the bar and the roll of condensation down the window was so painfully familiar it made Al's heart clench.

This would be a lot to lose, he realised. Even this.

9

The Catacombs

In one day Guil had gone from captivity to freedom. It was too quick to register, and without some demand on his attention he slipped too easily back into the memories of his cell in the basement of the duc's palace. Comtois had explained his plan, and so Guil had focused on it like a marksman, the world reduced to a single point. He did not claim to understand the science behind it, but the tactic he saw at once.

Guil worked alongside Comtois all day while Camille rested, until his hands and back ached, his muscles unused to work after months trapped in the cell. It felt good to move, clear and simple, yet demanding enough that there was no space for other thoughts.

Now, the evening opened up before him, too much space for his mind to roam.

He found himself thinking of Olympe.

Since he had fled the duc's palace, he was always thinking of Olympe.

The last week kept playing in his mind's eye, retreading each conversation, to look for the moment he had made his fatal mistake. Had he been wrong to court Clémentine's sympathy? He had brought her closer to Olympe, rekindled their trust. He should have known that would hold its own complications.

Or perhaps he should have made his move long before, in the early days of their capture, before Olympe's spirit had been broken. Before her faith in a future had been crushed.

He sat alone reading a slim volume of Molière he had found among the duc's old things, when a voice called from one of the gloomy passages, a lamp bobbing in its wake. Guil sprang up, reaching for something to use as a weapon – then James's face resolved from the shadows and Guil relaxed.

'What are you doing here? Has something gone wrong?'

James shook his head. 'Where is Camille?'

In one cave Comtois continued his work alone. In another Camille was asleep, slumped forward over a scatter of femurs, a halo of short golden hair glowing in the candlelight. Her skin seemed stretched too taut over the bones of her skull, her eyes sunken and bruise-dark, lips pale and chapped. As fragile as porcelain, dress hanging loose, she was living on borrowed time.

Guil swallowed the lump in his throat.

She deserved something to raise her crushed spirit. To renew her broken faith in the future.

He woke her with a gentle hand on her shoulder and she blinked at him, confused.

'James is here.'

'James?'

James came to sit beside her, a gentle hand on her arm. 'Hello, my love.'

Tears brimmed in her eyes, and then she thumped him. 'You *left* me.'

He cupped her face and brushed away her tears with his thumb. 'I could never leave you.'

'You didn't say goodbye. I thought I might never see you again.'

Guil faded into the shadows to give them privacy.

James pulled Camille into his arms and stroked her hair.

'Listen to me, Camille du Bugue. Wherever it is we both go next, you will always carry a part of me with you and I will always carry a part of you.' He twined their fingers together. 'I'm so happy Ada loves you. You are so loved, Camille.'

Tears slid down her cheeks and he pressed a kiss to her forehead.

Guil let a moment pass, then asked the question that had arrived with James. 'What of Olympe?'

'I'll tell you about everything.' He rose and offered one hand to Camille and one to Guil. 'First, come with me,' said James. 'I have a surprise.'

Guil pulled the blinds down over the carriage windows, closing off the rain-spattered streets and the lamps swaying in the wind. A storm had been gathering on the horizon for several days now, casting the city in grey gloom and buffeting the surface of the Seine into frothing crests.

Camille sat on the opposite bench, wrapped in a heavy greatcoat that smelled like wet sheep and lanolin.

'You know I'm not a fan of surprises,' she said, but her lip was curling in a smile of curiosity. 'Won't you at least tell me where we're going?'

James smiled and said nothing.

The roads were slow, and with the blinds down he couldn't track their progress. He thought they were crossing the river, when some of the clamour of the narrow streets dropped away, and then traffic picked up on the left bank.

A short while later, the carriage stopped and James jumped out first, opening an umbrella. Guil followed and held a hand out to help Camille onto the pavement.

'Cover your eyes.'

With a look of amusement, Camille complied. Guil shook his head. He wanted to know what he was walking into. So he followed behind as James opened the door to the Au Petit Suisse and guided Camille in, then shook off the umbrella and closed it, tucking it under his arm so he could take over covering her eyes and steering her to the table at the back of the restaurant. Guil sucked in a breath.

James held a finger of his free hand to his lips.

A seat was pulled out, and he helped Camille into it.

James took his hand away.

10

The Au Petit Suisse

Camille opened her eyes and it was like a blow. A rush of emotion so strong it took the air from her lungs.

Warmth. Music. Laughter. A meal of roast guinea fowl, pottage, a dish of anchovies and a plate of pickled greens was spread upon the table.

And her battalion. Guil on one side, James on the other, Al, and opposite, Ada. Oh, Ada. She thought when she died, this might be what she saw. Only love, warmth. Family. And her face. That beautiful face.

The only gap where Olympe had once sat, timid and trusting.

Camille covered her face with her hands, worked to set her breathing steady. When she looked again, she saw Ada was crying too, quiet, bright tears that flecked the deep brown of her eyes with warm light.

'Thank you,' she whispered. 'What is this?'

'Think of it as a happy coincidence,' said Al.

They explained how James had followed Ada to the Au Petit Suisse, and Al had found them, then James had decided to fetch Camille and Guil.

'Not that he cared to tell us before disappearing. A surprise for both of us,' said Al.

Camille squeezed James's hand in gratitude. She didn't deserve him.

'Will someone hurry up and be Mother?' said Al. 'The food's getting cold and I'm starving.'

James rose to carve the chicken and dishes of samphire were passed around to fill plates. Beneath the table, Ada had extended her legs so her feet hooked snugly around Camille's. It was such a small, intimate gesture that it hurt her heart to think she might have no more left to come.

After they had eaten, Al ordered coffee and they came with the same tiny biscuits wrapped in twists of fine paper. Camille took one, curling it into a loose cylinder and touched the end to a candle flame. It caught at once in a flare of orange and yellow, and rose like a leaf on the wind. It burned so beautifully, and so quickly. Its short flight was swallowed up in seconds, leaving only a patina of ash over the table.

Tomorrow, Camille would light the last flame she had left within her.

She only wondered what she would leave behind.

When the plates were cleared away, Ada came to her side, and whispered in her ear for her to follow. With a wink from Al, Camille let herself be led through a door at the back of the room.

'I don't have the key to the roof any more,' said Ada. 'We can't see the stars. But I thought this might be okay.'

The courtyard at the back of the restaurant was as cramped as Camille remembered it, stacked with crates from the market, potato peelings and cabbage leaves stamped into the cobbles, a smell of vegetal rot rising from the sewer grate – and cold, painfully, bitterly cold.

But it was private.

Ada held out her hand and Camille let herself be drawn close. Her greatcoat hung open and she wrapped it around the both of them. The sound of the fiddle player filtered through from the restaurant, bright and beautiful and they began to dance.

The sway of their bodies was intimate and familiar, like a melody remembered from childhood. Like coming home. Camille rested her forehead against Ada's, savouring the warmth of Ada's breath on her skin, the flush of breast against breast, hip against hip. This was where everything made sense. This was where she fit.

'Are you okay?' asked Camille. 'I didn't think you'd find another chance to leave before tomorrow.'

Ada was quiet for a while. 'I had not thought I would either. The duc…' She stopped herself. 'I needed some space.'

'I can understand that.'

They drifted over the cobbles together, snug in the greatcoat as rain drifted down in the windless air of the sheltered courtyard.

'If you can't … do it.' Camille couldn't bring herself to say the actual words. 'It's okay. We'll find another way.'

Ada was tense in her arms, the rise and fall of her breath shallow. 'No. I will not fail. Not now. Not after everything I have done.'

Camille wanted to ask Ada to let her share the burden, to tell her what had passed in her time with the duc. But she knew what it was to have a horror that could not be voiced for fear of it being seen, and in being seen becoming indelibly real.

So instead she kissed her, and hoped in the heat of her skin and the softness of her touch Ada would know she was loved, no matter what. That she was the star by which Camille navigated, the anchor holding her steady, the compass needle pointing her home. No love was unconditional, but Ada, in her very nature, met every condition Camille could ever have. She was salvation. She was home.

She was the future, if Camille had one.

The kiss grew heated, Ada's tongue slipping into her mouth and Camille's hand finding Ada's breast.

Then the restaurant door banged open and Al stuck his head outside.

'God's teeth, it's freezing out here. Stop being romantic heroes and come back inside before Camille drops dead like the tragic gutter orphan she is. We need to discuss tomorrow.'

Camille came back to earth.

Tomorrow.

The duc.

Al was right, she couldn't let herself be distracted yet.

Inside, a fresh pot of coffee waited for them, and the chairs had been pulled together in a conspiratorial huddle.

'Ada, tell them what happened,' said James. 'I only overheard the end of it. Tell us what happened with Clémentine. And Olympe.'

Guil frowned. 'Clémentine?'

Ada slipped from lover to spy in a breath, her posture shifting and her face growing sharp.

'There's a rift between Clémentine and the duc. I don't know how deep, but today she stood up to him for the first time. Refused to let him run another experiment on Olympe.'

Ada explained what had happened outside the ballroom earlier that day.

Camille felt a spark of hope flare in her chest. 'You think she'll turn on him?'

'I don't know. But it was enough for her to take Olympe from the cells, which allowed Guil to escape. Today, it saved a life. But I worry if we move too quickly, she'll panic and go back to where she feels safe.'

'Too bad,' said Al. 'We've run out of time. She's either an asset or a liability, and that sounds like too much of a risk for me.'

'I thought you liked a risk?' said Camille.

'That was the old me. The reformed me is looking forward to a long retirement somewhere by the sea with many handsome servants to feed me grapes.'

'I agree with Al,' said Guil. 'We can't push Clémentine. If she's loyal to anyone, it's to herself.'

'Fine,' said Camille. 'If we see an opportunity, we take it, but we cannot count on her.'

'I've some better news,' said James, drawing the conversation to him. 'The duc has hired security to control the aftermath, but he's also had to hire a lot of extra servants to staff the event. There are so many people coming and going through the kitchens no one will notice a few more. I'll leave a door open for you.'

He took a candle stub and used the sooty tip of the wick to draw a rough outline of the palace to show them where.

'Guil and I will go that way,' said Camille.

Al interrupted. 'Don't be ridiculous.'

'Excuse me?'

'Everyone here is being too polite because they think it's kind, but I think being kind is telling you that under no circumstances can you be involved in anything strenuous.'

Camille went hot. 'I'm fine. I need to—'

'Guil is far cleverer than us, he doesn't need you to do anything but come with me as a guest and waft around delicately with plenty of opportunities to sit down.'

She scowled. 'I'm not an invalid.'

Her battalion regarded her with a mixture of looks from pain, to pity, to incredulity.

'Okay, fine. I'll wear a dress and play the stupid bourgeoisie again.'

'Good,' said Al. 'So Camille and I will be in the ballroom – and, I suppose, Ada, you'll be there too?'

Ada nodded. 'Have you got the vitriol of copper?' she asked James.

He patted his pocket. 'I'm not letting it out of my sight.'

'They'll do a toast with champagne,' said Ada. 'I saw Clémentine finalising the menu.'

'That's a lot of glasses to spike,' said James, a note of worry creeping into his voice.

'You don't need to do them all, just a critical mass. He can't risk showing his hand unless he's confident he can eradicate all guests at once.' Ada swallowed, twisted her fingers together so tightly her knuckles pressed pale against her skin. 'Please. You all need to be extremely careful. If you're inside that room and he can get a charge through the wires… You haven't seen what it can do.'

Camille exchanged a conspiratorial look with Guil and Al.

'Ah. That's the last thing we haven't told you: we're working with Comtois. He's helped us form a plan.'

'I thought he died in the explosion,' said Ada in confusion.

'So does everyone. He hid out long enough for everyone to write him off.'

'But he came back? I still don't understand why you would work with him in the first place.'

'He did come back.' Camille leaned in closer, drawing her battalion tight around her. 'Here's the new plan…'

The Countryside Beyond Paris

Ada sat in silence for the entire carriage ride back to the duc's palace.

She had to have faith. In Camille's plan, in her own courage.

God help them, all they had was faith.

At the front of the palace the carriage drew to a halt and James leaped down from the footman's perch to let her out. Night lay so thick he was nothing but a warm body in the shadows. She took his hand to dismount; he tightened his grip to stop her from going inside.

'Ada.'

'Yes?' she whispered. There was no one except the well-bribed driver around but it still felt a frightening risk to talk to him so openly.

For a moment he said nothing. There was only the crush of his fingers, the soft rush of his breath.

'Take care of her for me.'

'What?'

'I trust you.'

She thought she saw him smile, the edges of his eyes crinkling, and she felt choked.

Ada nodded. 'I will. Always.'

And then he was gone, hopping onto the carriage that drove away across the gravel, leaving her alone before the vast edifice of the palace, with the ghost of his touch on her skin and the promise on her lips.

11

Paris

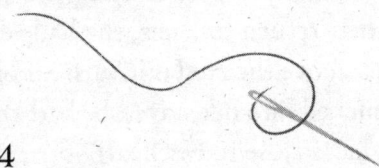

16 October 1794

The day of the duc's electrical demonstration dawned dark and feeble. Night slipped over the horizon only far enough to turn the sky from black to deep grey, a sheet of rain scudding across the city in waves as people ran, heads ducked from shopfront to doorway. The church bells tolled out the hours, each as dull as the next. Dusk came as unremarkable as dawn. Lamps were lit by men in waxed coats slick with rain, and candles glimmered behind shutters.

Camille sat at her dressing table in Al's hôtel particulier. There was nothing left for her to do. Her cheeks already burned with colour, her eyes already flashed too bright. A midnight-blue satin ballgown had been hastily taken in to fit her disappearing frame. Her collarbones stood out too starkly. Her hair, now short, took little dressing, Al helping only to use a pot of his pomade to tidy the worst of her cowlicks.

There was no need to evade the duc's men any more: she would deliver herself to him presently. Comtois's preparations were complete.

From a box on the table, Camille drew a necklace. A fine silver chain with a locket hanging from it. She had carried it safely from hideout to hideout when she had fled her home after her parents' execution. On their return to Paris, she had retrieved it from the rooms above the Au Petit Suisse. Folded within a cloth and tucked into her stays, she had kept the memento of their faces close to her heart.

She fastened it around her neck, the metal warming quickly against her skin.

It felt right to keep them near, despite all the anger she felt towards her father and his betrayal, the confusion she felt over her mother's affair. She thought of James and Ada and the mess she had made of her battalion. Her friends. Perhaps now she understood her parents a little better.

After all, she would join them soon.

Guil slipped the hammer into the waistband of his breeches, letting the handle lie flush against his leg. The footman's uniform was slightly too big, despite his height, and hid the weapon well. Comtois slipped a chisel inside his own clothes. Everything was borrowed from Léon's theatre troupe; it made Guil happy to see Al at ease with Léon.

At least one of them had made good choices.

On the country road outside the duc's palace, an army of staff were arriving, drays pulling carts loaded with beer barrels, women carrying baskets of fresh fruit and vegetables, pails of milk hanging from heavy yokes across their shoulders, kitchen maids in well-worn dresses and wooden clogs, stable hands pushing carts of hay. Guil and Comtois took their places among them, in matching blue frock coats and white powdered wigs.

In the stable yard, Guil caught sight of James in conversation with someone whose back was angled to the crowd. Guil touched Comtois's arm and they hurried towards the coal door James had marked on his sketch the night before.

Above them, the palace was impossibly vast. A light shone in one window, then the next, and the next, as servants went room to room touching burning tapers to the candles. A cold, glittering beast just beginning to wake.

Al tightened his grasp on the leather strap hanging from the carriage ceiling as they jolted over the cobbles at Port Saint-Antoine and out into the countryside. The city disappeared in a haze of rain and light. Beyond the city walls lay only darkness, and the rattling lamps hung at each corner of the carriage.

Camille sat next to him so still and quiet that only the weak squeeze of her hand reassured him she was still alive. That he wasn't alone in the dark, and the cold, and the fear. He could feel her pulse fluttering in her wrist through the leather of his gloves. Too fast, too faint.

As the last of the city died away, he wondered if he had made a mistake. He meant to live.

In the darkness, it was as quiet as the grave.

Henri had been difficult to distract, and James had been forced to resort to flattery. The man had overseen the arrival of the temporary staff like a drill sergeant, scrutinising each face and barking orders at the slow or sloppy. James had first tried concocting a disaster with the silverware, but Henri had been dismissive.

So James had done what he had always done, become pleasant and blank, ready to reflect back whatever people wanted to see in him. And after a moment, it was clear that Henri was frightened he wouldn't accomplish what he set out to, that humiliation lay in wait behind every smeared glass or spilled drink. James told him it would never happen. That every preparation was masterfully thought through, that without Henri they would be floundering.

Guil and Comtois edged past unnoticed and James finally returned to his primary task. In an anteroom by the crystalware storeroom hundreds of champagne flutes were being set on trays and filled from ranks of bottles. James coopted overseeing procedures by dropping Henri's name, and under the guise of checking for chips in the glass, he shook the vitriol of copper from the sleeve of his jacket, a little one into the base of each flute before it was filled.

The line of trays stretched before him.

Time was running out, and there were so many left to go.

The storm cloud of Olympe's skin was still. She stood by the window, watching the next band of rain roll in across the fields that spread beyond the palace gardens. It was too cold for the assembly to spill into the formal grounds, so no lanterns had been lit. She could only hear voices somewhere distant below; the crunch of carriage wheels and slamming doors.

Olympe flexed her hands, looking at the swirls of purple and blue and grey. So still. With a nudge of power, she sent a ripple of blue sparks along one finger to burn in a single bright point.

Her mother said that after tonight things would be over. But they never would be. While she wielded this power, none of it would ever be over.

Her life was a prison, and there could only be one escape.

The copper floor and ceiling of the ballroom shimmered in the candlelight like molten flame, a jewelled cavern lined with hidden wire teeth. Death would move on silent feet here.

Ada tugged at the cuffs of her long-sleeved winter gown. Red silk glowed warm against the brown of her skin, the waist cut fashionably high and the train of the sack back trailing on the floor behind her. She had tucked her knife up her sleeve so many times that there was a thin slice of skin on the underside of her arm littered with nicks and cuts that never quite closed. She could feel one opening now, the sting and pull of flesh rending.

It felt good.

Al was right. The fear kept her sharp.

It kept her true target in view.

The duc stood before the double doors in an elegant tailcoat and britches after the new, plain style popular in London. He had even shed his wig to let the salt and pepper grey of his hair show.

He raised his hand, and footmen drew the two huge doors open.

'Welcome!' he called to the waiting crowd, 'to the greatest spectacle of our age. Step inside.'

Guests in silks and gauze, velvet and pearl, flooded into their metal cage.

The doors of the trap snapped shut.

PART SIX

Après Moi le Deluge

16 October 1794

1

The Kitchens of the Duc's Palace

A sea of glass glimmered with golden liquid as footman after footman carried their polished silver trays through the kitchens and up the stairs to the palace above. James watched them go, feeling sick to his stomach.

He hoped the guests would feel worse.

The bottle of vitriol of copper had seemed laughably tiny for the number of glasses he had attempted to spike, one clumsy movement between making too few people dangerously ill or too many only a little nauseous. It was too late to do anything now, the champagne disguising the rime at the bottom of each flute. He should take a tray himself and see if his handiwork had come good.

But he wasn't finished yet.

He couldn't believe Olympe had truly chosen the duc's side. She would never agree to what he wanted her to do tonight.

She just needed another chance.

She needed someone to believe there was hope.

This time, he had finessed his cover. Alongside the food being prepared for the assembly, James found what he was looking for: a single tray set out with a portion for one. Generous, a glass of claret and the finest white bread.

'Is this for the Dauphin?' he asked imperiously.

The maid preparing the tray looked at him, wide-eyed. 'Not so loud.'

James huffed, a busy man about his business. The maid was scared, and for her, he would be the person who took the fearful task away.

'That's a yes, then. Is it done?'

She nodded and he took the tray.

Instead of following the other footmen up the stairs to the ballroom, he crossed the length of the palace through the basement passageways to the concealed servants' staircase at the far end.

The end closest to the Dauphin's rooms – and Olympe.

The Ballroom

Al kept Camille's hand tucked firmly into the crook of his arm as they entered the ballroom. Passing from marble floor to metal, another jolt of misgiving shot through him. It had been far easier to feel confident about the future when he wasn't standing on a surface designed to murder him by lightning strike. Several hundred guests were already amassed, laughing and talking like they were in a perfectly normal country that hadn't spent the last three years chopping the heads off their friends and neighbours. All the good and the great of Revolutionary Paris were here, all too happy to believe they had won.

Al clamped down on the hysterical laughter that threatened to spill out of him. This was a *farce*. How on earth did the battalion think they could do a thing to stop this? The tides of history were too strong.

They could stop this massacre but another one would come along; it was like throwing a thimble of water on a house fire.

If they wanted to save France, they were horribly, horribly too late.

'How pleased I am you could join us, Comte de Périgord, though I do not remember sending you an invite.'

The duc arrived with Ada, Clémentine and Charles in tow. Camille's hand squeezed Al's arm painfully, and he came back to himself in time to give a shallow laugh.

'You didn't, but I won't take offence. I borrowed one off a chap who had a nasty accident in a back alley.' He smiled in the inscrutable way he had perfected over the years. 'We thought we'd come and see what this was all about.'

The duc assessed them with a glimmer in his eye.

He must know they came with an ulterior motive, but the duc thought his trap foolproof, and that his enemies had walked directly into it.

His hunger for victory outweighed his suspicion.

'How fortunate – for me. To have the pleasure of your company,' said the duc.

A fleet of footmen came in bearing trays of champagne. The duc made the smallest gesture to Clémentine, who looked sickly beneath her powder. She excused herself and hurried from the room.

As the footmen passed through the guests distributing drinks, the duc smiled wider.

'I believe it is time for a toast.'

The Depths of the Palace

The covered moon gave no light as Guil and Comtois searched for the door James had left open. They were alone, fumbling across flagstones and gravel, hands tracing the outline of barred cellar windows and solid stone walls.

Guil found it in the end by almost breaking his neck. What James hadn't said was that it was at the foot of a narrow flight of steps cut into the stone terrace, almost invisible in the dark. Comtois steadied him at the last moment, and together they crept down to the sightless void below.

There was no need to light the storeroom – a naked flame could be dangerous with all the coal dust in the air – but logic dictated that there would be a corresponding door to the interior of the palace somewhere. Moving by intuition around the heaping piles of coal, until there – the tiniest glimmer, a line of paler dark around the outline of a door. This handle was unlocked too, and Guil and Comtois wasted no time in putting themselves on the other side of it.

Here was a corridor, colder than the coal hole, walls moist with damp and moss, a gutter cut down the centre of the floor. Doors were set off either side, solid wood with slots cut into each at eye height, left over from when the palace had been a medieval castle, before wealthy aristocrats had had the resources and security to turn their defensive structures over to pleasure seeking.

Guil knew these cells.

He felt too cold and hot at once, a clammy sweat on his palms. Time folded in on itself and he was in two moments at once, the mission Camille had set him overlaid by panic and desperation. The sound of a cell door thudding shut, the turn of a key. Olympe screaming.

Guil shut his eyes and dug his nails into his palms.

Comtois rested a hand lightly on his shoulder. 'Are you okay?'

Guil swallowed, nodded. 'Yes. I know where we are. At the end of this passage is the servants' quarters.'

It wasn't what Comtois had meant. They both knew Guil understood the real question.

He turned away as they passed his cell and Olympe's. Beyond the next door they could hear voices, life. They made a quick attempt to clean the worst of the coal dust from their clothes.

'The thing I am afraid of has already happened,' said Guil softly. 'I can live my life alert to the threat of it happening again, but nothing I do can change the past. The worst happened, and I survived. So I cannot let fear rule me.'

Comtois thought about this. 'You are right. But the thing I fear is still happening.'

He set his hand to the door knob and turned.

'I must ensure we survive it.'

2

Olympe's Room

She was waiting for him, dressed simply in white silk with her hair loose around her shoulders, standing in the middle of the room as though there was nothing left for her to do but wait.

Her door was unlocked. If she'd chosen her mother's side, what need was there to lock her in any more?

'I didn't know who would reach me first,' said Olympe. 'It's you.'

James set down the tray of food and nudged the door shut to keep their conversation private.

'Who else would be coming?' he asked.

'You know.'

'Your mother? The duc?'

'I heard the guests arriving.'

She held herself so still, braced for the worst. He could only imagine what she had been through these past months, on top of all she had been through before. That she had kept fighting so long was a miracle.

'Are you here to kidnap me again?'

'No.' He sighed, sat down at the table where he'd

put the tray and drank some of the claret. 'Maybe I should. Maybe that's what would save everyone. But I won't. I want this to be your choice.'

'I made my choice.'

'Yes, Guil told me.'

'Then you know I'm not going with you.'

He pushed the wine glass in front of the chair opposite, and began to portion out the food. 'Come on. Eat some of this. We might as well take the opportunity while we can.'

After a moment's hesitation, she joined him, taking a piece of the soft white bread, her eyes trained on James.

'It's not a trick,' he said.

'I know. You don't do tricks like this.'

He warmed, despite himself, at the thought she felt she knew him. 'So. Tell me your plan,' he said. 'How does this work?'

'What do you mean?'

'You do what your mother and the duc want. We're defeated. The duc puts a king back on the throne. Then what?'

'Does it matter?'

James shrugged. 'Of course it matters. None of us can escape the consequences of our actions.'

'Stop it. Stop acting like I've had any meaningful say in this.'

James rolled a boiled egg on the tray, cracking the shell. 'That's fair. A lot of it hasn't been. But you *chose* not to escape with Guil. What happens next is at least in part on you.'

'So. What? You want me to make the *choice* that

means I'm running for my life, for the rest of it? That means I am never safe? That I can never let my guard down even for a minute because if I do someone will hunt me down and not all of them will be as willing to keep me alive as my uncle? You think I should *choose* that future?'

'You don't know that's what would happen.'

'Don't I?' she narrowed her gaze. 'The Revolutionaries took me, and then I'd barely escaped them for five minutes before you did the same. And then Wickham and then the duc again. I'd be stupid not to see a pattern.'

'I won't deny it's a risk. But it's not the only thing that could happen. You could meet someone like Camille, like the battalion. You could travel. You could learn about medicine, like you wanted to in London, learn English.' His cheeks heated as he said the next words. 'You could fall in love.'

Olympe folded her arms. A purple flush threaded through the storm clouds of her cheeks. 'What a nice dream.'

'It's only a dream if you stay here. The only guarantee of failure is if you never try.'

'You think I'm failing?'

James set down the fork he had been using to pick through the stewed quail. 'I think you are choosing to survive. I am asking you to choose to *live*.'

Olympe held the challenge in his gaze. 'I can do that better with someone who'll keep me safe.'

He tried another tack. 'Do you know what the duc wants you to do tonight?'

'Yes.'

'Really?'

Olympe faltered. 'Sort of.'

'He has built a machine into the structure of the ballroom that can pass an electrical current through every person inside it at once.'

Olympe went grey, the blue and green and purple bleaching from her skin. 'What do you mean?'

'It's a killing machine.'

She shook her head. 'No. No. I'm just – a power source. Like the fire in a kiln or water in a mill. That's all.'

'No.'

'You're lying.'

'Why would I do that? We both know he wanted you as the muscle behind his coup. Tonight he will execute every single figure in the Revolutionary government, and the path will be clear for the return of a king. You are the axe he will swing.'

'Stop it – stop—' Olympe ran her hands through her hair, twisting her fingers in their wild strands.

'Is that the price you're willing to pay for safety?'

'Shut up.'

'Safety in the shape of a gilded cage?'

'So kill me!' she yelled, grey smudged swirls raging across her face. 'That's the only way this all ends. Get rid of me so no one can ever use me as a weapon. If I run, I will only ever be hunted. If I stay, I will be used for slaughter.' She trembled where she stood, breath shallow. 'What other way is there? So go on, kill me. Get it over with.'

James stared at her, dumb with shock. 'Is that really what you think I'm here to do?'

But Olympe wasn't looking at him any more.

Her wide eyes were fixed on the door behind him.

James bolted up, grasping for the candlestick as a makeshift weapon.

Clémentine stood on the threshold, her expression steely. 'I swear on my life, while there is breath in my lungs, no one will kill.' Her gaze landed on James and narrowed. 'No one.'

The Ballroom

'Today is the beginning of the future of France!'

The duc's voice carried over the hush of hundreds of silent bodies. Camille held her glass tightly at the stem. She couldn't look at the people around her knowing what was at stake, so instead she focused on the bubbles in the champagne, countless tiny specs of air struggling to the surface, crowding each other out in their escape. She thought the colour seemed a little different and hoped it was a sign James had been successful.

'You have gathered here to witness the power of science. That flag bearer of the future. That noble art. That glory. Our great ship of state has foundered in choppy waters. Our crew have gone overboard, one by one. We are lost. How can we right ourselves? How can we take everything precious with us as we move forward?

'Mesdames and messieurs. I say we have failed. We have failed France, we have failed our children. We trample on their heritage, bringing them only rags and burdens. You came here today curious about what the future might hold. I offer only this: trust in the power of science, and France will be glorious once more!'

Camille swallowed. Cheers came from around the room, glasses raised. They did not hear the message beneath the duc's words. They did not know they toasted their own death.

Champagne flutes clinked together on every side as people drank. Charles knocked back his glass. The duc was too close. He would see if she did not drink. Camille raised the wine to her lips. Tipped the brim so it swilled against them but did not enter. Al did the same.

The duc watched them both, and frowned. He did not lift his own glass. Camille's stomach twisted into a knot and for a moment she thought she must have drunk James's poison.

Then the retching began.

Charles doubled forward, spewing the rotten champagne onto the floor, face flushing puce. All around the ballroom, people lifted their hands to their mouths, grimacing in disgust. Some fled the room, others vomited onto their shoes, smearing the polished floor. Voices raised against the duc, cries of Royalist tricks, glasses went smashing to the ground. Less than half the guests were sick but it was enough to sow panic. A stampede headed to the doors that had not yet been closed. Two of the duc's men were trying to force them shut but the tide of people was too strong. It burst the doors open, and the balance of fortune tipped away from the duc.

He rounded on Camille and Al.

'What have you *done*?' he snarled.

But Camille was already running.

3

Outside the Ballroom

Guil and Comtois arrived seconds before the doors blew open and a crowd of people in vomit-splattered finery poured from the room. Comtois grabbed Guil's arm and pulled him to one side, where a velvet curtain hung from floor to ceiling. At first Guil thought it must hide another doorway, but when Comtois pulled it aside he realised they had reached their target.

A large wooden panel was set into the painted wallpaper, the height of a man and an arm-span wide. With an intricate series of switches and wires, it looked like a figment of a fevered dream. It frightened him that something so innocuous could cause the horrors he had seen. Was this the future? Death from a sanitary distance, mechanical and impersonal. The gun, the guillotine, what did they do but remove you from the act of killing? Then it hardly felt like killing at all. Just the pull of a trigger. The drop of a rope.

Guil took the hammer from within his clothes. Comtois palmed his chisel. As more and more people forced their way screaming from the ballroom, they set to work prising away the wood that protected the wiring behind. But it was no good, the crowd was too many and they barely had space to manoeuvre.

'Wait till they've passed,' yelled Comtois. 'It's quick work once we get the panel free.'

Guil nodded, and pressed himself as close to the wall as he could. A memory came to him of the fire at the Théâtre Patriotique, the terrified crowd driving themselves further into the crush. The swollen bodies lined up on the street outside.

He held the hammer tightly, shut his eyes, and waited.

Olympe's Room

Clémentine shut the door behind her.

'Who are you and what are you doing in my daughter's room?' she asked, eyebrow arched as though he were a normal suitor snatching a moment of privacy. Then her expression changed, her head cocked. 'Wait, I know you. You're the boy from England, the one at the wedding.' She frowned. 'The one who stole Olympe away from France.'

James brandished the candlestick, hot wax dripping over his hand.

'You've come to take her again.' Clémentine reached for the summoning bell.

'Mother, no.' Olympe snatched her mother's hand away. 'I trust him.'

Clémentine looked between them. 'What is going on?

James steeled himself, replaced the candlestick, clenching his fist to break the coating of wax across his fingers.

'I'm not here to force Olympe to do anything,' he said after a moment. 'But I wanted to give her another chance to make a different choice.'

Clémentine studied him so closely he felt like a specimen in his surgical lectures. It was as though she could peel back every layer of his performance, his self-doubt, his shame, and see to the snivelling core.

'You care about her, don't you?' she said with curiosity. 'So much that you'd face down people with more money and power than you can dream of?'

James swallowed. Nodded.

Clémentine raised a hand to her throat. 'I think I have made a mistake. Philippe is not who I knew him to be before.'

Olympe searched her face. 'Mother, what are you saying?'

The words seemed to be a struggle for Clémentine, each one given up only after a fight. 'He changed while I was imprisoned. He has become … twisted.'

'You said we were better off with him.'

'I know. I thought it was true.'

James made an offering. 'I made the same mistake with someone I thought I knew. Someone I thought I trusted.' The memory of Wickham changing from mentor to monster still waited for James when he closed his eyes at night. He had made his own grievous, arrogant errors. He could not judge Clémentine for hers, though he might not forgive her for how she had treated Olympe. 'It is never too late to take a different path.'

Clémentine was pink with discomfort.

'I shackled myself to a monster, and I refused to see it,' she said. 'But I see it now.' She went to Olympe, held her face in her hands. 'Beloved daughter. Go. I won't stop you.'

'Where will I go?' Olympe was reduced to a child in her arms, asking for the world to be made simple, safe.

'I do not know. But I know that the rest of your life doesn't start with mass murder.'

Olympe began to cry and James felt that slither of guilt in his gut again. He had brought this on her. Taking her from Camille in the bowels of the Madeleine church, he had set in motion the events that put her in this position now.

'I'm frightened,' sobbed Olympe. 'I don't want to be alone.'

She looked at James over Olympe's shoulder. 'You won't be.'

'I can't do it. I tried before and I failed. I'm too scared.'

Clémentine stroked her hair. 'Yes. But being frightened doesn't mean something is impossible. You are stronger than I wanted to acknowledge. *I* was frightened you wouldn't need *me* any more. But that's right, isn't it? Children grow up and don't need their parents.'

'No,' said James. 'We always need them. Just in different ways.'

Clémentine drew back to look Olympe in the eye. 'Well, then let me need something different from you, my girl. I need you to *run*.'

'Mother, come with me.'

'No. I have made my choices and now I must bear the consequences. You have your friends. A future. I have my brother. I will do what I can to protect you tonight, but I cannot leave him.' She closed her eyes again, summoning strength. 'He is my monster so I will be his keeper.'

James took Olympe's arm, helping her from one life to the next.

'You must be quick. They're expecting you in the ballroom.' Clémentine removed the shawl pinned at her shoulders and wrapped it around Olympe's hair to hide her face, then enclosed her in another embrace. 'I hope you can forgive what I have done, one day. I hope I can be worthy of your forgiveness.'

She held the door open, and hand in hand, James and Olympe walked away.

Outside the Ballroom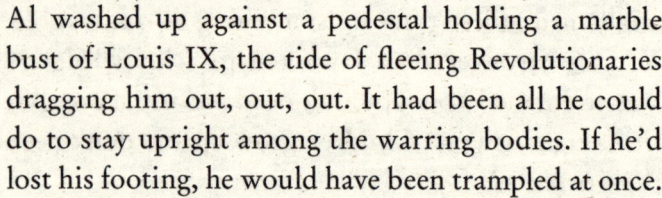

Al washed up against a pedestal holding a marble bust of Louis IX, the tide of fleeing Revolutionaries dragging him out, out, out. It had been all he could do to stay upright among the warring bodies. If he'd lost his footing, he would have been trampled at once.

The chaos was magnificent.

The duc had thought himself invulnerable, the battalion self-righteous children, ants he could crush under his boot. His own arrogance had blinded him to their strength. Across the anteroom, a velvet curtain had been pulled aside to reveal the control panel – not that the fleeing guests noticed – but Al saw. Guil and Comtois poised with their hammers ready to strike, stalled only by the crush of people.

A worry interrupted his revelry with a jolt: where was Camille? He'd thought her directly behind him, but he was alone. Had she been dragged further along? He searched the fast-moving crowd for her shorn head but there were too many women who had attempted the same style. Each face he found was not hers.

He imagined her fallen below the thundering feet, her fragile body crushed against the floor.

'Camille? Camille!' He called her name but the screaming crowd was too loud.

Then he saw her. In the distance, beyond the trailing rear of the herd.

She had fallen, tripping on the hem of her dress and struggling for breath. She didn't even try to run.

She knew it was too late.

The duc's hand closed around her arm, yanking her up. Al's heart stuttered.

They had been so close. So close.

The crowd thinned. If he meant to escape under their cover, he would have to go now. Guil and Comtois swung the hammers towards the control panel.

He should flee. That was what he had wanted, wasn't it? To live?

He watched as the last of the guests stumbled down the staircase.

Then he looked back at Camille. Alone. Defiant.

Al swore, at length and creatively. He was an absolute idiot. Doomed.

He hopped down from his perch, considering his options.

It was the hesitation that got him. That moment, stood in the open, debating how to save Camille.

The hand closed over his mouth at the same time as he saw two heavyset men pull Guil and Comtois from the panel, yanking their tools away.

Al felt strangely calm.

It made sense, really.

Had he really believed he could make it through the end? People like him didn't.

He had always known his fate.

Now had to finally face it.

4

Outside the Ballroom

da trembled so badly the knife concealed inside her sleeve caught against her skin. A hundred rivulets of blood seeping down her arm and into the lines of her palms. Her hands were red with blood.

The duc dragged Camille from the ballroom with one hand clamped around her slender arm. She struggled to catch her footing, smashing her knee and hip into the floor, before giving up and going as limp as a doll.

Ada followed behind, leaving Charles kneeling with his head over a vase. She wished she could enjoy his momentary defeat but they were nowhere near through yet. The duc's men were scattered through the anteroom. One held Al, a hand over his mouth and his arm behind his back. Two more stood around Guil and Comtois. The wooden panel covering the electrostatic generator had been ripped off, but the wiring was still intact.

They had failed.

The duc sneered. 'Pathetic. Crude violence and party tricks.'

He dumped Camille on the floor and pinned her to the ground with his foot.

'Did you really think you could stop me?'

From within his tailcoat the duc pulled a pistol. Ada's stomach flipped.

'You are a stone in my shoe. Irritating, but easily got rid of.' The duc registered Comtois. 'Another traitor.'

Comtois squared up to him. 'You are the traitor, Philippe. You have betrayed science for your own gain.'

The duc snorted. 'Do you hear yourself? Betrayed science? Our work is a tool, to be used how we see fit.'

'What you see is monstrous.'

'You worked with me on it, once.'

'And I was wrong to. Philippe, this is not the way. If the Terror showed us anything it is that violence begets violence. If you want a future for France, you must engage with your fellow citizen and—'

'Oh, do shut up.'

The duc lifted the pistol and shot Comtois between the eyes.

A puck of blood burst from the back of his head, and he dropped to the ground, a neat hole singed between his eyebrows.

Al cried out, his voice muffled by the hand of his captor. Guil said nothing, only looking at the dead man by his feet, and the pool of blood spreading over the parquet.

'He always did talk too much.' The duc tucked the

gun inside his coat and ground his heel into Camille's back.

Before he could say anything more, Clémentine arrived, an unreadable expression on her face.

'Olympe is gone,' she announced.

'What?' snarled the duc.

He kicked Camille over and pushed her chin up with the toe of his boot. Ada's heart hammered; she let the knife slip from her sleeve into her hand.

'What have you done, you little vixen?'

Camille smiled and said nothing.

'You think yourselves so clever.' He brought his foot to rest on Camille's throat, applying enough pressure that her smile vanished. Feebly she tried to push him away but he pushed down harder, a look of grim satisfaction on his face.

Ada had waited as long as she could. She could spend the coin she had earned over months of horror at the duc's side only once. She had stood by and watched so many awful things done. But not to Camille. She could not watch this happen to Camille and do nothing.

Soundlessly, she leaped forward, stabbing the knife towards the duc's kidneys.

The moment before the blade cut cloth, he spun, grabbing her wrist in a crushing grip. With a cry she let go as bones ground together under the strength of his fingers.

His blue eyes were as sharp and brittle as ice.

'This nest is full of vipers,' he said. 'Oh, Ada. Did you really I think I would trust you with my life?' He dragged her to his side so she could see the window that reflected them. The reflection that betrayed her attack.

At their feet, Camille began crawling towards the door.

The duc flung Ada on top of her, knocking the wind out of them both.

'My patience has run out! You are tiresome. If you want to play with the grown-ups, then be my guest.'

He smoothed out his tailcoat, straightened his cuffs.

'I will see this finished tonight.'

The Duc's Palace

Olympe took James's hand as they sneaked through the corridors towards the ground floor, and his heart lifted.

Perhaps Olympe wasn't so far gone as he'd feared. Her skin was cold and smooth as marble, but he held her tightly, like a talisman that would see him through this night.

They found signs that the vitriol of copper had worked as soon as they left the quiet upper floors. They stepped one moment from peace into chaos. Guests were scattered around, collapsed on chairs, sweating and waxy, hunched over chamber pots, throwing up, and more running towards the entrance, lifting their stained skirts to step over the bodies. Servants hurried to and fro with buckets and bowls, but they were wildly outnumbered and unprepared. James spared a thought for Henri, his worst fear come true.

It was easy to find the ballroom by going against the flow of people. With all the uproar no one looked twice at a footman and a girl with her face in shadow. The first thing James saw was the glimmering hall still lit by a thousand candles across the two huge candelabras suspended from the ceiling. Empty now, the floor was stained with vomit and wine.

Then he saw the body. Face down in a pool of blood, the coat of the footman's uniform spread out like wings. Olympe rushed forward but James held her back. The duc's men could still be here.

Once he was sure they were alone, he came closer to see the mess of bone and grey matter at the back of Comtois's head. Olympe let out a soft cry and buried her face in his shoulder. He held her to stave off his own fear. He harboured no warm feelings towards Comtois, but his death made the threat they faced suddenly real.

When Olympe pulled back, she asked, 'What was he doing here?'

'He was helping us.'

Olympe looked wary, so James quickly explained Camille's plan, guilt mounting. Comtois held some responsibility for what had happened, but Camille had roped him in. Another death on the battalion's hands.

Blood had seeped up the hem of Olympe's dress.

'Was this part of her plan?' she asked, pulling away.

He shook his head. 'It wasn't supposed to go like this. We should get out of the palace.'

'No.' She drew herself up to her full height, short though it was, and squared her chin. 'If I'm doing this,

I'm not starting by leaving our friends behind. We're doing this together, or not at all.'

It would be so simple to leave. The palace was in such disarray they could take a carriage and be back to Paris in an hour or two.

But Olympe was right. He couldn't leave Camille and the others.

They had to see it through.

He took her hand again and smiled.

'Together, to the end.'

'To the end.'

5

The Laboratory, the Duc's Palace

S ince work had finished in the ballroom, Ada had not had cause to return to the laboratory she had been confined in for the last three months. Unlike the duc's workrooms in the abandoned abbey and the catacombs, this had been turned over entirely to the study of electricity. Ada had thought the lack of specimens in jars and resin model arteries would make the space somewhere more tolerable, but that was wishful thinking. The cold, clinical precision of the experiments. The single-minded drive of the duc. The knowledge of what evil her work wrought.

All had haunted Ada every day in that room.

It made a miserable backdrop now she had failed in her one true mission. Her hands were bound behind her back where she was dumped on the floor in a line with Camille, Guil and Al. All four original members of the Bataillon des Morts captured, their reign of chaos come to an end.

She shook herself. It wasn't over yet. She couldn't think like that.

Next to her, Camille let her knees drop sideways so their legs were pressed together and Ada was impossibly grateful for the comfort. The corner of Camille's mouth curled in a smile, and she winked.

Ada tried to draw strength from it. Her Camille, who held the line even as her body failed her.

The duc paced. His men guarded the door. Charles had emerged from the ballroom, pale and sweaty but gleeful to see Ada trussed up with the others. The duc had sent him to track down Olympe.

Clémentine hovered near her brother. When she caught Ada's eye, she mouthed something Ada couldn't catch but then the door opened and Charles returned.

'Well?' asked the duc.

'We looked for her but it's madness out there.'

The duc shot the battalion a look of hatred.

'Are you guarding the exits? The carriages? The gates?'

'Yes. But no one has seen anything.'

In a wave of fury, the duc swept everything from his desk, sending ink and quills, bundles of wire and pieces of metal clattering to the ground.

'Then. Keep. Looking,' he snapped.

Ada held onto the small kernel of hope still alive. James had been right to try Olympe again. They had achieved their first goal: the duc's slaughter would not happen that night. If Olympe was on the run, all was not lost. They could deny him victory for ever.

The duc paced before the bound battalion and came

to a halt in front of Guil. Ada remembered his threat against Guil should Camille interfere with his plans and icy fear sluced through her.

Then the duc turned.

And stood before Camille.

His expression was the analytic, calculating one he'd worn when he and Ada had worked together late into the night. The human mask had slipped completely, and now he was only predator, assessing his prey and calculating his attack.

'Bring a bucket of water,' he ordered.

A man left at once.

The entire time he was gone, the duc remained by Camille, staring at her, unblinking. She looked back, chin tilted and eyes burning with fever. Ada nudged her knee, but Camille didn't break their gaze.

The man came back with the bucket of water and Ada grew uneasy.

The duc set the bucket in the middle of the room where he and Ada had placed the scaled-down models of the electric cage they had tested on small animals. Then he summoned two men to haul Camille over, positioned so she was facing her line of friends. The duc fisted his hand in her hair and wrenched her head back, crouching so he could hiss in her ear.

'You have done something with Olympe. You staged the mass poisoning of my guests as a decoy while you took her. Yes?'

Camille said nothing.

'The English boy is missing, so I assume he is who you sent. You knew I would be guarding the building, so you must have some plan for how to get her out. I would like you to tell me what it is.'

Camille said nothing.

'For your own sake, tell me now.'

Camille looked only at Ada, her mouth crooked in a smile but her eyes, oh, her eyes were so sad Ada's breath caught in her throat.

'Very well,' snapped the duc.

He forced Camille's head down, holding her underwater. It sloshed out of the bucket as Camille struggled.

Ada jerked forward, but the men gathered round to keep her and the boys in place.

'Stop it!' Ada yelled. 'Get off her!'

Clémentine rushed over, wrenching at her brother's hands.

The duc let go and Camille lurched up, gasping for breath.

'Philippe, what are you doing?'

'Get out of my way. Or do I have another traitor on my hands?'

Clémentine faltered. 'No. I only implore you as your sister, do you really think this course of action is wise?'

The duc's eyes blazed. 'I *think* your opinion on the matter is entirely unnecessary. You've been happy to accept my money, my food, my protection and turn away from the work I do ever since our parents died. I do not see why I should entertain any last-minute change of conscience from you.'

Clémentine was at war with herself and Ada urged

her to say something more. But she only stepped back. Hung her head.

The duc returned to Camille. Her hair was stuck to her forehead and temples, droplets of water catching on her lashes.

'Well? Are you ready to talk or do you need more persuasion?'

Camille only smiled.

The duc forced her under again.

'We don't have a plan!' cried Al. 'I swear. We're not that organised. Surely you can believe that.'

'Lies!'

The duc pulled Camille up, sending a spray of water across the floor.

'Give up, little girl. Your friends cannot get you out of this. Tell me everything and I let you live.'

Camille sucked in desperate breaths.

Then nodded.

Ada's stomach was in knots. They'd lost. This was the moment.

The duc dropped her and she only just caught herself before her teeth smacked the rim of the bucket.

'Speak.'

Camille said something too quiet to hear.

'What?'

The duc drew close but Camille's voice was too hoarse. He drew closer again.

'I said, go to hell, you monster.'

Camille spat. The spittle caught his cheek and eye. For a moment he froze.

Then with a roar he grabbed her head and pushed it deep into the bucket. Camille struggled, bound hands unable to help as he held her under.

'Stop—stop—' Ada screamed, yanking so hard against the arms holding her that her shoulder wrenched. 'Please – stop.'

All three were yelling; even Clémentine came to her brother's side, pulling at his arms.

'This is enough!' Clémentine smacked the bucket away and Camille collapsed onto the floor as the duc stumbled back. He seemed flustered by his own violent outburst.

The room went silent.

Camille lay unmoving, face down.

'Camille. Cam. Get up.' Ada studied the pale strip of face she could see.

The silence extended.

'Camille?'

Trembling, Clémentine kneeled beside Camille and turned her over. Eyes, glassy and wide, stared unseeing at the ceiling. Clémentine lowered her ear to Camille's mouth, pressed two fingers to her throat.

A loud roaring filled Ada's mind. Her heartbeat a deafening drum played inside her head.

Clémentine glanced at Ada, and shook her head.

The world winked out.

Ada felt as though she'd stepped outside of her body. As though she were floating somewhere above them all, looking at this scene like a tableau at the theatre. It was all unreal, happening to someone else.

She was aware Al and Guil were yelling; she could

see Al's face slick with tears and knew in some distant way that her own cheeks were wet too. They were being moved, arms hauling her up by her bound hands so her shoulders screamed in protest, but Ada felt nothing.

She could not let herself feel anything, for if she did her pain would destroy her.

Camille was dead.

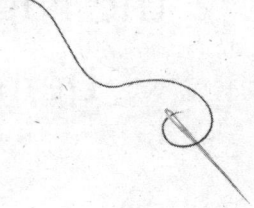

6

The Au Petit Suisse, the Night Before the Demonstration

A fat drop of rain landed on the back of Ada's neck, running down the inside of her collar, as she crossed the threshold from the courtyard into the restaurant. She shrieked at the shock of it, slapping her hand to her nape in a vain attempt to prevent its course.

Camille caught her hand and drew it away. With a chuckle she pressed her warm lips to the cold, wet patch and slid her other arm around Ada's waist to pull her flush. Ada relaxed into her grip.

'Better?' mouthed Camille against her skin. The graze of her tongue sent a shiver down Ada's spine and heat flared in the pit of her stomach.

'You are a public menace,' said Ada, turning in Camille's arms. 'But, yes. Better.'

She closed the distance between them in a kiss,

letting herself be distracted by the rising fire inside her. Camille pulled away first.

'Plenty of time for that after.'

Ada frowned, less willing to stop what they had begun. 'After what?'

'After I tell you all how to save the day, of course.'

A wild grin flashed across her face, and then she was leading Ada back to the battalion's table tucked into the smoky recesses of the restaurant.

Hands entwined beneath the table, Ada told her friends of the split between the duc and Clémentine, James explained how Guil and Comtois could slip inside, and Al argued Camille round into attending the demonstration as a guest.

Then Camille gathered them closer.

'Here's the new plan. We can't just stop the duc for one night, we need to stop him for ever.'

Al arched an eyebrow. 'Well. Yes. But that's never really turned into a plan yet, has it?'

'Because we've been scared,' answered Camille.

'Really? I hadn't noticed,' said Al.

She continued as though he hadn't spoken. 'None of us have been willing to take the risks we need to in order to play the hand we have.'

'What hand do you speak of?' asked Guil.

Camille looked at them each in turn.

'Our weakness, of course.'

Al snorted. 'Oh, thanks very much.'

James looked miserable, but he said, 'She's right. He's Goliath. We have to accept we're David.'

'Ada has tried it, and it worked, didn't it?' said

Camille. 'His arrogance has blinded him to the possibility that she's a spy. He can only see her as a vulnerable girl open to exploitation.'

Ada felt queasy to hear herself described that way but she couldn't deny that Camille was right.

'After we get the guests from the ballroom, we have to let ourselves be caught,' said Camille.

The table sat in silence.

Al spoke first.

'Uh. No? The world's biggest, loudest no?' Nobody said a word. He put his head on the table. 'I hate you all.'

Guil folded his arms, expression intense. 'I understand. We let the Trojans bring the Greeks into Troy.'

'That's too many literary allusions. Just say you're dragging us to hell with you and be done with it.' But Al's tone was resigned.

Camile nodded. 'We've evaded his lackeys so far – if we show up at the demonstration tomorrow he'll be suspicious but the opportunity to assert his strength will be too tempting. So first we give him what he wants: us. Helpless. Then Ada can make her move. With any luck, Clémentine will take our side, and unlike the last two times we've gone up against him, we don't have another enemy to worry about.'

Under the table, Ada squeezed Camille's hand harder.

'We have one final ace to play: Comtois. The duc doesn't know what he has been working on. We cannot destroy the machine beyond repair now he knows how to make it. We cannot keep Olympe from him for ever. There is only one way this ends. I know we can succeed. I know—'

The Duc's Palace. Now.

Ada squeezed her eyes shut. Pushed the memory of last night at the Au Petit Suisse away.

Camille looked sightlessly towards the ornate fresco on the ceiling. Her hair lay in wet tendrils around her face. She was like some sea creature, distorted beneath the refracted light of the water.

Ada stared at Camille's dead body as two men dragged Ada through the doorway and back to the ballroom. She had barely been listening as the duc barked orders, recovering himself from the shock of murder. Oh, he had killed before, but even for a man like him, bringing death by his own hand was something new. Something unsettling.

Servants were mopping the vomit from the ballroom floor and the duc waved them away. Ada, Al and Guil were dumped in the centre, still bound. She turned to the open doors, back towards the room where Camille had been abandoned.

Her attention only came back to their present surroundings when Al elbowed her in the ribs.

Charles had returned empty-handed and the duc was pulling at the short tufts of his grey hair.

'Bring the Dauphin,' he ordered. 'Bring everyone. Olympe and the English boy are here somewhere.

They will not leave without their friends so we must stay closely guarded. Recovering the girl is our first priority, but be cautious. She is more dangerous than she looks.'

There was a light of fear behind his eyes and Ada thought of England, where Olympe had slipped her moorings and unleashed a lightning storm into the duc. The memory of that pain must live in his mind like a brand.

Charles looked nervous. 'The mechanism will still work. The floor is…' He looked at the copper beneath his feet. 'It is dangerous.'

'Don't be stupid,' sneered the duc. 'This is the safest place in the palace. If they tried anything they'd kill their friends too. They won't do that.' He looked at the battalion members scattered on the floor. 'They're too *noble*.'

Then a spark of inspiration lit his expression and he turned to the battalion.

'We have built a trap. Perhaps all it needs is different bait.'

7

The Duc's Palace

With the stampede from the ballroom over, it became difficult for James and Olympe to move around the palace undetected. The corridors were patrolled by a mixture of the muscle the duc had hired for the demonstration and his cadre of scientists and assistants. They weren't helped by the fact that the palace was ridiculously large and one ornate hallway looked much like the next.

James wondered if they were on a wild goose chase. Maybe the others had abandoned the plan to let themselves get caught and fled, Comtois an unfortunate casualty, and James and Olympe were putting themselves at risk for no reason.

But it was wishful thinking. She was still here, he knew it.

He couldn't leave her. Just like he couldn't leave Olympe.

Olympe was getting harder to hide. Her anxiety manifested in crackles of current rolling across her skin, sparking on metal fixtures and door handles, illuminating her like a candle in the dark. She snuffed them every time they heard footsteps, but her reactions were unpredictable as she grew more afraid and James felt painfully aware he was walking around with the greatest weapon the world had ever produced.

They looped through the palace, floor by floor, ducking around corners and into rooms to avoid being spotted. On the top floor, the Dauphin's room was empty, and Olympe's had been ransacked. James tried to think what Camille's plan would be now. What the duc would do with them. But his mind kept running blank. They were too close to the end and he was running out of ideas.

In a quiet corridor near the ballroom, three men patrolled, shoulder to shoulder. Olympe noticed too late, her current still blazing. Without thinking, James barrelled her through the nearest door and slammed his back against it, expecting footsteps hammering towards them at any moment.

But nothing came. He stayed, ear pressed to the door, breathing hard, but they must be investigating further along the corridor. They would reach this door eventually. All he had done was trap them.

'Olympe – we need to go. Now.'

But Olympe had left his side, and was walking slowly towards the centre of the room that was set up like a laboratory. On the floor was a collection of silk rags. No, a dress.

Olympe kneeled beside it, reaching out a hand.

'What are you doing?'

He stared at the body in confusion.

James didn't understand what he was seeing. It looked like Camille, but that didn't make sense because Camille was alive and this person was clearly dead.

'Olympe, come away.'

He reached for her shoulder, but yanked his hand back when he got a shock from the current swirling like an aura above her skin.

'Olympe.'

'She's dead. I trusted you and she's dead.'

'I don't understand.'

Olympe whipped around, eyes blazing blue and a cloud of static swirling in her hair.

'Camille is *dead*. You told me to have faith in you, to believe that good things are possible, but you were *wrong*.'

James looked at the body again. It had Camille's face, her piano player's long fingers and her smattering of freckles on its waxy skin. Somewhere in the struggle, one shoe had come off. He knelt down and gently put the satin slipper back on. Camille would get cold in bare feet.

A crackle of lightning snapped his attention to Olympe. She had risen, standing over Camille like a vengeful demon. The light in the room dimmed, as though all the power had been sucked into her. Shadows spread from the corners and the rain hammering at the windows was quiet as the hum of charge grew.

'There is no escape. Nowhere I can go where death won't follow. I was a fool to believe you.'

James was on his knees at her feet, looking up at her with tears sliding down his face.

He knew now. He knew.

Camille was dead.

'I'm sorry,' he whispered.

'Get out of my way,' growled Olympe.

James drew back as she loosed the first flood of electricity into Camille's body. Camille jerked, then fell still when the current died.

'Olympe.' Quiet tears blurring his vision. 'Stop it. Please.'

'No.' She held both palms before her and let the current build so bright that James had to shield his eyes. She sent a second pulse. Again, Camille's corpse writhed then fell still. Olympe looked at her hands in horror. 'Why won't it work?'

'It's too late,' said James.

Olympe screamed.

A flare of white lit the room, arcs of electricity jumping from her body, gouging burns in the walls and floor. James didn't try to escape. A storm spilled forth from Olympe to rival the storm outside the palace, and James let it wash over him. His teeth ached and his hair bristled. He could taste blood. Arcs of blue grounded in a ring around him. Even in her heartache and despair, some part of Olympe was keeping him safe.

Pulse after pulse burst out, cracking the windows and shattering mirrors, setting papers on the desks on fire. And in the centre, Camille's limp body. The current surrounded her like weeds, snagging on the stone of her body as the tide rolled forward. Her body jerked as the power contracted her muscles, twitching grotesquely like the experiments James had witnessed in London. Like Edward had contorted when James and Wickham had brought him back after the carriage accident.

But she wasn't an experiment. She was Camille. His first love. His family.

And she was dead.

Little by little, James crawled towards the detonating bomb of Olympe, the circle of protection shifting with him, splinters from the shattered wood catching in his palms, the soles of his shoes smoking from the heat, his hair burning at the tips. He reached Olympe's legs, curled his fingers in the hem of her dress and pulled himself slowly to stand.

'Olympe!'

Her face was that of a god. Eyes blazing white like starlight, face and throat and hands and every inch of bare skin forked with currents arcing and grounding, a net of electricity covering her as completely as her mask.

He called her name again. Her face was upturned to the storm, arms outspread. The circle of protection around him had shrunk to a matter of centimetres above his skin. The fine hair on his arms had begun to crinkle, scorch marks marring the hem of his frock coat. The wall hangings had caught fire.

There would be no coming back soon.

There was only one thing he could think of.

James wrapped his arms around Olympe.

It was an instant of agony, white hot fire coursing through him from scalp to toe. Death would be a mercy.

Then that instinctive protection Olympe had cast spread; because he was curled tight around her, it spread around him too. Like a candle being snuffed, the electrical storm guttered and died, and the blue sheen faded from Olympe's skin. Around them, charred plaster and wallpaper floated down like ashes from a bonfire. The smell of smoke was everywhere.

Beside them, Camille's body was splayed and still.

James cupped Olympe's face in his hands. Her eyes had faded back to black, pinpricked with stars.

'Camille is dead,' he said.

'I can fix her.'

'No.'

Tears slid down Olympe's cheeks. 'I brought back a mouse. You brought back Edward.'

'She was sick.' He was crying too. 'And I couldn't save her. She was always going to die.'

Olympe shook her head but said nothing, only clung to James harder. He rested his forehead against hers and let their tears mingle. He wasn't sure when her lips met his but the softness was like a blessing. A moment of hope to hold onto.

He came back to himself and pulled away abruptly.

'Olympe. What was that for?'

'Because I'm terrified I won't get another chance to.' She disentangled herself from his arms, scrubbed her face clean of tears. 'I'm sorry.'

'That's not what I meant.'

'I shouldn't have done that. Not here. Not like this.'

They both looked down at Camille.

James took off his charred coat and covered her with it.

'We'll come back for her. We will. But first we need to find the others.'

He held out his hand and Olympe took it.

8

The Ballroom

Ada sat alone in the centre of the metal floor. Blood trickled down her face where she had been struck about the head with the butt of the duc's pistol. It was still trained on her, from where the duc was concealed to the side of the open doors. Not that she looked like she was going to run. Guil had never seen her like this. Like a light had been snuffed out inside her and now there was only the shape of a girl left.

Guil and Al, Clémentine and Charles, and the Dauphin and the rest of the duc's people had been corralled against the wall so they would not be seen from outside.

Al leaned his head close to Guil. 'We have to do something,' he hissed.

'What do you have in mind?'

'I don't know! You're the one who comes up with the plans with Camille.'

They both paused at the spike of pain her name brought.

'We have to do something,' Al said again. 'She would have.'

Guil turned their situation over in his mind. Outnumbered. Outgunned. Their only advantage was that James and Olympe were still at large, but he knew better than to hope they'd already fled. The duc's people were patrolling the corridors, sweeping through them to force James and Olympe towards the ballroom.

Clémentine wouldn't meet their eye. Perhaps hope that she would come to their side had been misplaced. Al was right, they needed to think of another way to make Camille's plan work. They were close to the duc. His attention was distracted by the search for Olympe.

There had to be a way they could use this to their advantage.

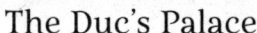

The Duc's Palace

The corridors were too quiet.

James and Olympe crept through the palace, finding every door locked. At each landing and stairwell were guards blocking one way. It filled James with unease. Olympe's outburst could not have gone unnoticed; he had the sinking feeling they were like mice in a maze, being flushed towards the prize.

Or the punishment.

When they were spat out by the ballroom, he felt it like some anchor at the base of his spine. Of course it would end here. Through the doors, he could see Ada placed like the lure at the end of a fishing line. It was all too neat.

'Ada!'

Olympe darted forward but James caught her.

'It's a trap.'

Olympe glared at him. 'So?'

'Let's not run directly into it?'

'Why not?' She ran a glove of current over both hands. 'Just get me close to the duc and I'll cook him alive from the inside out.'

'Unless they shoot you first,' he said. 'Or me. Or Ada.'

Olympe snuffed the current. 'So what do you want us to do? Stand out here at an impasse until we all die of old age?'

James hung his head. Camille had been right. This had to end tonight, one way or another. Every path held its own risks.

'No.'

'So, let's go.'

She turned and he pulled her back.

'What?' she snapped.

Colour rose in his cheeks. 'Before. You said you didn't mean to do it there, like that. So. Uh. Did you mean to do it another way?'

A flush of purple rushed over her face like a tide. 'Maybe.' Then after a beat, 'Yes. Would you rather I didn't?'

James thought about it. 'No. I'd rather you did it again.'

'Oh,' she whispered.

It didn't make sense, and it did. He didn't deserve her forgiveness, but he couldn't bear the idea of losing her again. He didn't know when his feelings had changed, but they had, and seeing her tonight was like an epiphany.

So he kissed her. Barely a brush of lips against lips. Something small and quiet budding, a flower growing in the ruins.

In the laboratory, beneath the burned frock coat, a blue spark arced from point to point. The hum of electricity hung in the air.

Camille's finger twitched.

The Ballroom

Once, when Al was small, he had found his brothers with a stray cat. He couldn't remember what they were doing with it, only that they held walking sticks and clubs. Heavy things that would hurt. He thought perhaps his memory had scoured any further detail from his mind in a moment of generosity. He didn't need to remember what they had done, because he had felt that pain himself.

He had survived around his brothers by making himself small and quick and quiet. But this time he knew he couldn't do it. He couldn't slip away. He couldn't carry what they would do on his conscience. So he had stepped among them, distracted them long enough for the cat to escape. They had been angry, of course, to lose their target. Al had known what would happen before the blows rained down on him instead. All through the next two weeks as he winced at the bruises, he wondered what had possessed him to do it.

Al wondered what possessed him now, here, in the duc's ballroom when his friend was dead and their odds miserable. He didn't know what it was, but he knew he couldn't do anything else. Camille wouldn't have hesitated.

James and Olympe entered the ballroom cautiously, Olympe holding a bright white charge gathered at her palms, ready to strike. The duc shifted the trajectory of his gun to track their approach, Clémentine standing to attention at the sight of her daughter. Al realised she had thought Olympe long gone and now didn't know how to play the cards she still held. The Dauphin stood casually, as though it were all an interesting play put on for his entertainment. Al hated him then, this arrogant boy who thought a country should bow to him.

James spotted the duc first, and raised his hands in submission. Olympe turned and bared her teeth, her own raised to attack.

'You cannot use your power here,' called the duc.

'You think I'm not strong enough?' replied Olympe.

'I think you're forgetting what this room is.'

Olympe looked around her, at the metal floor and up at the ceiling. James's face fell.

'Olympe. Get rid of the current. Now.'

'The boy is right. You'll kill your friends as fast as you'll kill me and your mother.'

Olympe's eyes flickered to Clémentine as if noticing her for the first time. She lowered her hands and the light around them died.

The duc's shoulders relaxed in victory.

Al chose his moment then.

He pounced on the Dauphin, throwing his bound hands around the boy's throat to choke him.

'Let her go!' he yelled. 'Let the whole bloody lot of us go or your precious prince dies.'

The duc spun on his heel, a snarl on his face. Charles, meant to be guarding him, fumbled for his weapon. The Dauphin's fingers scrabbled at Al's hands, drawing blood, but he kept his grip tight. This was the only chance they had left.

For a moment, one single, hopeful moment, he really thought it would work.

Then the duc brought his gun to point at Al.

'You can't shoot me,' he said, suddenly unsure of himself. 'You'll kill your Dauphin too.'

The duc shrugged. 'I can find another.'

The world went cold.

All Al could see was the muzzle of the gun too close to miss.

Oh, he thought, this was it.

It was over.

He thought, then, of Léon, and the dimple in one cheek that only showed when he really, truly smiled. Never onstage. But for Al.

The duc curled his finger around the trigger.

A crack of thunder rolled through the room. The ballroom doors slammed back against their hinges, and half the candles blew out as a figure appeared.

Camille stood on the threshold limned in white lightning, frightening and terrible to behold.

'Get the hell away from my friends.'

9

The Ballroom

er voice was a shock to the heart.

Ada had been so very far away. Locked somewhere deep inside herself, fractured out of reality by what she had seen.

Camille's voice brought her back in a breath.

Ada flung herself towards where Camille stood, but James caught her by the waist and held her back. 'Ada, no.'

Al let go of the Dauphin and stared at Camille in fear and wonder.

Ada scrabbled to get free, then caught sight of the duc, who swung his gun from Al first to Ada, and then Camille, wavering between the two. His face was grey, as though the day of judgement had come and the ghosts of his past sins had risen to confront him.

Perhaps that was not so far from the truth.

'What is this?' he hissed. 'Some sort of trick?'

Camille looked at her hands. 'I don't know.' There was a white radiance around her eyes, veins glowing beneath her skin. No – Ada looked closer – lightning forked through her. A jagged tracery of power.

'But he killed you.' Clémentine clutched a hand to her throat.

Camille's looked at the current sparking from her fingertips. 'Didn't stick.'

'Impossible,' whispered Guil.

Olympe came to stand beside James and Ada, staring at Camille with tears in her eyes. 'It worked.'

'What worked?' asked Ada, but she knew the answer. The only person who could have done this was Olympe.

The duc settled his gun on Camille.

'Dead or alive, you've lost!' he yelled.

She drifted to the control panel and its tangle of wiring and the cuffs meant for Olympe.

A note of panic entered his voice. 'I'll tell you the same thing I told the girl! You can't do anything here without killing your friends.'

Camille regarded him calmly as she put one crackling hand up to the panel, fingers centimetres from the wires. 'If we let you go, you'll build this evil thing again. The only way to stop this is to stop you.'

The duc sneered. 'I call your bluff. You won't sacrifice your friends to get what you want. You don't have it in you.'

The unholy light around Camille shone blue-white, her hair rising around her head like a halo.

'You have no idea what I am capable of.'

And she let the current burst forth.

Outside the Ballroom

The current flowing through her was like nothing Camille had ever experienced. A thousand pinpricks bristling beneath her skin, her flesh become sound and light. It was so overwhelming she lost any conscious comprehension of the world around her. She could feel the wiring in the control panel like an extension of herself, the expanse of metal ceiling stretching away and each individual point where the current grounded in the floor below. Each fleshy path of least resistance.

The torrent that flowed through her slowed to a trickle, and then she was done. Where the wires passed through the wall, the paper was charred black and licked with flame.

The smoke cleared.

The ballroom was littered with bodies, clothes burned from their bodies, skin bubbled like wax. Charles and the Dauphin had dropped side by side, burned almost beyond recognition.

Olympe stepped forward, hand covering her mouth.

The electricity had flowed through her like the blood in her veins, traces of it wreathing her arms and throat.

'Camille, what did you do?'

Camille disentangled herself from the cuffs and drifted into the ballroom.

One by one, her battalion emerged from the smoke, terrified, but alive.

Ada pushed past them all and ran to Camille, putting her fingers to the still-crackling skin of her cheeks.

'You died. I watched you die.'

Camille saw the horror, the unbearable sorrow in her eyes, and briefly the memory of the duc holding her underwater came back to her. Her own fear; the moment she knew she'd miscalculated and death faced her, not in some nebulous time, but immediately.

Her final thoughts had been of Ada. Her own mother.

Pushing her panic far down, she reached for Ada instead. 'I know. I know.'

Ada smacked her shoulder. '*Never* do that again.' Then she burst into tears and clung to Camille with great, heaving sobs.

Olympe looked between the battalion. 'I don't understand. How did you survive?'

Shaken, Al pulled off his shoe, carefully standing on one leg to avoid touching the floor, and showed her the inside. 'Rubber. It was Comtois's idea.'

'Clever,' said James. 'An insulator. The current can't pass through rubber, so it didn't touch us.'

That had been the last piece of the plan Camille had

explained to the battalion at the Au Petit Suisse last night, the ace up their sleeve that would allow them to get close enough to the duc to strike.

Camille looked around the dead bodies and frowned. Nameless faces she had taken the life from. If she let herself think about it, it would become as insurmountable as the memory of her own death. 'Where is the duc?'

James pointed to the concealed servants' doors that, when closed, lay flush with the wall.

'He grabbed Clémentine and ran a fraction before the current hit.'

Dread pooled low in Camille's stomach.

She had done the worst thing she could think of, and it was still not over.

Of course it wasn't.

It was never going to be that simple.

'Er. Fire? Fire!' Al pointed to the antechamber where the small fire Camille had seen around the wiring had caught hold and spread like oil, flowing over the ceiling and up the paint-rich walls and thick drapes.

They drew back as flames curled around the door frame, reaching for the wall hangings.

'We need to raise the alarm,' said James, pale-faced. 'There are so many people still in the building. A place like this will burn quickly.'

Camille snapped into action.

'Al – you and Guil make sure everyone gets out. Now, while you can still get through. Take Olympe and get out of here.'

'We're not leaving you,' said Guil, face firm.

'No way,' agreed Al.

Camille glared, a flash of blue in her eyes. The weakness that had dragged her down for so long was gone, and she felt painfully, vividly alive. 'No.'

'What do you mean, no?'

'Who are we?' she asked.

Al blinked. 'What?'

'It's a simple question.'

'The Bataillon des Morts,' said Guil.

'Correct. And what do we do?'

Al looked embarrassed. 'Save people. In theory.'

'Correct again.' The blue flared brighter. 'So go and do that.'

Al and Guil nodded. 'Yes, ma'am.'

Al reached for Olympe but she shook out of his grasp.

'I'm going with Camille.'

Ada touched her arm. 'Olympe, please. We need you somewhere safe.'

'No. I can't. I *can't*. He has my mother. Without him gone, I have no future.'

It was simple and stark, and Camille knew she was right.

James positioned himself alongside Camille, Ada and Olympe. 'I'm coming too.' He caught Camille's eye and she softened. 'You don't have to do this alone.'

Ada reached for her hand.

'We need to go now – the fire – the duc—'

Camille nodded.

As Al and Guil hugged her, she felt in the tightness

354

of their grip that they were willing her to come back alive. Seeing her die once was enough.

She had been granted another shot.

She wasn't going to throw this one away.

11

The Staircase

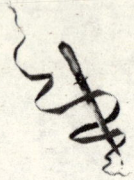

The door the duc had fled through led to a staircase. The way down was blocked by a stack of wood and metal, a broken ladder, bundled cloth: detritus from the building work to the ballroom.

There was only up.

Camille went first, followed by Olympe, Ada and then James. At each floor they checked the door and found it locked. The duc must have known it, but there had been no other options.

Camille swallowed, her mouth dry and tasting of zinc. Fate drew her upward like a tug at her navel. Since she had first met the duc in the Jardin des Tuileries, every path led her here. There had been chance after chance to flee, but to save herself would have meant turning away from Olympe. From the fate of her country. From doing what was right. She could have gone now with her family reunited, the duc thwarted for the time being. But her own stubborn nature refused to let her take the easier path.

So instead she turned towards the climb, and the impossible choice at the top.

Olympe gripped her hand, cool and tight.

The staircase opened onto the palace roof. Rain lashed the tiles, a solid wall of black cloud spread overhead. A crack of lightning illuminated the scene: a narrow walkway ran the length of the building, slate tiles angled sharply down on either side, and squat-roofed turrets marked the corners.

Standing at one end, the duc.

A boom of thunder followed. The storm was close.

Camille advanced on him, holding her hands up. He was cornered, so he would be desperate. They had Olympe. He was out of options.

Or so she thought. When she got closer, she saw that the duc held Clémentine in front of him like a shield, an arm around her waist and his hand at her throat. Olympe gasped. Again, she could not act without risking the life of someone she loved.

'Careful,' said James. 'He still has the gun.'

'He can't use it in this weather,' Ada explained. 'The powder would get wet.'

The storm raged around them. Rain plastered Camille's hair to her skull, the gauze of her dress to her legs. Keeping her hands up she edged closer.

'It's over!' she called. 'Let Clémentine go!'

'Why? What will you do? Arrest me? Kill me?'

She ignored him. 'The palace is burning. We must leave now.'

'A trick,' he sneered.

'It is no trick.' Behind him, the grounds were lit by

a fierce orange glow. The fire had spread. 'Look below. The rain may slow it, but the passage out will soon become impossible.'

'Get out of here, then, if you're so afraid.'

Camille sighed. 'I can't let you go.'

Olympe pushed past her, hands crackling with current despite the wet. 'Neither can I. Get your hands off my mother.'

'Run!' cried Clémetine before the duc put his hand over her mouth.

'You are petulant, self-righteous children,' he bellowed. 'You do not know what you've done.'

Ada stepped beside them, squaring her jaw. 'We know exactly what we're doing. Stopping a monster.'

'Traitor,' he spat. 'All of you. Even my damn sister. Why are you all too stupid to see I am only doing what needs to be done? I am trying to make a better world.'

'You tortured me,' said Olympe. Her voice was unnervingly steady and the bright light of the current was seeping into her inky eyes. 'You locked me in a metal mask. You tried to force me to commit mass murder. You have no idea what a better world is.'

Storm clouds gathered over Olympe's head, swirling in a vortex that funnelled power into her outstretched hands.

'Anything worth fighting for requires sacrifice,' said the duc, but a note of fear had crept into his voice.

Olympe was wreathed in a net of stars, charge crackling around her like mist.

'This time we will sacrifice you.'

Before she could strike, the duc threw Clémentine at them.

Olympe instantly extinguished the charge to stop her mother tumbling into it, but Camille caught the brunt of the blow, and Camille and Clémentine went rolling down the rain-slick tiles. Camille scrabbled desperately at the roof, struggling to find purchase. The ground was so far below, hidden by smoke from the fire.

A turret brought them up short and the two clung to each other and its bulk.

James, Ada, Olympe and the duc were still on the walkway.

Lightning flashed and Camille saw an image in fractals.

The duc forced to the very edge of the roof, open air at his back.

Flash.

Olympe drawing power from the storm clouds above.

Flash.

The glint of a knife in the duc's hand as he stabbed low.

Flash.

Olympe surging towards him.

Flash.

James moving to intercept the knife.

A boom of thunder and all Camille saw was the jagged image of someone barrelling into the duc and going over the edge.

Outside the Palace

The chaos of the palace had spilled out to become chaos on the lawns. Between throwing up in the rain or throwing up in a building on fire, all but the most addled made the obvious choice. At first, the staff hadn't believed their reports; it had taken the bursting of a window on the first floor sending flames shooting into the sky to persuade them to evacuate en masse. The fire spread quickly, swallowing the central staircase and moving between floors. Al and Guil combed the building using the servants' warren of passages, bypassing the richly upholstered rooms and corridors that burned more easily, to look for servants or guests who'd retreated to quiet rooms to nurse their illness, making sure no one was left behind. More carriages were readied, so the guests who'd recovered enough left rapidly. Guil and Al stayed with the others while help was sent for from the nearby village, and a bucket chain was set up to douse the flames.

But Al could see it was too late to save the palace. While the rain would stop the worst, it would be gutted by morning.

His hands shook the entire time they worked. It felt unreal. All of it.

He had survived.

It made no sense. He wasn't the one who got to live. But he had.

Guil came over with a cup of water that Al took gratefully. They were both smeared with ash and soaked with rain.

Side by side, they looked up at the burning building.

'They should have come out by now,' said Guil.

Before Al could reply, movement caught his eye. Through the smoke and rain he could see figures but not make out who, or what they were doing.

Al's breath caught in his throat with fear.

Then two people at the roof's edge toppled over, and went crashing into the burning orangery below.

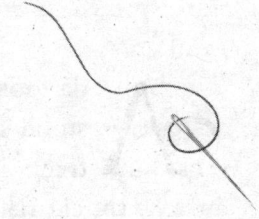

12

A Graveyard in England

Ada took Camille's hand in her own as they stood side by side beneath the ancient yew tree. The graveyard was small, tucked around the church like a garden of stones. The Harford mausoleum had only been built fifteen years before, on the death of James's grandfather.

No one had thought his grandson would be the first to join him.

The vicar stood by the open door, watching over the interment. Guil and Al had joined Lord Harford as pallbearers, shouldering the coffin from church to tomb.

Ada hadn't been to many funerals, but they all made her think of her mother. Even the quiet memorial for Camille's parents, who had been consigned to the common pit with the other victims of the guillotine, had brought back memories of the humid air and white stone of her mother's resting place. Under a blazing blue sky her father had stood apart from her, weeping over her mother's casket. There had been a Latin mass, and countless people bringing food, people she didn't recognise coming to press their hands to her face and declare her mother's spirit lived on in her.

James's funeral was a quieter affair. Ada was unfamiliar with the Protestant rites, but she sat with Camille in the pew behind James's family, rising and sitting when called and singing the hymns as best she could. Olympe, hidden under a heavy veil, sat on Camille's other side and remained silent the entire duration.

The coffin was stowed safely in the mausoleum and the funeral party broke into muted conversation. Ada left Camille kneeling before Lady Harford, their hands folded together as they passed whatever quiet words that needed to be said, and went to join Al, who had slunk off to the lychgate to smoke. Guil went with her. Neither of them wanted to intrude on private mourning.

After a moment's silence, Al said, 'I never knew a coffin was so heavy.'

Ada waited for Al to make his way through whatever difficult thing lay around him.

'I don't think I really believed he was dead, until I felt that weight. There was a body in there, Ada. It was James and we buried him.'

His eyes were limned with tears and Ada felt her own spill onto her cheeks. None of it had felt real to her. She had seen Olympe lunge for the duc, and the knife he'd pulled ready to gut her when she got close. But she hadn't spotted James until the last minute, barrelling into the duc just in time to save Olympe and send himself and the duc toppling over the edge into the flames and glass of the orangery below. She saw that moment when she shut her eyes at night. When her attention slipped. When it rained, when night fell, when she saw candlelight glinting on metal. She saw the determination on James's face.

To save Olympe, to save Camille. To save all of them.

He must have known he was going to his death.

The flames had burned so hot they had only identified his body by the healed bone in his arm from a childhood fracture.

Olympe had never accepted it. It was impossible to her that she could revive Camille, but not James. Ada didn't have to understand her powers to see why she couldn't. Camille had only been dead a few moments. A brief pause of her heart, her flesh still warm and pliant.

James had fallen into oblivion.

Al tried to relight his pipe, but fumbled the tinderbox and dropped it with a curse. Ada bent to retrieve it. Al had scrubbed the tears from his eyes hard enough they were red and raw.

'Thanks.' Then, so quietly she almost couldn't hear, 'I thought it was going to be me. I always thought it was going to be me.'

'Oh, Al.' She wished she could take his hand, but here in the polite society of James's family, the familiarity the battalion shared had to be held at a distance. 'You can't blame yourself.'

'I don't. I just don't understand. It makes no sense that, of all of us, it would be him.'

Olympe joined them, walking stiffly in her black bombazine and crêpe over the uneven ground of settled graves. She held out her hand for the pipe.

Al passed it over. 'I didn't know you smoked.'

'I don't. I just need something to destroy.' She flung it to the ground and smashed the pottery bowl with the heel of her shoe.

Al looked down, dismayed. 'I was enjoying that.'

'Sorry.' Olympe leaned against the wall next to him. 'I hate everything.'

'I get that,' said Al. 'Everything is terrible.'

'I just want to shake James and ask him why he would do something so completely stupid, only I *can't* because he's *dead* and I am so furious at him about it.'

Ada didn't know what else there was to say because Olympe was right. Death made no sense. Grief was a madness.

By the mausoleum, Camille had her head in Lady Harford's lap, and by the faint shaking of her shoulders, Ada knew she was crying too. James's little sister Hennie was folded over her mother like a wilting flower. Lord Harford looked as blank with shock as he had the day they arrived bearing the news. Camille had written to them before they left Paris with James's body packed in ice and straw, but it had been an even bet which would arrive first. Ada couldn't let herself think of that awful meeting again. She had seen and done many terrible things with the battalion over the last year, but that had been among the worst.

The mausoleum was closed, and the funeral party filtered out of the graveyard. With a final embrace

Camille left the Harfords and came back to the battalion. A heavy veil hung over her face from the brim of her bonnet, and she tucked her gloved hands under her arm.

'What now?' said Guil. 'Whatever you need, Camille, you need only ask.'

She took a shuddering breath in, held it, then slowly exhaled, standing a little taller.

'Let's go home.'

In the early, mist-wreathed morning the next day, Ada slipped away from the commotion at the door of the Harfords' house. Their trunks were being packed to take them first to London, then on to the coast and a ship back to France.

Ada only had one more chance to do this.

With the fur-lined hood of her cloak pulled down low and the dew soaking into her skirts, she walked across the rolling parkland to the churchyard. The sole sign of their presence the day before was the churn of mud and the first few flakes of snow. It promised to be a cold winter.

The crypt had been locked. An area was cleaned ready for the stonemason to add James's name. Ada rested her hand over the blank space and closed her eyes.

'I promise I'll look after her.' Her voice was soft enough to disappear on the wind, an echo of the promise she had elicited from her father when she thought everything was going to end so very differently. The promise James had asked of her in the quiet before their final mission.

'Do you?'

Ada startled and turned.

Camille stood a few paces away, black dress stark against her pale face. She had been crying. The tears froze on her lashes like jewels.

'Always,' said Ada. 'Always.'

Camille came silently to her side and raised her fingers to the locked door of the crypt. 'He always said the same thing. He's such a fool, and I love him so much.'

Her voice broke on the final words, and the sobs she'd held back at the funeral came out now, made her double over. Ada wrapped her arms around Camille, held her up, held her close.

'I've lost everyone, Ada,' cried Camille.

Ada stroked a gloved hand over her hair, wrapped her cloak around them both.

'I've lost so many people, I don't know how to go on.'

'Neither do I.' Ada drew back so she could hold Camille's face in her hands and kiss the tears from her cheeks. 'All I know is that we do go on. Step by step. Even if there's nothing else we can do but take one more.'

Tears brimmed, but she nodded and held onto Ada harder.

'And I'll be there for all of them. I promise.'

'I'll be there for all of yours too,' said Camille, her voice barely above a whisper. 'I promise.'

Ada smiled despite herself. She still loved Camille so much it made her giddy. What a world it was to visit upon them so many horrors, and so much unrepentant joy.

'So, my darling Camille, what is our first step?'

'I don't know.' But the ghost of a smile crossed Camille's lips in return. 'Let's find out what happens next.'

POSTSCRIPT

The Harbour, Marseille

January 1795

Aship creaked in its moorings, swaying with the rise and fall of the sea that churned dark grey in the winter harbour. The twin forts Saint Jean and Saint Nicolas lay on either side of the narrow sea mouth, flat against the dull sky. Winter came even to the Mediterranean and Camille pulled her wool pelisse close as they waited for their turn to board. She still wore her veil from the funeral. Though she and James had never married, she wanted to observe mourning. It felt important to keep him with her a little longer, even while his memory slipped inexorably into the past.

The veil served another purpose: since Olympe had used her powers to bring Camille back from the cusp of death she had found herself covered in a filagree of forked lightning scars that mirrored the path the electricity had taken through her body. Like the roots of a tree. Like the branches of her lungs James had shown her in his books. The charge she had carried in the palace had faded over time; now she only occasionally caused a spark when reaching for a metal doorknob or when a storm passed over. The strangest change had been in her lungs. She had seen several doctors since and each had returned the same verdict: she was healthy, but her lung capacity was reduced. It was like something had scourged her insides, turning the diseased branches of her lungs to scar tissue and leaving the rest whole and healthy. Her illness was halted, for now, at least. No one could say what might happen to her next.

Ada had broken down crying in relief at the news. Camille had only shut her eyes and focused on her shallow, but easy breaths, and thought of James when he had first told her she was going to die. She wished he could have known she was going to live.

A carriage arrived and Guil hopped out, followed by Al and Léon. Several travelling trunks were strapped to the roof and the rear, and Guil tossed a coin to a few loitering boys to help unload them and bring them to the ship.

Al bounded over and clapped Camille on the shoulder.

'You know, if one of us was going to flee the country under an assumed name, I'd have put good money on it being me. I'm actually quite jealous. Imagine going somewhere with decent weather and some proper culture to look at. Say hello to the Romans for me.'

Ada's mouth curled in a smile. 'You could always come with us.'

'No chance. Seems like too much hard work. I have found someone who can keep me in the manner to which I have become accustomed.'

He held his hand out and Léon came closer, slipping an arm around his shoulder. 'These days that's constitutional walks around the Tuileries and bed by nine. You've been domesticated.'

Al bristled. 'I certainly have not. I am simply committed to being a socially spurned eccentric well into my old age.' He turned to Ada and Camille. 'Seriously, though, don't stay away too long. That hôtel is far too big for two people.'

Al flung his arms around Camille in a rare gesture of affection. 'I mean it. Come back.' He hugged Ada with just as much force.

'We will,' said Camille and she hoped it was the truth.

They had no plans for where they were going, only away. Paris held too many difficult memories. The Harfords had invited her to England, but she couldn't do it. She couldn't go backwards like that.

'They're ready for you,' said Guil, bringing word from the ship.

He had returned to his family in Marseille soon after they'd come back to France, and for the last week the battalion had stayed with them, squeezed into the joyful, busy townhouse over his father's business. Guil had been welcomed without any questions. If he'd deserted, that meant nothing to them. They were only happy to have their son home again, even if he did sit quietly, his gaze far away, more often than before.

Camille took Guil's hand. 'Not quite the quiet town in the mountains with a garden to tend,' she said, remembering the exchange they'd had about his future back in the duc's first hidden laboratory.

Guil smiled. 'There's a yard and some flower boxes. That is more than enough for now.'

The last to join their reunion was Olympe. Clémentine was with her. They had gone to one of the tea rooms for a final conversation. Olympe had been bristling with nerves beforehand – Camille could only imagine what she needed to say to a mother who had done what Clémentine had. But Olympe seemed calmer, and Clémentine thoughtful. She had taken over the duc's estates after his death and had been good to her word to leave Olympe to choose her own future. After the disastrous demonstration and the fire at the duc's palace, his death had been accepted as a fortunate tragedy. The rumours the battalion had seeded that Olympe had died too had taken root, and anyone with an inkling of the duc's secret weapon were hastily distancing themselves from the man who had tried to murder half of the government of France.

The only thread left to tie up before they departed had been Ada's father. Camille had said nothing when Ada visited him one final time, explaining she was alive and well, but he wouldn't see her for a while. Camille still harboured anger and pain that Ada had continued to meet with her father after he'd reported Camille's parents to the Revolutionary Tribunal, which had led to their death. But after everything they'd been through, she couldn't begrudge Ada the last connection to her mother she had left. Perhaps if they did make it back to Paris, Camille would have enough distance from her feelings that the different strands of their life wouldn't need to stay so far apart.

Clémentine embraced Olympe, and then Olympe came to the gangplank with Ada and Camille. The sails of the ship had been unfurled and tied, billowing above their heads in the wind like their skirts that swirled around their ankles. Seagulls turned on the updraughts, wings spread wide, and a litany of different languages came from the vessels filling the port.

The horizon ahead was a flat line; somewhere beyond was the south-east coast of France as it curved around Montpellier, Narbonne and Perpignan, before giving way to Spain and the Balearic Sea. Half a year ago, Camille had been leaving the coast of Normandy behind as she'd sailed with Al to England in pursuit of Olympe. The world had turned on its head since then, and she knew not what coast awaited her next.

The future was an unknown country. But she wanted to see it.

Ada offered her hand and smiled, warmth in her eyes.

'Ready?'

Camille took it.

Acknowledgements

Finishing a trilogy is to come to the end of a long journey. The way was so much harder than I could have expected when I set out with the battalion in 2017. Pandemic, death, lost years, trauma and grief. As I write this, my grandfather has died only a day ago. If the battalion grew a little darker with each book, it is only because I had little light to offer them. Leaving the battalion, and leaving these books, is a heartbreak I didn't see coming.

Thank you to my dad for over thirty years of listening to me ramble about my writing. To Kiran for being my sister-pal for life. To Chelsey for holding my brain in your hands and taking such good care of it. To Kirstin, it's been so long. To Jane and Tasha and the goblins, sorry I didn't resurrect zombie Robespierre. To Harry, max gatty and s.orm made it a lot further than we thought, huh.

To my agent, Hellie Ogden, who has had a hell of a job holding me together this last year. Thank you for not giving up on me.

To my east London pitchwars gang, Kate Dylan and Sarah Underwood: thanks for all the long, freezing walks, coffees and dinners. It's been one long emotional breakdown for all of us, but you can't get rid of me.

Thank you to all my writer friends who've suffered with me online or in person: Tasha Suri, Tori Bovalino, Saara El-Arifi, Maddy Beresford, Laura Stevens, Kylie Schachte, Ava Reid, Daphne Lao Tonge, Stevie Finegan, Helen Corcoran, Chloe Seager, Amber Chen, Pascale Lacelle, Samantha Shannon, Catherine Johnson, Melinda Salisbury, Kiran Millwood-Hargrave, C.L. Clarke, L.D. Lapinski, Peta Freestone, Non Pratt, Darran Stobbart, Yasmin Rahman, Sophie Cameron, Bex Hogan, Danielle Jawando, Lizzy Huxley-Jones, Emma Theriault, Allison Saft, Sarah Corrigan, Ciara Smyth, Ciannon Smart, Kes Lupo, Jess Rigby, Jess Rule, Leena Normington, Franceseca May.

Thank you to my Sheffield family: Tim, Saskia, Jack, Lottie, Kai, Coco and Tony (and Sula!), and Brian and Rynagh. And, Kate, if you didn't want to be family you shouldn't have moved so close.

Thank you to my editors and the whole team at Zephyr and Head of Zeus: Fiona, Lauren, Meg, Jade, Polly, Clémence and Ben. And thank you to Laura Brett for my wonderful covers.

Thank you to the booksellers, bloggers, booktubers, bookstagrammers and booktokers who've supported the battalion over the years. It means the world to me.

It's no secret that I've struggled hugely since *Dangerous Remedy* was published. Debuting is always hard, but the last few years have been among the worst in my life – and the best. A dream realised in the setting of a nightmare. Writing these final words is bittersweet; I'm not ready to mourn another loss.

All we can do is let something go with love.

One step forward, into an unknown world.

Kat Dunn
London
March 2022